SUSPECT RED

First Edition, September 2017
10 9 8 7 6 5 4 3 2 1
FAC-020093-17216
Printed in the United States of America

This book is set in 11-pt ITC Caslon 224 Std, Baskerville MT Pro,
Arial MT Pro, American Typewriter ITC Pro, Minion Pro/Monotype;
Erased Typewriter 2, Vtg Stencil US No. 72/Fontspring
Designed by Maria Elias

Library of Congress Cataloging-in-Publication Data
Names: Elliott, Laura, 1957– author.
Title: Suspect red / by L.M. Elliott.
Description: First edition. • Los Angeles : Disney–Hyperion, 2017.
Summary: In 1950s Washington, D.C., teenaged Richard, a bookworm
whose father works for the FBI, experiences effects of McCarthyism,
beginning with book banning and ending with a threat to his half-
Czech friend. • Includes bibliographical references and filmography.
Identifiers: LCCN 201604182 • ISBN 9781423157540 (hardcover) •
ISBN 1423157540 (hardcover)
Subjects: • CYAC: Family life—Washington (D.C.)—Fiction. •
Loyalty—Fiction. • World politics—1945–1955—Fiction. • United States.
Federal Bureau of Investigation—Fiction. • Cold War—Fiction. •
Washington (D.C.)—History—20th century—Fiction.
Classification: LCC PZ7.E453 Sus 2017 • DDC [Fic]—dc23
LC record available at https://lccn.loc.gov/2016041824

Reinforced binding

Visit www.DisneyBooks.com

For Peter and Megan,
standard-bearers for integrity, eloquence,
and freedom of thought

"Communism . . . is a malignant
and evil way of life . . . akin
to disease . . . so long as school
boards and parents tolerate conditions
whereby communists and fellow
travelers, under the guise of academic
freedom, can teach our youth a way
of life that eventually will destroy
the sanctity of the home, that
undermines faith in God, that causes
them to scorn respect for constituted
authority."

—FBI Director J. Edgar Hoover

"This is the time of the Cold War . . . when all
the world is split into two vast, increasingly
hostile armed camps . . .

When a great democracy is destroyed, it will not
be because of enemies from without but rather
because of enemies from within . . ."

"There are no degrees of loyalty in the
United States; a man is either loyal or he is
disloyal . . ."

"We must be sure that those who seek to lead us
today are equally dedicated. We cannot survive
on half loyalties any more than we can find the
facts of . . . conspiracy with half-truths."

—Senator Joseph McCarthy

"[McCarthyism] is the corruption of truth, the abandonment of . . . the due process of law. It is the use of the big lie and the unfounded accusation against any citizen in the name of Americanism or security.

"It is the spread of fear."

—former president Harry S. Truman

Chapter 1:

Julius and Ethel Rosenberg are executed in the electric chair for espionage, despite appeals to the Supreme Court and President Dwight D. Eisenhower for clemency. Their trial follows a string of spying cases involving British and American diplomats and other federal workers. The Rosenbergs are convicted of giving U.S. atomic-bomb technology to the Soviet Union. Many believe the Soviets would not have developed their A-bomb without the Rosenbergs' help.

Reporters follow their sons, Robert, six, and Michael, ten, to Sing Sing prison for their final good-byes, while newspaper headlines shout: "Atom Bomb Spies Die Silent to the End: Couple Display No Emotion As They Pay for Betraying Their Nation."

(Opposite top) Julius and Ethel Rosenberg • (Opposite bottom) Their sons, Robert and Michael, leaving Sing Sing prison

Workers in East Berlin go on strike.

They also march for reunification of their city, calling for an end to the Soviet Union's control of the German capital's eastern sector. The policed dividing line between democratic and Communist Germany had been established after the defeat of Hitler, in a post–World War II stalemate between the two new superpowers—Stalin's Soviet Union and the United States (with its NATO allies Great Britain and France).

Soviet tanks crush the East Berliners' plea for democracy and reunion with their families, friends, and neighbors. The symbolic Iron Curtain becomes a deadly barrier. Within a few years, the Soviets will build the fortified Berlin Wall. More than one hundred East Berliners will die trying to cross it.

Germans facing Soviet tank in East Berlin

The Red Scare spreads to books. Convinced that hidden Communist themes could pervert American thoughts, aides to Red-hunter Senator Joseph McCarthy remove "subversive" books written "by Communists, fellow travelers, etc." from State Department and embassy libraries overseas. Hundreds of books are torched in bonfires. Across the United States, librarians pull suspect books from shelves. Some civilians also burn novels by authors who focus on the plight of the working class, such as John Steinbeck.

The *New Republic* magazine runs a cover story explaining who is being censored: "The following Americans have been mentioned unfavorably in testimony before the House Un-American Activities Committee (HUAC) or cited as belonging to one or more 'fronts.' Present directives indicate that their works should be withdrawn from U.S. libraries overseas and that they should not be subjects or authors of feature articles or broadcasts."

The 64 names include physicist Albert Einstein; novelist Ernest Hemingway; Pulitzer Prize–winning author Upton Sinclair; and *New Yorker* columnist Dorothy Parker.

(Opposite center) 1954: A film still from the 1989 documentary *Comic Book Confidential* showing the burning of comic books • (Clockwise from top left) Dorothy Parker, Upton Sinclair, Albert Einstein, and Ernest Hemingway

RICHARD settled down at the kitchen table. Under his armpit was a book, in his hand a cup of Chase & Sanborn he'd poured himself, curious. He took a sip and made a face at the instant coffee's bitter taste. *Good grief! Why the heck does Dad drink this junk?* He shoved the cup aside and put his novel on the table.

School was out, summer was on, and Richard had a stack of books he planned to read. Stuff that would obliterate all the crumb-bum melodrama of junior high school, including the cliques that froze out a kid who liked to read and couldn't roller-skate; the girls who went steady with dopes who greased their hair into duck butts and who turned their pretty freckled noses up at a guy who talked about the Holy Grail or Sherlock Holmes or Sam Spade.

In September, Richard would wade back into that donkey manure. But this summer? Richard was going to escape. He'd travel universes brought to life by *his* books—no moldy old mush dictated by school wardens. Good stuff—heroes, spy intrigues, quests, underdogs winning the day, private detectives cracking crime cases, and a couple of dames in distress. He'd even squirreled away a copy of that novel all the parents hated, *The Catcher in the Rye*.

He was reading Salinger's story in chunks at midnight with a flashlight, knowing it was dangerous stuff. Last night, the sixteen-year-old narrator—Holden Caulfield—ran away from boarding school, after getting his nose busted by a jerk in his dorm. Richard pulled out the pocket-size spiral note-book in which he jotted down things that he really liked. He re-read some Holden truths he'd copied.

"*. . . you can always tell a moron. They never want to discuss anything [intelligent]. . . .*"

Richard nodded. *Exactly.*

"*What really knocks me out is a book that, when you're all done reading it, you wish the author that wrote it was a terrific friend of yours and you could call him up on the phone whenever you felt like it.*"

Right again. Sometimes books could be better friends than kids. No joking.

Richard ran his hand along the forest-green cover of the novel he'd brought to the kitchen table. *Robin Hood.* Classic stuff. He'd love to talk to the guy who wrote it. Richard had read the book before, but the story never got old. How could it? A former knight, now outlaw, hanging out with forest desper-ados, taking down a bully, and winning the prettiest maiden in the land.

Richard smiled down at the cover and its N. C. Wyeth illustration of the legendary Merry Men. Standing among a thick grove of trees, they glowered out menacingly. Robin leaned on a longbow, and a green feather festooned his emerald cap, illuminated by an arrow of light piercing the dense forest canopy. Richard opened to where he'd reluctantly left off the day before, when he'd been called down for dinner. (Tuna casserole. The worst!)

Now it was early morning. Everyone was asleep. No interrup-tions. Richard began to read. Instantly, he no longer sat in a tidy, perfectly symmetrical brick colonial in northwest Washington,

DC. Instead, he stalked the gloam of Sherwood Forest in the age of the Crusades. He came upon an ambush.

"It was a wild spot: and only the notes of the birds and the rush of the falling water disturbed it. But ere they had proceeded a quarter of a mile up the bank of the stream a sudden bend in it brought them the harsh noise of desperate and near fighting. . . .

"'Our arrows must do duty for us, then,' muttered Robin, grimly, soon as he understood this. 'Fit shafts across your bows, friends, and aim with all your hearts in it. . . .'

"They dropped to their knees and . . ."

"Richard!"

Richard flinched. Sherwood Forest vaporized.

His mother stood in the doorway in a hot-pink bathrobe, her blond hair a crown of neatly bobby-pinned swirls. "What in the world are you doing up this early, honey?" Abigail asked. "It's summer vacation."

"Reading," Richard answered without looking up, trying to recapture the forest battle.

"You should have woken me so I could fix you some breakfast." She went to the stove and pulled out a frying pan. "Scrambled? Fried?"

Richard shrugged to indicate he didn't care which and tried to focus on the page as she threw bacon into the pan and cracked eggs.

"'Smite them, Warrenton,' cried he, suddenly and excitedly. 'Speedily, instantly—or they will end this fight against us. Now!'

"Their arrows flew together, marvelous shots, each—"

His mother set down silverware. Again, the battle between Robin's men and the sheriff's villains disappeared.

"You were drinking coffee? That'll stunt your growth, silly." She ruffled his honey-colored hair. "What are you reading? Must be good."

Keeping his place with his hand, Richard flipped the cover over so she could see.

Abigail gasped. "You can't read that!" She slammed the book shut on Richard's fingers and then pulled it off the table.

"What the heck, Mom!" He tried to reach for it, but she turned, cradling the book in her arms.

"What if Mr. Hoover knew you're reading this?"

Richard's dad, Don Bradley, was an FBI agent, a G-man—as gangster Machine Gun Kelly had dubbed "government men"—a tough-guy title Richard loved. Mr. Hoover, the agency's director, lived on the next street. Sometimes Hoover had his driver stop in front of their house so he could talk with Don. His dad always got the weirdest look on his face when that happened, and then he just mysteriously disappeared—no matter what the family was doing. Richard had decided those quick conferences with the director must involve some top secret work to rid the country of bad guys and commies. He'd convinced himself that his dad was a secret agent of some kind, a total hero.

That's why he was always thrown by his mom's anxiety about impressing Hoover. He knew Abigail's concern came from love for his dad, but Richard couldn't help it—her being such a worrywart annoyed the heck out of him. It made him question his belief that Don Bradley was in good with the director.

"Why would Mr. Hoover care about what I'm reading?" he asked. "Especially *Robin Hood*?"

"Well . . . maybe he wouldn't." Abigail hesitated, her grip on the book loosening. She looked down at Robin's face. "I remember reading this when I was about your age. I loved Maid Marian."

Seeing her soften, Richard reached for the book again. But Abigail stepped back, pulling *Robin Hood* with her. Her voice had that grating, nervous tremor: "These days, Mr. Hoover seems to agree with everything Senator McCarthy says. And Senator McCarthy says a lot of books are subversive. Hidden commie propaganda. His staff just burned a whole pile of books they found in our Berlin embassy."

"Like Hitler did?" Richard asked with a twinge of sarcasm. Well, at least his History teacher had taught him something useful last year.

"Don't give me that flak, honey." Abby shook her head. "Senator McCarthy is really serious about certain books being dangerous. He's calling into his congressional hearings all sorts of authors suspected of being Reds, or somewhere in between, left-leaning, liberal-sympathizing pinkos." She lowered her voice. "I bet they'll be blacklisted, like all those Hollywood screenwriters were."

"But what's that got to do with *Robin Hood*?" Richard reached for his book a third time. Abigail refused to budge.

"You know how I volunteer at the library? Well, the librarians are all scared silly. A librarian up in Massachusetts refused to take a loyalty oath and a group called Alert Americans raised such a ruckus about it that the county actually fired the poor woman.

"So to be safe, our librarians made a list of books we might have to pull from the shelves. It includes *Robin Hood*."

"But why?"

"Because Robin Hood takes from the rich to give to the poor." She added in a whisper, as if they could be overheard, "That's a *Communist* concept."

"You gotta be kidding me!" Richard's voice cracked on *kidding*, adding to his aggravation. Would his voice ever deepen and stay put?

"Hey! That's no way to talk to your mother." Richard's dad entered the kitchen, dressed for work, his ever-present pipe clenched between his teeth. "Is it?" But Don smiled at Richard nonetheless.

"No, sir." Richard couldn't help eyeing his dad's pipe. A few days before, Don had been sharing some pretty wild war stories about FBI cases and divulged that the agency had pipe pistols that could fire a small projectile and kill a person at close range. As soon as he had the chance, Richard was going to pull open his dad's to see if he had one.

"So, can I negotiate a peace?" Don asked before adding, "I swear I'll bring home a dozen roses for you, Abby, if I could get a cup of joe right now. I was up late writing a report." He frowned. "Um, dear, I think those eggs are burning."

"Oh, for pity's sake, Abby!" she scolded herself and hurried to the stove, still clutching Richard's book.

"So, what's up?" Don looked back and forth between Richard and Abigail.

"It's nothing, Don, really." She glanced at Richard, making her eyes big in that look—the look Richard and his sister, Ginny, knew meant to remain silent. That look that kept them from ever saying anything against Hoover.

"Yeah, it's nothing," Richard said reluctantly. He hated fibbing to his dad.

"Well, just for the record, I don't believe you two." Don pointed at them with his pipe. "But as long as there's a truce. And . . ." He grinned. "That coffee?"

● ● ·

When he had his cup of inky, strong brew, Don switched on the new high-fidelity radio that crowded the windowsill. He spun the dial to news. A broadcaster boomed:

"Today, inside Sing Sing prison, Julius and Ethel Rosenberg await their fate. Unless their attorneys win another stay in court or President Eisenhower grants them clemency, they will be executed tonight in the electric chair for their crime of organizing atomic espionage for Russia."

"So today's the day," Abigail said quietly as she cracked new eggs. "I can't believe it. I thought for sure President Eisenhower would show Mrs. Rosenberg mercy and lower her sentence to jail time."

Don's typically upbeat expression turned grim. "Yeaaaahhh, I know, honey."

"Well, I don't understand it." Abigail started beating the eggs with some furor. "My heart just broke when the TV showed her two little boys arriving to visit her for the last time. Honestly, Don, I couldn't believe how cruel the news announcer was. It was so callous, I remember it word for word. He said, 'The boys' suffering is a small price to pay for the irreparable damage done by their Communist spy parents.'

Those boys are only six and ten years old! Not exactly a small price for them."

Don shifted in his seat. "The evidence of their parents' espionage is overwhelming, Abby. Her brother worked on the Manhattan Project. He had access to designs for our atom bomb. He gave Julius Rosenberg the drawing of its implosion device. Julius passed on that information to the damn Soviets. And Ethel saw that happen. She typed up letters for Julius."

"Oh, Don, any good wife would do that."

Don took a long drink of his coffee like he wanted to be done with the conversation. Richard noted that his father's hand had begun to tremble as he held the cup—a nervous tic he kept watch for to read his father's mood. Seeing it told Richard to keep silent. Boy, he'd give just about anything to know what that tendency for Don's hands to suddenly start shaking was all about.

At the stove, Abigail kept pushing. "But if all the FBI has on her is that she played secretary, why electrocute her? And I think it's fishy, don't you, that her brother changed his original testimony? He didn't give evidence against her at first, did he?"

"No, you're right. He confessed after we promised him clemency *if* he cooperated." Don put down his cup abruptly, with a loud *clink*, and clasped his hands to still them.

"Well, that sounds pretty coerced to me."

Don shot her a look—heated with a flash of discomfort or defiance or aggravation, Richard couldn't decide which. Then Don stared down into his coffee. "Ike can't let her off, honey. Too many people think the secrets her husband passed on caused the Korean War. And too many of our boys are coming home from Korea in coffins right now for America to be forgiving of two Reds who spied for Stalin."

With that, Don turned up the radio, signaling he wanted to hear the rest of the news report without further interruption:

"At noon, the Supreme Court hears the Rosenberg arguments. Their supporters parade in front of the White House, singing in protest. Passing cars honk and drivers shout at them to go back to Russia."

It was only when the commentator broke for a commercial about Tootsie Rolls that Richard dared join the conversation. That was the closest his parents ever came to a squabble.

"Dad." He hesitated, fearing the question might sound flippant, but he really wanted to know. "How did the Rosenbergs cause the Korean War?" Two fathers he knew had died in the fighting, and their sons, his only real friends at school, had moved away.

"I know it sounds ridiculous to say two people could start a whole war, Rich, but it's a domino effect. Joseph Stalin was a real sonuvab—"

"Don!" Abigail interrupted. "Language, please!" She nodded toward Richard.

He itched to let his mom in on some of the language Holden Caulfield used. Her hair would pop right out of her bobby pins!

Don laughed. "I think he's heard that term, hon. He'll be fourteen in a couple of weeks, you know. I had a paper route and was working a job after school when I was his age. He's almost a man." He winked at Richard. "Here's the deal, son. Stalin sent millions of his countrymen to die in Siberian gulags—their version of labor prison camps—in his purge of disbelievers. Some of those poor people simply had ethnic backgrounds he didn't like. Frankly, he was as bad as Hitler. And he wanted to spread Communism everywhere.

"But Stalin didn't take risks. Without an atom bomb of his own to match ours, Stalin would never have dared to give North Korea weapons or train its army. Without Soviet tanks and guns, the North Korean commies never would have invaded South Korea. And the Russkies were able to build their own atomic bomb that set all this in motion because of the secrets the Rosenbergs gave them."

As Abigail put plates of bacon and eggs on the table, Don reached out and caught her gently by the wrist.

"I love your big heart, honey." Don looked at her with such a desire to please that Richard could feel it. "The trouble is, the most clear-cut evidence we have against the Rosenbergs is just too top secret to be entered into their trial. You'd be convinced, too, if you knew some of it."

"Really? Like what, Dad?"

Don turned to Richard. "Well . . . I suppose it wouldn't hurt to tell you this one little thing. As long as you swear not to tell your friends. I trust you to protect national security, son."

Richard smiled and sat up taller, proud, although he also thought: Friends? No danger there.

Don nodded in approval. "For starters, the Rosenbergs used all sorts of safe codes to communicate with their spy ring—like passing empty Jell-O boxes as signals."

"Jell-O boxes?" *What the heck?!* Richard had read plenty about the tricks of the spy trade, but he'd never heard of that method before.

"Yeah. Isn't that something?" Don smiled. "I'll never look at Jell-O the same way again. The KGB also had an official code name for Julius. You see, there was this Soviet codebook that we found near the end of World War II and . . ." Don stopped himself. "Well . . . forget what I just said." He rubbed his hand over his mouth. "Just . . . believe me. There are things that connect the dots. Also, some of the Rosenbergs' buddies let the Soviets know that we could decipher their communiqués. Suddenly, overnight, their codes changed. We couldn't read anything anymore. So when the North Koreans invaded the South, we were caught with our pants down. Thousands of American soldiers have died in Korea because of it."

He shoved his plate away, his eggs half-eaten. "And God knows what the NKA is doing to our downed pilots they've caught." Don's voice grew husky. "People don't understand what happens to POWs in the hands of political fanatics, the people who truly believe in their leader's demagoguery." His hands were really shaking now. "They don't get it at all."

Abigail sat down by the window, blowing on her cup of tea to cool it and watching Don's face. After a long pause she shifted the conversation back to the Rosenberg family. "Well, it's just so scary. The Rosenbergs looked like ordinary, nice enough people. It's beginning to feel like there's a commie lurking in every corner, just like Senator McCarthy says!"

"The truth is, Abby, there are spies among us." Don reached for his pipe and began puffing. A swirl of tobacco mist engulfed him and his hands steadied. "Then again, there are innocent people who simply like Russian music. Spotting the true troublemakers is our job at the FBI. Don't you worry."

"How can you tell the difference, Dad?"

But before Don could answer, Richard's little sister, Ginny, skipped in, trailing her enormous stuffed bear. She plopped down on the bench beside Richard, cramming the bear in between them. "Rufus says good morning." She grinned up at him, putting the bear's paw on Richard's elbow.

When he was younger, Richard had played elaborate hide-and-seek games with Ginny, leaving a string of clues that would lead her to Rufus. But Richard had outgrown that nonsense last year. The four-year difference between them now seemed as wide as the Pacific Ocean.

"Aren't you kind of old to carry that thing around with you?" he whispered irritably, peeved that the nine-year-old's entrance ended his man-to-man talk with his dad.

She stuck her tongue out at him.

"Oh, that's mature. You better not try that in fifth grade, even if you are smart enough to skip ahead a year."

"As it happens," Ginny began, "I have an important appointment today. Rufus"—she patted the stuffed bear's head—"is how I got it." She raised her left eyebrow meaningfully.

Richard laughed in spite of himself. Ginny's imitation of Abigail's official mom voice and expressions was dead-on. She was pretty cool that way. She should become an actress. No kidding.

"And how's that, sugarplum?" Don asked. He turned off the radio, seeming relieved to have lighter fare to discuss.

"We have an audience at the zoo. Rufus is getting his picture taken with Smokey Bear!"

Smokey Bear had been rescued from a wildfire and become the country's beloved mascot for forest fire prevention. He received more letters at the National Zoo than President Eisenhower did at the White House a few miles away.

"Why Rufus?" Don asked.

Abigail handed Ginny a plate while saying to Don, "Your daughter wrote a story to grab the zookeepers' attention—about Rufus saving Smokey's life in a forest fire that consumes Rock Creek Park."

"I made it real scary, too, Daddy. A Russian Bear named Stalin started the fire."

Don's smile faded. "Where did you get that idea, honey?"

Ginny tossed her ponytail. "Teacher was talking about Russia—oh, the Soviet Union, I mean—and she said they were gobbling up Eastern Europe and dropped a big old iron curtain to divide the people of Berlin from each other and that pretty soon the Russians—I mean Soviets—would want to come here, too. She showed us a map that had a big Russian Bear growling at Uncle Sam." She sipped her orange juice. "So the idea just came to me. And it worked, too!"

"She'll be in Congress before you know it," Don joked, but Richard couldn't tell if his dad meant it to be funny or not.

"Oh, no, Daddy, I want to be a newspaper reporter."

"Of course you do, honey," Abigail said with the same I'll-humor-her-fantasies look she'd had when Ginny announced as a six-year-old that she was going to grow up to be crowned Queen of England someday.

"Gotta go." Don stood and kissed Abigail and Ginny on their heads. He pointed his pipe at Richard. "You're in charge while I'm at work, son. Keep the women safe."

Richard saluted. "Yes, sir, Dad." They grinned at each other.

When he was gone, Abigail left the kitchen, taking *Robin Hood* with her.

She came back with a wrapped package. "I was saving this for your birthday, but I think today's a better day to give it to you."

Richard could tell it was a book. Did she really think another book made up for her swiping the one he *wanted* to read? "Gosh, thanks, Mom."

Abigail ignored his sarcasm. "Go ahead. Open it."

With little enthusiasm, Richard ripped off the paper, expecting some totally lame thing like a Hardy Boys mystery. But instead he found *I Led 3 Lives*, the best-selling memoir of an FBI agent who'd posed as a Communist to root out conspirators. Adman, commie, secret FBI informant—three lives. He'd become quite a celebrity after testifying before the House Un-American Activities Committee and exposing Communists with whom he'd pretended to work side by side. And it was exactly the life that Richard suspected his dad to be living.

"Wow, Mom, thanks. Seriously."

"I stood in line at the bookstore so he could sign it to you." Abigail opened to the title page: *Happy Birthday, Richard. Your parents expect great things of you.*

Richard smiled. Autographed by the country's best-known G-man. Pretty boss, he had to admit.

"I read in that new magazine, that *TV Guide*, that there's going to be a weekly show on Sunday nights about Mr. Philbrick's counterspying. I thought you'd enjoy reading his book beforehand. Like it?" she asked hopefully.

"Yeah, Mom, I do. Honest." She actually was really thoughtful that way—picking out good gifts.

Relieved, Abigail kissed his forehead. "Thanks for understanding about *Robin Hood*, honey. Now I better get ready to take Ginny to the zoo. Oh." She snapped her fingers, saying, more to herself than to Richard, "I better take a few things off the bookshelf, given all this trouble. I know Don loves *The Maltese Falcon*, but Dashiell Hammett went to jail for refusing to answer questions about some commie-front organization he'd been involved with."

Abigail headed for the living room. "Let's see . . . Hemingway was on McCarthy's list. Steinbeck's *Of Mice and Men* is supposedly proletariat. . . ." Richard could hear the scrape of leather-bound books being pulled from shelves and a *thunk* as she dropped each one to the floor.

He looked down at chapter 1:

"Nine years of conspiracy, uncertainty, fear. Nine years in the shadows where glances must be furtive, where I looked in vain for the face of a friend. . . . Secret meetings on darkened street corners, where automobiles drove up, swallowed me, and whirled away. Nine years with my face smothered in a mask that could never be taken off . . ."

Cool! Richard sat back. Maybe this wouldn't be such a bad substitute for *Robin Hood* after all.

Chapter 2:

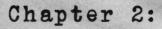

After three bloody years of American troops fighting to protect democratic South Korea from the Communist North, the Korean War ends in a cease-fire. A formal peace treaty is never signed, but a guarded 150-mile-wide Demilitarized Zone (DMZ) is established as a buffer between the two regimes, along the 38th Parallel.

A total of 36,574 American servicemen and -women died in the conflict, and approximately 8,200 remained missing in action at the cease-fire.

(Above) Korean children in front of M-26 tank in Haengin • (Opposite top) A soldier consoles a grieving friend as a medic fills out a casualty tag • (Opposite bottom) Gun crew near Kum River

In Cuba, Fidel Castro leads about 160 Communist rebels in an attack on army barracks in an attempt to overthrow the island's dictator, Fulgencio Batista, and his pro-Western government. The rebellion is put down within a few days. But the fear of a Communist, pro-Soviet Cuba, just 105 miles from Florida's shores, now haunts America. Government officials know what that close proximity could mean in terms of a deadly nuclear strike if Cuba ever housed USSR missiles.

Seattle

San Francisco

Los Angeles

Missile radius from Cuba

32740

"SPARKLERS? Are you serious?"

Abigail stood at the bottom of the hall stairs, holding up a fistful of the flammable sticks. Her dimpled smile crumpled. "But you always loved sparklers."

"Yeah, when I was a baby. For crying out loud, Mom, I'm fourteen now, in case you hadn't noticed!"

"Cool it, wiseapple!" Don leaned over the railing of the banister. He was knotting his paisley tie and his suspenders dangled down by his hips. "No sassing your mother, *kapish*?"

"Yes, sir."

Richard stomped the rest of his way down the stairs to his mom. He'd woken up in a horrible mood thanks to a phone call the night before from one of his crumb-bum classmates. "My parents are away for the holiday," the guy had begun, "and I need a ride to Jimmy's pool party. Can I catch one with you?"

Richard hadn't been invited. Worse, he could hear a bunch of sniggering in the background as the dirtbag said, "Geez, Rich, I'm sorry. I can't believe Jimmy didn't ask you. Everyone else is going." He rattled off ten names. "Didn't you guys use to be buddies?"

Yeah, until Jimmy started flunking out of History because he wouldn't do his homework and expected Richard to help him cheat. When Richard refused, Jimmy called him a traitor and a chicken goody-goody and followed him down the school's hall making a *clllluuuuuck-cluck-cluck-cluck* sound. Then he went out of his way to stab Richard in the back as many times as he could. Like Brutus attacking old Caesar. Jimmy was the snitch who spilled the beans during lunch one day about Richard playing spy games with Ginny. Jimmy, of course, didn't mention that he used to join in when he was over at the house. Richard had been laughed out of the cafeteria.

After hanging up the phone, Richard had tried to write one of his secret songs—a verse about the cruelty of pack mentality and teenage boys who had to be told what to think by a king-of-the-hill jerk. But he failed. He just couldn't come up with good rhymes for *bash*, *heads*, or *morons*. Around 2:00 A.M., Richard had given up.

So sparklers in his face first thing in the morning felt like the last straw. While every guy he knew would be lounging around a pool, talking about baseball and babes and the latest *Dragnet* episode, and probably sneaking their first beers, Richard would be babysitting his little sister with Tinkerbell sparklers.

Maybe he could convince Abigail to at least get him some actual fireworks.

"How about Roman candles instead, Mom?"

"I don't think those are allowed on the National Mall, honey. Besides, we'll be standing right underneath the best Fourth of July fireworks the country offers. I just thought sparklers would be fun during our picnic. I remember you looping them around in circles trying to write your name in a trail of sparks. You were so darling then, sweetie." She patted his face.

Darling no more, he knew. Richard was currently the prince of gangly, all legs and arms and pimples amid his freckles.

"I need you to do me a favor," she went on. "I completely forgot to buy sugar and all the stores are closed today. I need more for our pie. Please go ask Mrs. Emerson for a cup."

"Aw, Mom, can't you go?"

"I've got to fry the chicken. If I go, I'll be there an hour. Barb is so sweet, but I swear, everything takes forever with her. She always has some gossip she wants to pass on. She could talk the broad side off a barn."

"What about Ginny?"

"She's over at the Johnsons', playing with Lynda and Luci."

"Oh, sure. The Minority Leader's kids. Is she trying to get Rufus an invitation to the Senate or something?" Richard knew he was stepping over the line with that crack. But messing with his mom when he was cranky was like scratching a poison ivy rash, not caring that it'd only make the itching worse.

Abigail picked up a measuring cup she'd left on the front hall table and shoved it into his hand. "When you come home with that sugar, please bring back a better attitude, too, honey. It's the Fourth of July!"

● ● ·

Outside, hot summer sunshine drenched Richard. To acclimate to the heat, he stood in the shade of the cherry trees that lined the street, trying to cool down emotionally as well. He knew Abigail didn't realize what was going on in his head. And Richard just couldn't bring himself to tell her. How could he admit to his mom that he felt like such a loser? It'd make her cry. Only a turkey would be mean enough to knowingly make someone as sweet as Abigail cry. Besides, Don would be furious with him.

Richard sighed and shoved his hands in his pockets, staring at Mrs. Emerson's front door across the street. He'd be there all summer if he didn't come up with some story that could get him away from her chatter.

Hmmmm. Holden Caulfield wouldn't have trouble coming up with a believable fib—something impressive—and he'd be all charming as he told it. Or Philbrick, the double agent. Richard was about halfway through *I Led 3 Lives.* So far, it wasn't quite as exciting as he'd thought it'd be, but Philbrick was winning over commies left and right by saying stuff they wanted to hear.

Mrs. Emerson was real into DC's who's who. Plus, she organized some do-gooder committee of neighborhood ladies watching out for hidden Reds and their propaganda. Like that penny candy that was banned for having wrappers with miniature geography lessons because one was about Russia.

So . . . what about . . . Richard had a meeting. Sure! A meeting with the vice president. Yeah, that's right. The Nixons lived a few neighborhoods away, and the oldest Nixon daughter was Ginny's age. He'd seen them around. And Dick Nixon was a big Red-hunter going way back. He'd led the conviction of that former State Department guy named Alger Hiss.

That's right, Mrs. Emerson, he could hear himself saying. *Gotta pass on a top secret discovery. Following in my dad's footsteps!* That'd get her.

With confidence, Richard stepped into the street. But wait, Mrs. Emerson would ask a thousand questions to find out what his top secret discovery was. He stopped. *Darn.* Well, maybe he just had an appointment with the barber to get his flattop trimmed. He rubbed his head. His hair was getting kind of dandelion-fuzzy. She'd believe that.

He dawdled along Mrs. Emerson's walkway, taking a kick at the sun-colored marigolds marching alongside. They were peppered with weeds. He guessed it was too hard for her to lean over and pull them out. She was kind of old. Maybe fifty, even.

Richard wondered what had happened to Mr. Emerson. He'd never met the guy. In fact, he'd never heard anything about him. Maybe he didn't really exist. Or maybe she'd killed him like Lizzie Borden had hacked up her parents. *Yeah. Wow.* What could have been her weapon?

As strong as his imagination was, Richard just couldn't picture plump, short Barbara Emerson wielding an ax or sledgehammer or fireplace tongs or anything. He paused at the bottom step. He knew what had happened. She'd talked her husband to death! To hide her crime, she'd buried him in her marigolds. No wonder they were choked with weeds—it was a spooky symbol, like in Poe's *The Tell-Tale Heart.*

He looked at her front door. He could almost hear it warning him—*Run! Run away!*

Without thinking, Richard crouched down, sneaky-like, just as he used to when he was playing all those spy games with Ginny and pretending to be on a stakeout.

Of course, at that very instant, when he was playing cops and robbers like a baby, the door popped open. Startled, Richard fell back on his butt.

"Goodness, Richard, what happened?"

He tried to be nonchalant and waved at her from the ground. "Oh, hey, Mrs. Emerson." But he could feel his freckles and pimples burn red with mortification.

"Are you all right?" She pushed open the screen door and started down the stairs toward him.

Think, Richard, you idiot, or you're in for epic humiliation. Stupid weeds. If only he hadn't noticed them.

"Oh, no, Mrs. Emerson, I'm fine." In anger, Richard reached for a weed and yanked it. That gave him an idea. "I just noticed you might need a little help with these. I can come back tomorrow and pull them if you like."

"Lord love you, child. I would be so grateful. What a thoughtful boy you are, just like that handsome father of yours."

Forcing a smile, and feeling ridiculous for his wild imaginings that the sweet old lady was a murderer, Richard stood and held out the measuring cup.

"Can my mom borrow some sugar for her pie?"

"Of course, dear. Come in, come in."

As Richard stepped inside, Mrs. Emerson's poufy cats came running, the bells on their collars tinkling. They swirled around his ankles, leaving a hot cuff of fur.

"Mutt and Jeff certainly take right to you, dear. They don't like most men." Mrs. Emerson looked him up and down. She wore thick, rhinestone-studded, black-rimmed glasses tipped up like cat eyes. "Have I told you how they came to me? There was such a storm blowing up and I was on the porch reading the comics and . . ."

"Yes, ma'am, you've told me. It's a very funny story." Richard held up the measuring cup again. "I'm sorry, Mrs. Emerson, I'm kind of in a hurry. Mom's waiting for me."

"Oh dear, how silly of me, delaying you while your precious mother is waiting to make a pie for your big day. I'll be back in a jiff." Mrs. Emerson retreated to the kitchen with the cup, still talking. "My mama always made lemon meringue pie for the Fourth. It was my daddy's favorite. He always said . . ."

Her voice faded. But her cats remained, rubbing against Richard's legs, a small cloud of fur drifting up. By the time she returned with the sugar, Richard was sneezing so violently, he could barely say good-bye.

"Drink some chamomile tea for that sniffle, dearie," she called after him.

●　●　·

"Mom!" Richard bellowed as he burst back through their door, sneezing. "Here's your sugar. I gotta change my pants. Mrs. Emerson's stupid cats slimed me again!" Furious with himself for having to go back the next day to pull weeds, he slammed the cup down onto the table. It sprayed sugar along the week's mail.

Geez. Could this morning get any worse? Not having a full cup of sugar would earn him a trip back across the street. Hurriedly, Richard picked up the top letter and poured the spilled sugar back into the cup.

Underneath the letter was the most recent *Saturday Evening Post*. On its cover illustration, bursts of fireworks exploded above a row of cars as little children chased each other, holding sparklers. *Little* children. *Sparklers*. Exactly. Richard picked up the magazine as proof of his argument. He was about to storm the kitchen when he was racked with sneezes again. New pants first.

Upstairs, Richard looked more closely at the weekly's cover as he pulled on shorts. In its upper right corner was a teaser for an article inside. THEY CALLED HIM A "PSYCHO": THE CASE HISTORY OF A MARINE WHO CAME BACK FROM A WWII MENTAL CRACKUP.

As Richard pulled on fresh khakis, he skimmed:

"Nearly one million servicemen were diagnosed as psychoneurotics during World War II. What happened to them after they were discharged? Did they adjust? How many wound up as misfits—or even criminals? Here's the case history of a marine who cracked up after Okinawa. . . ."

The article opened by reassuring readers that an Army study found only 8 percent of veterans diagnosed as "psychoneurotic" were disabled "enough to be a real problem to themselves or others." Symptoms of being "psycho" or "frightburned" included headaches, jitters so bad a man had to use two hands to steady his fork when he ate, sudden irritability, stomachaches, and bad dreams.

Richard took in a sharp breath. Those were all symptoms that plagued his father. Was that what it was? "Fright burn?" Engrossed, he kept reading as he headed toward the stairs. The marine profiled in the article had returned home and "became something of a problem for a time," staying out nights, restless when home, and drinking heavily. Check. Check. Check. *Uh-oh.* Richard turned the page nervously.

"Whoa, son, look where you're going!" Richard felt a jerk on his collar. "It's not safe to walk down steps while you're reading!" Don laughed. "What's so interesting?"

Richard held up the magazine. Dare he ask his dad about his nervous quirks?

"Hang on a sec. I heard about this. It's about an old buddy of mine. He and I trained for the FBI together. I haven't seen him in years. We both joined up after some jerk saw us two good-looking, fit young guys"—Don jokingly flexed his muscles like Popeye—"and called us gutless draft dodgers for not being in uniform. It made us hopping mad. G-men are exempt from the draft, but most people don't know that. So we enlisted that very day. When I went to the Air Corps, flying over Europe, he went to the Pacific with the Navy."

Don shook his head and flipped through the pages. "I heard he had a rough go of it and was pretty much a lost ball in high weeds when he came home. I'm afraid a lot of our boys coming back from Korea will be, too."

"It says in the magazine that he's fine now, Dad, that he's a lawyer and belongs to a country club. Hey, Dad?"

"A country club?" Don got an odd look on his face. He didn't seem to hear the questions in Richard's voice. "Well . . . good for him." He clapped Richard on the back, kind of hard, and headed downstairs.

● ● ·

In the kitchen, Ginny was back. She twirled round and round as Abigail stuffed deviled eggs. "Dance on your feet, Daddy!" She skipped toward him.

"Not now," Don replied gruffly. He reached into the refrigerator for a beer. "Later. During the fireworks."

Abigail looked up from her work with a frown. But Ginny pouted for only a moment before starting to twirl again. "I'm not going with you tonight." She did a little curtsy before continuing. "I will be sitting with Senator Johnson and his girls. I'm going to interview him about his feelings during the fireworks."

"Wait, you mean it's just going to be me with . . ." Richard snapped his mouth shut. If anyone saw him alone with his parents, when every other boy he knew was at that pool party, he'd look so pathetic. With Ginny there at least he could claim his mom had demanded a family outing.

Abigail sighed and looked to Don for help.

He took a swig and eyed Richard for a moment before putting the bottle down on the counter. His dad got what was bothering him. "Tell you what, son. Let's get out of your mom's way. Today's the very first Fourth of July that the National Archives are open for viewing the Declaration of Independence. Just think, on this day a hundred . . ." He paused. "Hmmmm . . . 1953 minus 1776 is . . . is . . ." He squinted his eyes in subtraction.

"One hundred seventy-seven," Richard said, jumping to show off his quick math skills.

"Right! So let's celebrate the one hundred seventy-seventh anniversary of Americans thumbing their noses at the king!" He laughed at his own enthusiasm. "Then I'll treat us to lunch. Guy to guy. Patriots!"

"Really, Dad? Just you and me?"

Don grinned. "Yeah, and let's make it a steak and oysters at Harvey's. We'll go all in. That'll put hair on your chest."

Richard suddenly felt a foot taller. Who knew that a day that started out so awful could turn so great? He'd have to remember this the next time he felt like a total reject.

● ● ·

Within the hour, Richard and Don stood in the vaulted rotunda of the National Archives, surrounded by gleaming marble,

Corinthian columns, and two huge murals representing all the signers of the Declaration of Independence and the Constitution. People around them spoke in hushed whispers, reverent in such a grand temple to ideas.

"Ain't she gorgeous?" Don leaned over, almost pressing his nose to the glass to read the opening lines of Jefferson's bold words. "'We hold these truths to be self-evident, that all men are created equal, that they are endowed by their Creator with certain unalienable Rights . . .' Damn straight," he murmured and straightened up to look at the life-size founding fathers in the murals. "Way to go, boys."

As they descended the Archives' wide white marble steps onto Constitution Avenue, Don detailed just how God-awful Jefferson's punishment would have been had the revolution failed. He got all excited about historical stuff. "Before hanging him, the British would have drawn and quartered TJ and ripped out his guts and burned them!"

He paused, seeing Richard's look of disgust. "Sorry, kiddo. All I'm saying is those guys were brave."

He laughed at himself and gazed catty-corner across the street at the Pantheon-like National Gallery of Art. Then he turned to look up the wide boulevard toward the Capitol building. A cool dignity, a sense of destiny, emanated off all that polished white stone, built in such balanced symmetry. Richard had to admit it was pretty gorgeous where they stood.

"We Americans have our faults, son. But our bodacious liberties"—Don pointed his thumb back toward the Archives—"our respect for freedom of speech and religion and the rights of each individual—that's worth protecting." He nodded, almost as if convincing himself of something. "That's why I'm back at the FBI. We were supposed to have made the world safe for democracy by fighting World War II. That's what they promised us. But . . ." He trailed off.

"You were a tail gunner, right, Dad?"

Don startled out of his thoughts at the question. "Yup."

"See a lot of action back there?"

"Yup."

"Did you choose that particular gun, Dad?"

"Oh, the Air Corps put me there because of all that sharp-shooting training at the FBI, I suppose."

"Was it . . ." Richard hesitated. This was his chance to find out what bugged his dad so much. "Was it hard? Like how the *Saturday Evening Post* article described Okinawa?"

"What?" Don looked sideways at Richard and then away. "Well, let's just say it was no walk in the park, son. War is hell. That's why I'm back at the FBI, trying to stop threats to the United States before they snowball into another one."

His jawline twitched like he was grinding his teeth. "Let's get those oysters."

● ● ·

Richard had never been in the legendary Harvey's restaurant. But he knew it was where Washington's celebrities— congressmen and White House staff—went for lunch. He bet the place was crawling with spies, too. Vying to get a table close to some big-deal official, so they could eavesdrop during their shrimp cocktail.

This was swell! Maybe his dad would be eyeballing some foreign agents while the jerks checked out a senator. Don had said it was his job to know the difference between Reds and people who just liked Russian music. Maybe he'd witness his dad spot a pinko traitor!

Richard and his dad joined a long line of men in seersucker suits and ladies in white cotton gloves and little pillbox hats.

"Wow, I didn't think it'd be this busy today," Don said. "But it'll be worth the wait, Rich. You're old enough to appreciate all this now. Best oysters anywhere. And don't tell your mom, but their crabmeat Norfolk is as good as hers. I'll take the Fifth if you repeat that." He winked at Richard as two couples were ushered to a table and the line inched forward.

Richard could now peer around the bodies to see a slice of the activity inside. Propeller-big ceiling fans swept the rising cigarette smoke into drifting puffs of fog, as elderly Black waiters in white shirts, white aprons, and crisp bow ties took orders. Mahogany wood and brass fixtures were polished to a sheen, reflecting sunbeams spilling through the windows. The dining room was loud with clinking china, almost-shouted table conversations, and the scrape of chairs pushed back as men recognized one another and stood to shake hands.

Nobody looked like a Red. But that was the point, according to Philbrick. Subversives were supposed to blend in. Once they were seated, Richard would ask Don exactly what telltale signs he should be looking for.

The maître d' ushered in a large group, making Don and Richard only six people back from his podium. Now Richard could see that amid all that frenzied eating and delivering of food there was a calm pool of empty tables not far from the entrance and next to the stairway leading to the restaurant's second floor. Richard waited to see if that was where the group would sit, but they were led up the steps instead.

The aroma of hot butter, garlic, and steaming oysters was getting pretty irresistible. Richard's stomach rumbled. He started to ask Don about the empty tables when the maître d' waved in the last patrons ahead of them. He and his father stepped into the black-and-white–tiled foyer.

"We're next!" Don grinned. Then he stiffened. "Damn it. I didn't think he'd be here today."

Richard followed his dad's gaze. *Hey!* Wasn't that Mr. Hoover himself, sitting with his right-hand man at the FBI, smack-dab in the middle of all those empty tables?

Just as Richard was about to point at the bureau director, Don put his hand on Richard's shoulder. He gripped it tight. "I'm sorry, son. How about we—"

He stopped midsentence and plastered a fake smile on his face when Hoover spotted him and gestured for him to come over.

"Wait here." Don strode into the fray.

When Don approached the table, Hoover reached out and put his hand on Don's forearm. Seemed friendly enough, but a real courtesy would have been a handshake, Richard knew that much. Sitting there, Hoover looked a lot like the boxer dogs he owned—thickset around his middle, dark eyes and brows, and his nose kind of squashed like he'd walked into a door. Even as he smiled at Don, it looked like a weird little snarl to Richard.

Watching the scene, he noticed a number of patrons had stopped talking to eye his dad. The waiters looked pretty surprised he was standing there, too. Don had suddenly become the center of attention.

Richard felt himself swell up with pride, like a puffer fish. His dad had to be pretty darn important for the director to call him over like that. Maybe Hoover was telling him about a spy in a corner table he was supposed to tail!

Richard held his breath as he watched.

Don leaned down. The director spoke into his ear and handed him something. A top secret document? But as Don came back toward him, Richard could see it was a wad of money his father was stuffing into his jacket's breast pocket.

Why money? Maybe it was to bribe some stool pigeon, like in a Mickey Spillane detective novel.

"Come on, Rich," Don said, his voice hoarse, his face flushed red. "Let's go to Hot Shoppes. I have a hankering for an Orange Freeze shake and a Mighty Mo burger." He walked out the door.

Hot Shoppes? What? What about casing Harvey's for spies? What about their special man-to-man lunch? The drive-in was kids' stuff, a poor man's substitute for Harvey's. And Richard had been pretty stoked to try those oysters, just like tasting the coffee Don always drank.

"Dad, wait!" Richard called.

But Don was already halfway down the block. When he caught up, Richard could tell by the set of his dad's jaw that he shouldn't ask any questions. All of a sudden, Don was in one of *those* moods.

BANG. Bang, bang, bang!

Across the street a couple of kids lit a string of cherry bomb firecrackers and threw them into the air. Richard flinched and gasped and then laughed at himself as he watched the boys run off, shouting insults at each other.

Cherry bombs! Well, if he wasn't getting treated to Harvey's, maybe he could guilt his dad into buying him some cherry bombs to replace the stupid sparklers. "Hey, Dad, do you think we could stop at a fireworks stand on the way home and pick up some—" Richard broke off, seeing his father's reaction.

Don was searching the sky frantically, then looked over his shoulder. His face was ashen and his whole body quaking.

"Dad?"

Don shook his head, like a wet dog shudders off water. He turned to Richard. For a second, it was like his father didn't recognize him. Then Don's eyes cleared. "Step on it, son," he snapped. "I haven't got all day. I've got something I need to do now."

When they got in their green Chevrolet, Don's hands were shaking so badly, he could barely get the key into the car's ignition. Richard had seen that before, so many times—but now he put two and two together. Don's hand shook when he was startled by a sudden and loud, sharp noise. Or when he *really* didn't like something someone said. Just like the magazine article described.

Richard had always just chalked up such moments to Don having a big personality, a little bit of a temper—being a little jumpy, maybe. But now, according to the *Saturday Evening Post,* he had a scary new word for his dad's reactions: *psycho.*

Chapter 3:

AUGUST

1953

Senator Joe McCarthy, Republican from Wisconsin

Senator McCarthy investigates security leaks at the Government Printing Office (GPO). He targets a bookbinder accused of being a Communist and stealing a secret code from the Merchant Marines. The GPO's loyalty review board has cleared the bookbinder four times, but McCarthy's committee pursues the case.

During a closed session with McCarthy, the bookbinder answers questions freely, denying he is a Communist. But the next day, during the committee's public hearing, his attorney discovers that the transcript of the private conversation from the day before seems altered to more convincingly prove the bookbinder's "guilt." The attorney advises his client to take the Fifth Amendment—his constitutional right not to give self-incriminating evidence.

McCarthy is furious. "Your refusing to answer is telling the world you have been selling secrets," he barks. The senator has a smear term for witnesses refusing to answer his hostile questions by taking that constitutional protection: "Fifth-Amendment Communists."

Ultimately the bookbinder loses his job. FBI reports had questioned his loyalty, but the main justification for his dismissal is the fact he placed small bets at local horse races with coworkers. Gambling of any sort, even among friends, could make a person vulnerable to blackmail from the Soviets, according to McCarthyism.

Everyone on the GPO loyalty board that had previously cleared the bookbinder is fired as well.

The Soviet Union test-explodes its first hydrogen bomb. Soviet officials crow that the United States "no longer has a monopoly" on the hydrogen bomb or dominance in the Cold War face-off. The two diametrically opposed superpowers are now equal in their ability to annihilate each other with atomic weapons.

Hydrogen bomb test

RICHARD sprawled on his bed in front of the whirring window fan, breathless, nauseated. He'd almost gotten caught! He'd been snooping in his father's tall dresser, unscrewing his pipes to see if any of them were actually secret-agent pistols, when his mother came in with a stack of folded laundry. Thank God she'd been preoccupied with balancing all those towels so he could slip out without her spotting him.

The wild pounding of his heart slowed as Richard lay on his back staring at his bedroom's sky-blue wallpaper, dotted with fighter planes. Sometimes, when he couldn't sleep at night, or was really wound tight about something, Richard counted those tiny airplanes. His dad had hung the wallpaper, and there were lots of bubbles where Don hadn't rolled it down tight. But Richard didn't care. He loved that paper.

He flipped onto his stomach, rattling the twin bed. How could he have explained himself if Abigail had seen him? He replayed the scene in his mind, realizing he'd left some of the pipes unscrewed. He'd have to go back to put them together. And it hadn't even been worth the risk—they were all just plain old pipes.

What a dumb-bunny. What a baby. *You're entering high school—the big time—in two weeks, man*, he reprimanded himself.

Maybe there'd be some upperclassmen he could talk to. Guys who might have read some of the books he had that summer—like *The Count of Monte Cristo* or *The Sword in the Stone*. He was dying to talk to somebody about that book *The Catcher in the Rye* and the way Holden started out being a total piece of work and then turned all angsty and poetical. It was like the author, J. D. Salinger, could see right into Richard's heart. It'd been a great summer that way, at least—finding all sorts of truths written by authors who felt like friends, just like Holden said.

Richard had read a bunch of stuff. As soon as his mother stole *Robin Hood* and purged their bookshelf, Richard read *The Maltese Falcon* by that Red subversive Dashiell Hammett. Abigail had obviously forgotten that Don had given Richard a copy of his own. He didn't do it to be defiant. Honest. He just wanted to know what the big deal was. He was all in for watching out for commie spies. After all, he wanted to be a G-man.

But books? Come on. They were sacred.

Take Steinbeck's *The Red Pony*. He'd read that just to see how dangerous the author really was. Richard couldn't see a Red being able to write so beautifully. He'd even written down one of Steinbeck's descriptions, it was so well turned.

Richard hung over the edge of his bed and pulled out the notebook he filled with observations that impressed him, pieces of conversations he overheard, and lines from books he loved.

He flipped through the pages to find: *"He was only a little boy, ten years old, with hair like dusty yellow grass and with shy polite gray eyes, and with a mouth that worked when he thought."*

Richard had loved that way of describing a kid who actually thought as he talked.

He tucked the notebook back under the bed, into a shoe box he kept next to a shirt box full of songs he was writing. That one was top secret. No one knew about that box and its contents. Not even Don.

Philbrick would never have gotten caught unscrewing pipes. Sighing in disgust with himself, Richard reached to his nightstand for *I Led 3 Lives* and flipped the book to his favorite passage—the part where Agent Philbrick astounded the courtroom and horrified eleven Communists on trial with the revelation that he had been an FBI double agent all along. His testimony was the very first time the FBI had publicly acknowledged it had undercover agents working inside the Communist Party. Philbrick's statement drew gasps in the courtroom, glares from the defendants, and panic from their attorneys. *"I sat back in the witness chair"*—Richard read the phrases he'd highlighted—*". . . a great weight rolled off my shoulders. . . . Now for the first time . . . I was able to shrug off the burden of those nine years, and to square myself with my family, my friends, and the world."*

How cool was that? Braving all sorts of stuff, all alone, to keep the country safe. Richard could hardly wait for the TV show to start in October.

For the thousandth time, Richard mulled over the meaning of that wad of money Hoover had shoved at his dad on the Fourth of July. It had to be money to buy some info from Reds, or for Don to throw around at their gatherings to look like some big-time operator in DC that the commies would love to turn. Philbrick said he'd done that.

No wonder his dad was so tense and preoccupied and impatient sometimes—Philbrick said he'd been that way plenty, given the stress he was under. If he used Philbrick's experiences as the litmus test, Don wasn't a "psycho"—he had to be an undercover agent, a secret hero! That's what Richard loved about books—they provided insights that could be such a relief.

Maybe someday Richard would be watching his dad destroy a couple of Reds in court! And boy oh boy, wouldn't he rub that into Jimmy's face then!

"Richie?" Ginny knocked on his door with her foot.

Irritated at having his epiphany interrupted, Richard shouted, "Stop calling me Richie!"

"Okay, Dickie. Open the door."

"I'm reading!"

Ginny kicked again. "Mom sent me. It's very, very, *very* urgent."

Richard rolled off his bed. "You know, Ginny, it's dumb to use *very* with a word like *urgent*." He jerked his door open to find his little sister holding a laundry basket full of flashlights. "What gives?"

"Take one and put it on your bedside table. It's *urgent*." She made a face on the word.

"What for?"

"You know how Russia—I mean the Soviets—just exploded their own superbomb?"

"Yeah?" The news had sent the whole country's nerves ajangle.

"Well, if the commies drop the H-bomb on us, our electricity will go out. The blast might shake our house enough that it breaks our gas pipes and our house will fill up with gas. Then if we strike a match to light a candle to see, we could blow up!"

Richard snorted. "Sis, we live in Washington, DC. We're ground zero. If the Soviets drop their new bomb on our capital, we're toast before the flash."

Ginny shook her head. "And where will this negative thinking get us, mister?"

Richard laughed in spite of himself. How did she imitate their mom that well?

Ginny grinned back at him. "That's what our bomb shelter will be for."

"What bomb shelter, Gin?" Richard asked.

"The basement! Mom and I are filling the cellar with canned foods and first aid and soap and towels and water for a month, plus bedding and potassium tablets and batteries and a crank-up radio and books to read. Oh, and cards. Mom says if we have to stay down there for long it'll be the perfect time for her to teach us to play bridge."

For some reason, it was the idea of happily learning a card game during a nuclear holocaust that got him. "What the heck are you talking about?"

"Civil preparedness, silly! I just copied out a checklist from the *Saturday Evening Post* about what we are supposed to do when the sirens go off. Mom taped it to the refrigerator. You better look at it." Ginny raised her eyebrow before turning to head for their parents' bedroom with her flashlights.

● ● ·

Richard bounded down the stairs to the kitchen. Sure enough, in Ginny's perfect printing, on lined homework assignment paper, was a list of things to do during an air-raid threat.

BEFORE.

Turn off the pilot lights in the stove and water heater and furnace.

Close all doors and windows and curtains.

Shut the fireplace flue.

Put car in the garage and roll up windows.

If caught outside, lie in a ditch or behind a sign. Cover yourself with a raincoat or an awning or newspapers. Do not hurry to get up after the blast. Crawl out from under your covering so that no dust falls on you.

Cover your mouth.

Do not step in puddles.

Walk in streets with tall buildings and against the wind.

AFTER.

Do not touch anything that looks like ash. It could be bits of unexploded uranium.

Do not use silverware. It holds radiation.

Shower. Scrub skin and hair.

Drink only the water in the basement containers. Boiling water concentrates radioactive pollution.

Underneath the list was a crayon drawing Ginny had done of the White House with a set of circles radiating out from the famous building in blast zones. Each zone showed the time and magnitude of impact with each passing mile away from the president's mansion. She'd copied it from a real estate ad that promoted houses for sale just beyond the blast radius.

"Mom?" Richard turned to Abigail, who was pulling a meat loaf from the oven. She didn't hear him over the radio, blaring the daily broadcast of *Arthur Godfrey Time.* He snapped off the folksy commentator. "Do we have to keep this list on the refrigerator?"

Abigail looked up, her face red from the stove's heat. "It gives me the willies, too, honey. But it's very important to Ginny."

Willies seemed a mild term for how he felt about being cooked alive in a thermonuclear blast. "Where's Dad?"

"Mr. Hoover called him in."

"But it's Saturday."

"I know, but it seemed urgent to Mr. Hoover."

Urgent to Mr. Hoover? His dad must be working undercover!

But then he noticed Abigail was frowning. Distracted, she managed to burn her wrist on the scalding pan as she slid it onto a trivet. "Doggone it!" she yelped, and then muttered something else under her breath. She stuck her arm under running water to soothe it.

"Geez, Mom, be careful!" Richard pulled some baking soda from the cabinet for her to make a paste that would pull out the sting. "You okay? Why are you cooking meat loaf in the middle of the day, anyway? It's too hot to eat it."

"Oh, gosh. I hadn't thought of that." Abigail looked deflated. "Well, they can refrigerate it and use it for sandwiches."

"They?" Richard asked.

She stopped running the water to sprinkle some baking soda on the burn. "We have new neighbors! Mrs. Emerson told me all about them. They just came from New York City.

She thinks the husband was doing something connected with the United Nations. Before that, he was posted to our embassy in Czechoslovakia. So they must be State Department people. Hopefully they aren't closet Reds or pinkos, like Senator McCarthy claims most Foreign Service Officers are," she said with a laugh.

"The best part is—Mrs. Emerson says they have a son about your age! So . . ." She gave Richard a hug with her good arm and then tugged on his sleeve. "A new friend! Let's go meet them."

She picked up the meat loaf dish with oven mitts and headed for the door. "Come on!" She smiled at him over her shoulder.

"Aw, Mom." She made him sound so desperate. Was it that obvious?

As Abigail walked a block down and over, her meat loaf still steaming and the wide skirt of her pink-and-green plaid dress swinging back and forth like a willow in a gentle breeze, Richard followed, daring to hope.

● ● ·

A moving van was rammed up under the low-hanging cherry trees in front of the brick house. Its yard was littered with boxes, bicycles, a grill, shovels, hoses, and rakes the movers had unloaded and dropped there. At the front entrance was a woman nailing something into the doorway. Her black hair was cropped short in little waves around her head, and she wore a sleeveless red top over straight, narrow, to-the-ankle Capri pants.

"Oh, my goodness," murmured Abigail. "She's so glamorous. She looks like Audrey Hepburn." She cleared her throat and called, "Hello! Welcome to Forest Hills! Mrs. White?"

The lady turned abruptly, hammer in hand, and the object she had been trying to hang fell to the ground, bouncing under a thick azalea.

"Oh dear! I'm so sorry to have startled you. Let my son help you with that." Abigail elbowed Richard. "I always ask my husband, Don, to hang things for me. I'm all thumbs."

While Richard crawled under the bush, Abigail introduced them. "I'm Abigail Bradley. But please call me Abby. We live on the next street over. This is my son, Richard. I've brought you dinner. Unpacking is such a nuisance. No time to cook!"

"How very kind! Please, come in." The lady's voice was husky with a slight accent. She held the door open and added, "And please, no need for the *Mrs.* Call me Teresa." The two women stepped inside.

Under the azalea, Richard found a thin gold box, about the size of a pen. On it was painted a tiny candelabra and a six-pointed star. He brought it to the kitchen. His mother was already at work, putting teacups in the whitewashed cabinets.

"Ah, thank you so much, Richard." Teresa held out her hand. "That is very dear to me. My grandmother's mezuzah."

"What's that?"

"Oh, it's a very special thing. Jews believe God protects homes with a mezuzah at the door. I was raised Catholic. But my *bobeshi* really wanted me to have it when Mr. White and I had to flee Prague."

"You had to flee your home?" Abigail's face puckered with concern. "How terrible."

"I was lucky to be married to a member of the American diplomatic corps. I could get out, with my children, before the Nazis came."

"What's a *bobeshi*?" The question just kind of burst out of Richard. "Sorry," he added, seeing Abigail frowning at him.

Teresa smiled at Abigail. "I do not mind. I encourage our children to ask about such things. That is how they learn, yes? My husband says we forward peace by coming to understand one another's backgrounds. I personally believe talking to teenagers as if they are children keeps them children and doesn't prepare them for the real world."

Wow. Richard was liking this woman.

Teresa turned back to him. "*Bobeshi* is Yiddish for *grandmother*. Mine died in Hitler's concentration camps, so I put up the mezuzah in her memory. You've never seen one?"

Richard shook his head.

Teresa looked at Abigail with surprise. "Really? We purchased this home because the realtor told us this neighborhood did not have any restrictive covenants. I was quite horrified to learn many still did against Blacks and Jews. There was a lovely house we liked, but the deed actually said the owners could not sell to Semitics or Armenians, Persians, or Syrians. I just couldn't live in a neighborhood with such attitudes.

"Do you think it will be a problem if I hang my mezuzah? There has been such a horrendous spike of anti-Semitic rhetoric after the Rosenbergs' conviction, since they were Jewish."

"Oh, no. Richard just hasn't noticed them before." Abigail waved her hand at Richard and laughed lightly. "You know boys."

But he could tell his mother was taken aback by so much honesty. That wasn't her style at all. Her company conversation usually revolved around articles in *Ladies' Home Journal*, recipes, and garden-club tips for arranging flowers.

Abigail opened another box and began stacking plates onto the kitchen counter. She changed the subject. "I heard your husband was posted to Prague before the war. Did you two meet there?"

Teresa brightened. "Yes, I was a first-year student at the university. He was this young, handsome cultural attaché. We met at an art show and fell in love instantly. Natalia and Vladimir were both born in Prague. Of course, when Hitler invaded, the embassy closed and relocated to London for the duration. Is your husband at State as well? Is that how you know of us?"

"Oh, no. We just have a neighbor who makes it her business to be well informed. I'm sure she will be by soon. A Mrs. Emerson. She's very sweet, but take my advice and don't eat the Rice Krispies Treats she's sure to bring you. Hard as cement." Abigail shook her head. "Also, don't tell her anything you don't want the whole neighborhood to know."

"I'll remember that," Teresa said with a smile.

"No, my husband was a gunner on a bomber during the war. Then he rejoined the FBI afterward," Abigail continued. "By the way, you might see the director's car pass by here. Mr. Hoover lives right around the corner. On the same block as Senator Johnson and his family, as a matter of fact."

"The FBI's Hoover? Really?" Teresa paused. "I hadn't realized." She closed one of the kitchen's white cabinets with an oddly loud *snap*.

Abigail seemed disappointed that Teresa didn't ask for more gossip about the neighborhood's famous residents. To

Richard, at least, Teresa seemed a bit frosty suddenly. Or annoyed, maybe. Or . . . ? *Hmmmm*. He just couldn't really read her expression.

"Speaking of Vladi." Teresa was the one to change the subject this time. "He will be so pleased to meet you, Richard. Go ahead upstairs."

She was sending him up there without warning her son first? Richard looked to his mother, who would have called him down to the living room to meet someone new and overseen handshakes and proper cotillion-style introductions. Abigail shrugged slightly and nodded at him in permission to go on up, before saying to Teresa, "Now, what else can I do? Where do you want these pots?"

● ● ·

The house was laid out exactly as Richard's: a center-hallway brick colonial, a dining room and kitchen to the right, a long living room on the left, and a side porch off that. This porch was finished, though, to make it into a year-round room. He could see the sunroom was jammed with ripped-open boxes and piles of paints, brushes, palettes, canvases, and easels, all awash in bright sunshine.

Curious, he tiptoed into the living room. It was a jumble of dark antiques, carved cabinets and tables juxtaposed with bright-colored modular chairs and weird artwork that looked like splotches of color. Except one. That piece was actually a poster for a 1947 exhibit in Prague with a painting by someone named Robert Gwathmey. Three Black people looked horribly sad while one of them played guitar. The melancholy of their expressions was emphasized by the fact that their bodies were built with geometric shapes and thick black outlines. The effect was powerful.

But it was the books that made him really want to snoop. Open crates of them were everywhere. *The Beautiful and Damned* by F. Scott Fitzgerald, *The Sun Also Rises* by Ernest Hemingway, *Animal Farm* by George Orwell—those titles he recognized. But there were also things by people he didn't know at all: Truman Capote, Ezra Pound, Albert Camus, Gertrude Stein, D. H. Lawrence, and T. S. Eliot.

"Whoa, wait a minute." He picked up *Invisible Man*. It was a recently published novel that he'd heard about plenty. Its author, Ralph Ellison, was Black, and the novel was merciless in depicting white people as racists and fools. Richard's English teacher had been really worked up about it, and not in a good way. Richard dropped the book and headed for the stairway.

A kind of battle of the bands danced down its steps to him. First a piano and a delicate, lilting voice in slow song: *Good morning, heartache, here we go again. . . . You're the one who knew me when. . . .* Bursting out against that was totally different music: raucous, fast piano riffs, constant drumbeats, and alternating saxophone and trumpets tearing up and down the octaves.

The dueling records were playing so loud, the girl inside the room he passed first didn't even notice him. A replica of Teresa in looks but wearing an embroidered peasant-like blouse and jeans, she was packing rather then emptying a suitcase. Her room was the source of the blues singer. On her door was taped a pennant for UCLA.

Shy, Richard hurried past.

Across the hall came the rowdy tunes. Richard slowly approached, wondering how in the world to begin a conversation. He recognized the music as jazz. But he had no idea who the artist was. As he neared, he could hear banging and slaps as Vladimir kept his own drumbeat on his walls. Richard peeped around the open door. A tall, thin boy was waggling drumsticks and tapping in rhythm on the windowsill while wiggling his bottom to the music. LPs were strewn all over the floor. Richard couldn't even see the bed under a heap of clothes and books and magazines and sheet music. But balanced on top of all that was a saxophone.

He knocked, gingerly. Boy, he'd hate it if someone caught him dancing to music. Vladimir didn't respond. Richard knocked again. But all that did was prompt Vladimir to look at his record player as if it were malfunctioning. Richard tried a third time, louder. Vladimir stopped, cocked his head, and then threw down his sticks, shouting as he headed for the door, "Need something, Natalia?"

He crashed right into Richard. "Geez Louise! Who are you?"

"A . . . a . . . Your neighbor. Your mom sent me up here."

Vladimir made a face. "She's like that."

"Yeah. Moms." Richard shrugged. "Whatcha gonna do?"

"Well?"

"Well what?" Richard knew he sounded totally lame. He could feel his freckles heating up.

"Got a name, man?"

"Oh, right. Richard."

"I'm Vlad." They shook hands.

"Know Charlie Parker?" Vladimir asked.

"No, I don't. Is he a friend of yours?"

Vladimir laughed. "My buddies warned me Washington was square. Well, it'll be my job to change that." He pointed to his room. "That." He grinned. "That bebop. That's Charlie Parker. Do you dig jazz?"

This was a test, clearly. Richard knew he had already flunked the first question. He took a chance on stuff his dad listened to. "Don't know this. But I like Louis Armstrong." Seeing Vladimir's approval, he added, "Yeah, old Satchmo. Boy, can he can blow that horn. I like Count Basie and Duke Ellington, too."

"All right! The pioneers. There's hope for you." Vladimir punched Richard's shoulder before running his hands through his own thick, wavy black hair to get it out of his eyes. No way Don would ever let Richard grow his hair that long.

The record ended, and Vladimir rushed into his room to lift the needle and stop the *scratch-scratch-scratch*. He snapped off the record player.

"Soooooo . . ." Richard stayed awkwardly in the hallway. Now what?

"Soooo . . ." Vladimir countered. There was a long pause.

Richard looked around the room, trying to find something to spark conversation. His eyes fell on the pile of things on Vladimir's bed. "Hey, you've got a copy of *The Catcher in the Rye*." Out in the open!

"Yeah, you want to borrow it?"

Richard tried to stay cool. "Nah, I have a copy of it already."

Vladimir smiled with approval. "Don't you love the way Holden just goes out on the town in New York City on his own?"

"Yeah. And the way he talks to all the cabdrivers."

"Oh man, Salinger really gets those guys. That driver who's so worked up when Holden asks if he knows what happens to the ducks over winter? Spot-on. Talking to a teed-off cabdriver is like sticking your head in a lion's mouth. Ask a cabdriver an existential question like that and you'll get your head taken off. Stick to the Knicks with cabbies, I say. Old Holden Caulfield. What a character."

Richard had no idea what *existential* meant. But he nodded. "Yeah, what a hoot."

"Soooooooooo, any fields of rye around here?"

Richard laughed again. This was great! Someone he could really talk to!

"Seriously, though, man, what's there to do in this neighborhood?"

Richard thought for a moment. "There are great bike paths in Rock Creek Park. We can get to the National Zoo on them."

"Too hot for that today."

"There's a bakery and ice-cream counter not far from here."

"Hmmmm. Nah, just had lunch. Hey, is there a movie theater anywhere nearby?"

"Yeah, the Uptown is a ten-minute walk, maybe fifteen, on Connecticut Avenue."

"Swell! There's this new flick out called *From Here to Eternity*. It's got Burt Lancaster and Frank Sinatra. Wait. You know who they are, right?" Vladimir grinned.

Richard tensed. That was exactly the kind of question Jimmy would have asked, but it would have been all snarky. He realized with relief that this boy's teasing was good-natured rather than snide. "Yeeeaaah."

"Righto! Let's go check it out." Vladimir was already racing down the stairs, shouting, "Mom! Hey, Mom, where are you?"

Both mothers were still in the kitchen. Abigail was sitting on the floor in a snowdrift of crumpled newspapers, pulling out finely etched wineglasses from a box and handing them one at a time to Teresa.

"We want to see a movie, Mom," Vladimir announced.

"Of course, *miláček.*" She pulled open a drawer, fished out her wallet, and handed him two dollars. "Treat Richard in thanks for all this gracious help his mother is lending me. We'll be done with the kitchen in no time, thanks to Abby. Do you know where you're going?"

"Richard does."

"That okay with you, Mom?" Richard asked, dreading her answer. Usually Abigail wanted to know exactly what the movie was about and who was in it and if it had any bad language or inappropriate guy-girl stuff before she would decide yea or nay. It was so embarrassing. He plastered a plea on his face and prayed she saw it.

Abigail took a deep breath. "Be home by dinner, honey."

"Thanks, Mom!" He grinned his gratitude, but still made sure he and his new friend escaped from the house before she could change her mind. As the boys trotted down the front porch stairs, Vladimir said, "You're going to love this film. I hear there's a really steamy scene between Lancaster and Deborah Kerr on the beach!"

Wow, this guy is wild, thought Richard. Maybe high school wouldn't be so bad after all.

Chapter 4:

SEPTEMBER

1953

Lucille Ball, the wildly popular star of *I Love Lucy*, is called into a private hearing with the House Un-American Committee (HUAC). The nation's top TV comedienne admits that she voted in a Communist primary election in 1936. But she says she did so only because her socialist grandfather had insisted. At a press conference in their backyard, her husband and costar, Desi Arnaz, defends her, joking: "The only thing red about Lucy is her hair, and even that is not legitimate."

Unlike other Hollywood actors and artists, the much-beloved actress is not blacklisted. Perhaps because she freely "confesses" and perhaps because FBI director J. Edgar Hoover says Lucy and Desi are among his "favorites of the entertainment world."

(Opposite) Lucille Ball and Desi Arnaz

Eight years after the end of World War II, England is able to stop restricting the amounts of sugar people can purchase, finally ending its wartime food rationing.

Senator John F. Kennedy marries prominent socialite Jacqueline Lee Bouvier.

RICHARD shifted his weight back and forth on his feet. He, Abigail, and Don had been standing forever in the reception line at Senator Joseph McCarthy's wedding. During the first twenty minutes, he'd been pretty entertained, speculating who in the crowd might be some kind of double agent. This was a party for the world's chief Red-hunter, after all. The room was full of important people that commies would love to turn. Someone there was sure to be a Red up to no good.

Richard's fascination with conspiracy theories had been fueled by a book Vladimir lent him that so far was only published in England—*Casino Royale* by Ian Fleming. A friend from "across the pond" had shipped it over. "I know you like all that spy stuff," Vlad had said as he tossed it to him. It was a crazy-good story about a British secret agent named James Bond.

But Richard was bored now with searching all the tuxedoed men at the wedding party for a Le Chiffre–style bad guy or an M-like king of intelligence gathering. He glanced at his mom. She looked so happy to be in the Washington Club's ornate ballroom. Evidently, she'd made her coming-out-to-society debut there when she was seventeen years old. *Eons ago*, she'd joked. She hadn't known Don then. They'd met at a soda fountain right after that and fallen head over heels, despite her parents' objections that Don was "just" a G-man.

She looked really pretty right now, smiling softly and gazing up at the chandeliers. So Richard stifled himself from complaining about the wait.

"Don, half the Senate's here," Abigail whispered. "And a lot of White House staffers."

Don nodded.

She reached out to brush Richard's hair into company-presentable place. With his crew cut, it was a pretty unnecessary gesture.

"Mom! Stop embarrassing me."

Abigail giggled nervously. "Sorry, honey." She patted his cheek. "You look very handsome, son." Then, barely skipping a beat, she tugged on Don's tuxedo sleeve and whispered, "Oh look, isn't that the CIA director? I thought you told me that he doesn't like McCarthy."

Don shot her a *shhhhhhhh* look even as he smiled fondly at her. He lowered his voice and leaned in toward them to answer. "He doesn't. But people are too afraid of McCarthy to not come to something for him if invited. Even if they hate the guy." Then he straightened and plastered on a party smile.

Abigail peeped down the row. "Jean looks beautiful, don't you think, Don? She always was, even when she was bitty and I babysat her."

"You're the best-looking lady here tonight, honey." Don kissed her on her blond curls.

Geez, thought Richard, the two of them were so . . . What would Vladimir say? *Schmaltzy.* Richard liked how in love his parents were. But yeah, *schmaltzy.* That was the right word for it.

Time to change the scenario.

"Where's Gin? Maybe I should go find her?" Richard asked hopefully. Abigail had allowed Ginny to wander the ballroom as long as she came back in time to thank the senator and his new wife when the family reached the end of the line—the perks of being younger. "She might feel kind of lost in all these grown-ups, you know," Richard said. He sure would have been when he was her age.

Don laughed. "She's holding her own." He nodded toward the vaulted windows, framed with ornate sconce chandeliers, where Ginny was chatting up Senator Kennedy's new wife, Jackie.

"How does she do that?" Richard murmured to himself. His little sister was definitely becoming a force to be reckoned with, and he wasn't so sure how he felt about it. She was so weirdly smart and starting to monopolize their parents' attention. Every once in a while he got a hot stab of jealousy about her. It felt awful—making him mad and sorry at the same time.

Like now, as Don said, "That girl sure has pluck—just walking up to Jackie Kennedy like that."

Ever since *Life* magazine did a cover story about her, Jackie had become the darling of the country—young, eloquent, fashionable, and aristocratically gracious. The adults vying for her attention were looking pretty peeved at being upstaged by a nine-year-old. Finally, Ginny shook Jackie's hand and skipped back to her family.

"What in the world were you two talking about, sugarplum?" Don asked.

"I was asking her advice about getting a job at a newspaper when I grow up," Ginny said matter-of-factly. "You know, she used to be the Inquiring Camera Girl for the *Washington Times-Herald*. She was telling me how she just roved the city, taking pictures of people and asking them questions about the day's issues for her column. And guess what, Mom?

She interviewed Vice President Nixon and drew sketches of President Eisenhower's inauguration and even covered Queen Elizabeth's coronation! Isn't that astonishing?"

"You don't say!" answered Abigail. She smiled slightly with amusement before echoing, "Astonishing!"

"It's too bad she can't do it anymore, now that's she's married," said Ginny.

"Maybe you need to take her place, then, until some lucky dog steals your heart. But now," Don said, turning her to face forward, "to meet Senator McCarthy."

"Hey, Dad?" Richard tried to get into the conversation. "Wasn't the senator a tail gunner during the war, like you?"

Don grunted. "That's what his campaign slogan said."

"Did you ever meet—"

"*Shhhh*, honey," Abigail interrupted. "We're next."

● ● ·

There he was. The self-proclaimed man of the year, looking very uncomfortable in his formal morning coattails and striped pants. He had dark, thinning hair, greased back flat on his large round head, and black, cigar-thick eyebrows. Even as he joked, the senator's meaty face seemed slightly sinister.

"Yes, yes." McCarthy was nodding as he shook the hand of the man ahead of Richard's family. "We're off to the Caribbean for a month. But I'll swim back if I have to, if there's trouble." He clapped the guy on the back and the man staggered forward a little.

"Oh, surely, dear, your committee can take care of things while we're away." His new wife smiled sweetly.

McCarthy ignored her. "Make no mistake, we're dealing with an epidemic. Even a day with our guard down is dangerous. Since the war ended and those lily-livered Democrats let Stalin take over Eastern Europe, the number of Communists in the world has multiplied four hundred times, I tell you— as fast as alley cats breed." McCarthy was getting wound up, his famous baritone whine getting louder as he spoke. "Millions upon millions of people have become Reds in the last eight years. And they are just as sneaky and invasive and diseased in their thinking as feral fleabags."

McCarthy started bobbing his head up and down to emphasize certain hot-button words like he did on TV. "Communists call God a hoax! They kill all dissenters. They build bombs to obliterate us. And if those left-wingers—those East Coast boys born with silver spoons in their mouths—had their way, we'd invite them in for dinner and give them all our cream."

The man laughed and said, "Not while you're around, Joe!"

McCarthy shook the man's hand enthusiastically, splashing him with the whiskey in his glass.

But before he could say anything else, Mrs. McCarthy suggested the man be sure to try some of the shrimp cocktail as a way of easing him along. "Abby!" She brightened at seeing Richard's mother.

The women embraced as Don thanked the senator for having them.

"Jean planned the whole thing." McCarthy shrugged. "She keeps me straight. Damn near runs my senate office, too." He smiled at Ginny. "And who is this little lady?"

Richard's skin kind of crawled as the senator leaned over to speak face-to-face with his little sister. But when he shook hands with the senator himself, Richard felt weirdly energized as McCarthy said, "I see a young patriot in front of me. A boy who will spot the enemy within. Am I right?"

"Yes, sir!" Richard answered.

"You come see me, son, if you ever want a summer internship. All right?"

Don put his arm protectively around Richard's shoulder. "Congratulations again, sir. I wish you and your missus much happiness. Let's get some punch, Rich."

As they walked away, Richard looked up at his dad. Don's face was a mask. "You don't like the senator much, do you, Dad?"

"I believe in the cause. I don't believe in the man."

Don looked like he was about to add something when the band started playing.

Abigail clasped her hand to her heart. "Oh, listen, Don. It's that Tony Bennett song."

Take my hand, I'm a stranger in paradise, all lost in a wonderland. . . .

"How about a whirl on the dance floor, beautiful?"

Abigail beamed.

Sweeping her into his arms, Don waltzed them into the crowd of couples dancing cheek to cheek.

"Oh, look, there's Vice President Nixon!" Ginny pointed. "I'm going to go ask him what it was like to be interviewed by Jackie Kennedy!" She skipped away.

Richard was left alone. Again.

● ● ·

Arming himself with a plate of ham biscuits and some ginger-ale punch, Richard backed himself toward the gold brocade–papered wall. Boy, did he wish Vladimir were at the reception to hang out with.

The two of them had been almost inseparable for the past few weeks. Besides waiting together for the city bus that dropped them near Wilson High School and finding each other in the cafeteria during lunch, Richard had shown Vladimir all the sights along the National Mall. Their favorite had been the Museum of Natural History and exhibits of fossils and dinosaur bones and stuffed game animals—some of them bagged by Teddy Roosevelt himself.

Richard also had lent Vladimir his collection of Rudyard Kipling stories. "First, read *The Man Who Would Be King*," Richard had said. "That's the best."

In return, Vladimir had told Richard all about growing up in Czechoslovakia and then London during the war, and what being in New York City was like. He had such boss stuff—a lump of charred flak and a fragment of a Nazi bomber that he'd picked up out of the rubble of the Blitz, and hand-carved wooden toys and marionettes from Prague. He'd introduced Richard to the crazy snaking rips of jazz pianist Thelonious Monk and trumpeter Miles Davis. And, of course, the bittersweet melodies of saxophonist Charlie Parker. He talked about wanting to form his own jazz trio.

"Bummer you're not a musician," Vladimir had said, genuine disappointment in his tone. "But hey, you're hip, you read."

No other boy had ever said that to Richard!

That's when Vladimir lent him Jack London's *The Call of the Wild*, jokingly warning him to be careful with it. "Jack

London was a socialist, you know." He also told Richard about a bunch of new writers calling themselves the Beat Generation. And about one of Teresa's closest friends, a woman writer named Jane something, from Brooklyn Heights, their old New York City neighborhood.

"You know what?" Vladimir had said. "Jane's written a play that's premiering on Broadway in December. You should come with us."

Thinking back on all that, Richard got even antsier watching old people fox-trot or whatever the heck they were doing. He went back to daydreaming about *Casino Royale* and how 007 might act at a reception like this, full of big-wigs, all of them potential saboteurs or con men or traitors. He put down his plate, crossed his arms over his chest, and forced a swaggering stance. "Yeah," Richard whispered to himself, nodding and mimicking the hero. "Bradley. Rich Bradley."

A tap on his shoulder shattered his suave. He whirled around. There stood Dottie. Dottie Anne Glover. The girl he had worshipped and followed behind like a puppy in third grade, the girl who played Laurey last year in their school's production of *Oklahoma!*, the songbird every boy at Wilson High School would gladly do a thousand days of yard chores to have one date with. Just one.

Immediately, a song he'd written about her when he was twelve years old started buzzing in his ear. It was a stupid takeoff on a Stephen Foster song his mother played on the piano, "Jeanie With the Light Brown Hair." His lyrics were ridiculous: *I dream of Dottie with the light golden hair, borne like a goddess, I do declare. I see her skipping rope in the school playground. Beautiful and sweet with a pretty face round.* What a dork. No, what a schmuck.

"Richard?"

He felt his mouth drop open and forced himself to shut it. God, she was gorgeous. She was wearing a sky-blue satin dress, her strawberry blond bangs perfectly straight and neat under a matching blue flowered headband. Her blue eyes shone bright through the delicate, nose-length veil that all ladies' cocktail hats had. *Fascinators*, his mother called them.

"Lady's choice?" Dottie's dimples deepened as she smiled and held her hand out.

"D-d-d-dance?" Richard stammered. Dottie Anne Glover wanted to dance with him? *Wow! Maybe he should pretend to be James Bond more often.*

"Yes, silly! We used to dance together at cotillion. Remember?"

Constantly.

His own hand suddenly very sweaty, Richard took hers, thankful she wore sky-blue gloves up to her elbow so she couldn't tell.

Step right; slide. Step back; slide. Step left; slide. Step forward; slide. Richard looked at his ridiculously big, brightly polished shoes as he led her in an awkward box, sort of in time to the music.

"Richie, you can look up at me. I know you know how to do this."

Haltingly, Richard dared to gaze at her face. Her skin was creamy, her eyelashes like butterfly wings when she blinked. And her lips. Her lips looked like sweet red rose petals. An intoxicating scent of citrus and lilies floated around her as they moved.

Richard felt his legs get wobbly as the singer crooned.

See the marketplace in old Algiers. Send me photographs and souvenirs. . . .

"This song reminds me of that boy you're hanging out with all the time now."

"Vladimir?"

"Yes." Dottie smiled. "I hear he's been all over the world. I wonder if he's seen the marketplace in Algiers. That's in the Middle East, isn't it?"

"Ah, North Africa."

"Oh! Has he been there, too? One of my girlfriends told me she'd heard that he drove a sleigh through Siberia."

"What? No, he didn't. He lived in Prague."

"Poland? Do you suppose he saw Mozart's home? Oh, it's all so romantic, don't you think?"

"Yeah, I guess." Mesmerized by her eyes, Richard decided to not correct her geography. Only girls like Ginny knew stuff like that anyway, he figured.

"All the girls have been talking about him. Marilyn's dad is a chief of staff on the Hill. I forget which congressman." She paused for a moment, trying to remember the name. "It doesn't matter. Anyway, Marilyn's dad said that Vladimir's dad is in the State Department. Is that right?"

"Yes."

"Right before I saw you, my parents and I were in the receiving line congratulating Senator McCarthy on his wedding. He and Daddy got into a big political discussion. I guess it's impossible not to with Senator McCarthy.

Although Mrs. McCarthy seemed pretty annoyed since there were a lot of people waiting in that line to shake their hands."

Richard nodded.

"Daddy was asking the senator who was next up to testify in front of his committee. And Senator McCarthy said, 'A bunch of Red Foreign Service Officers.' He said the State Department was just riddled with commie sympathizers—like a big, old house with termites. And that he was going 'to find them and get them.' A couple of people even applauded."

She lifted her lips to Richard's ear so he could hear her whisper, and his heart almost exploded, it started beating so fast at the brush of her breath on his earlobe. "So I'm guessing Vladimir's family is"—she almost crooned the next word—"subversive."

Dottie pulled back, and there was a wicked little smile on her face. "Daddy forbid me from trying out for cheerleading this year. He said my grades weren't good enough. Well, when I spotted you just now, I had a brilliant idea." She giggled. "I can't think of a better way to get back at Daddy than going on a date." She paused. "With a real Red. And besides, Vladimir is such a dreamboat."

The song ended. Dottie took Richard's lapels in her hands and pulled him close, very close. *Oh . . . my . . . Lord*, his soul gasped. His imagination ran wild with hope. Could this be his first kiss? He could feel her breath on his lips. It smelled of peppermint. He could almost taste it.

"So, do you think you could introduce us?" Dottie asked. She let go of his coat, patted his chest, and stepped back.

"Wh-wh-what?"

"Can you introduce me to your friend next week?" She clasped her hands together and held them under her chin, batting her eyelashes at him. "I'm hoping to get to know him before homecoming. Pretty please?"

Richard felt slapped with ice water. The intoxicating spell of peppermint and wishes evaporated. *What an idiot.*

"Richie?" She smiled sweetly.

He shrugged and mumbled, "Sure."

Dottie squealed, clapped her hands, kissed him on the cheek, and then practically twirled off the dance floor, just as the band started playing the latest radio hit:

How much is that doggie in the window?
[Bark-bark]
The one with the waggly tail . . .

Chapter 5:

OCTOBER

1953

President Eisenhower announces that 1,456 government employees have been deemed potential subversives and removed from their federal jobs under his loyalty program.

He amends Executive Order 10450 to include automatic dismissal of any federal worker who invokes the Fifth Amendment and its constitutionally guaranteed protection against self-incrimination.

The order also says: *"The interests of the national security require that all persons privileged to be employed in the departments and agencies of the Government, shall be reliable, trustworthy, of good conduct and character, and of complete and unswerving loyalty to the United States."*

Reasons for investigating or dismissal include: *"immoral, or notoriously disgraceful conduct, habitual use of intoxicants to excess, drug addiction, sexual perversion.*

"Any illness, including any mental condition . . . [that] may cause significant defect in the judgment or reliability of the employee . . .

"Any facts which furnish reason to believe that the individual may be subjected to coercion, influence, or pressure which may cause him to act contrary to the best interests of the national security."

(Opposite) President Dwight D. Eisenhower

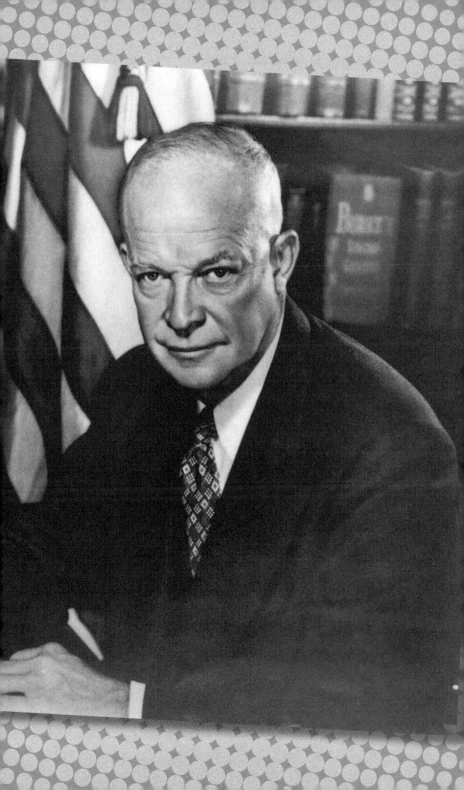

Edward R. Murrow and CBS newsmagazine

See It Now report that a World War II veteran and ten-year reservist named Lieutenant Milo Radulovich was deemed a security risk and dismissed from the Air Force because his father subscribed to Serbian-language newspapers. His sister was also a self-proclaimed progressive, a radical.

The Air Force points to Code 35-62, which states that a man is a security risk if he has a close and continuing relationship with those thought to be Communists. The evidence against Radulovich is hidden in a sealed envelope and never shown to him, his attorney, or the court. He is told that he might be able to keep his job or receive an honorable discharge if he denounces his own father and sister.

During the broadcast, Radulovich's father—a Serbian immigrant who served the United States during World War I and then worked in American coal mines—says that he took the Serbian newspaper because he liked their Christmas calendar.

Decrying the current national tendency to assume someone is guilty because of association, his sister adds: "My political beliefs are my own private affair. . . . Since when can a man be judged . . . because of the alleged political beliefs or activities of a member of his family?"

NATIONAL BOOK AWARD

DISTINGUISHED CONTRIBUTION TO AMERICAN LETTERS

RAY BRADBURY

FIRE

FAHRENHEIT 451

(Top) Ray Bradbury's dystopian novel that decries book-burning and government thought-police is published

BOUNCE ... *swish* ... *bounce, bounce* ... *swish.*

Vladimir sank his shots at the free throw line and then bounce-passed the basketball to Richard. The two of them were in the high school gym, surrounded by a crowd of other boys just hanging out or fooling around on the basketball court, prepping for team tryouts the next week.

Richard missed Vladimir's pass entirely. He chased the ball into the bleachers, where a bunch of underclassmen sat lacing their black high-tops and yanking up their white athletic socks. They had all been favorites of the gym coach in junior high school. Fast, strong, and cunning, killer dodgeball players. Of course Jimmy was among them.

"Catch much, spaz?" he asked. His buddies laughed at the sarcasm.

"Give it up . . . Dick," Jimmy's new best friend added, his tone dumping a not-very-nice meaning onto Richard's name.

Why did his parents have to name him that? *Bounce, bounce, bounce.* Richard dribbled the ball angrily and came back to the key, his face as orange as the ball with mortification.

"Don't listen to those turkeys," Vladimir reassured him. "You know what? Your dribble is decent. Maybe you can learn to be a ball handler."

Richard looked at Vladimir blankly.

"A point guard. Geez. How can you not know anything about basketball? Kind of un-American, don't you think?" he joked. He clapped his hands together and then held them out at chest level. "Throw me the ball."

Richard tossed it. "I know about baseball. Dad loves the Washington Senators. Maybe I can get him to take us to a game. How did you get so good at basketball?"

Vladimir passed the ball back, and Richard actually caught it. "There you go! I guess I learned a lot just playing in the neighborhood. There was a lot of pickup ball in Brooklyn Heights. And I loooooove the Knicks."

Richard's next throw was loopy, and Vladimir had to jump up to snag it. "Pop it when you pass, like this." Vladimir flicked his wrist as he threw, giving the ball a stinging speed. "It keeps the direction straight."

Richard imitated him and the ball made a *slap* when it hit Vladimir's upheld hands.

"Better!" Vladimir grinned. "Stick with me, kid! I'll get you ready for tryouts. Let's keep practicing your pass." He threw the ball at Richard's chest.

It bounced off Richard and ricocheted under the bleachers. He had to half crawl under the seats to pull it out and came back up sneezing from the dust, expecting Vladimir to ridicule him, too. He would if he were trying to help someone and that kid kept screwing up.

But Vladimir didn't. "Maybe you're thinking too hard about this. Let's talk as we pass. Deal?"

Well, that certainly was better than focusing on how unathletic he was.

Richard tossed the ball to Vladimir, who zinged it back at him.

Wouldn't it be swell to actually make the JV squad with Vladimir? To be on par with Jimmy? Richard had never even considered trying out for a team before—which is part of why his classmates never had time for him. To belong, really belong, to the world of fourteen-year-old boys seemed to require a good uppercut or a linebacker's hulk or a solid bank shot.

Vladimir, on the other hand, was a shoo-in for the team. He had a great arcing shot he sank from the outside over and over with a clean *swish*—all net, no rim. He hadn't missed a foul shot yet, either.

Richard might as well kiss this new friendship good-bye. Once Vladimir made the team, no way the jocks would let him hang out with Richard. It'd mar all the guys' social standing to have one of them be friendly with a loser. Richard had experienced that brush-off a dozen times in junior high school.

Lost in these despairing thoughts, he totally missed the ball again. This time it rolled up to the toes of a pair of saddle shoes.

Dottie's.

Please God, can the floor just open and swallow me now, he prayed.

"Hi, Richard." She smiled meaningfully at him. "Who's your friend?"

Richard was so flustered that he started to say "But you know who he is," when Vladimir sauntered up.

"Vladimir White," he introduced himself and held out his hand.

She took it. And then, rather than shaking it, Vladimir bowed a bit, turned over her hand, and kissed the back of it. "Charmed to meet you, Miss . . . miss?"

Dottie's mouth popped open, then closed. She pressed her lips together as a pink glow lit up her cheeks like a sunrise. Finally, she giggled and murmured, "Dottie Glover."

Vladimir smiled.

She smiled.

He still held her hand.

Boy oh boy, the guy is smooth as apple butter, Richard fumed.

● ● ·

WHAM. Bounce, bounce, bounce.

WHAM. Bounce, bounce, bounce.

WHAM. WHAM.

The three of them turned toward the noise.

"What a bunch of morons," muttered Vladimir.

The bleacher boys were hurling their balls against the backboard to see who could ricochet it the farthest back onto the court. They were laughing and egging each other on.

Then Jimmy tried to jump high enough to grab the rim and hang on to it.

One after another, the others followed his lead—all missing, since they hadn't had a sufficient growth spurt yet to reach that high. But Jimmy was the biggest and strongest. He actually managed to grab the hoop and hang, just as two of his buddies' shots pelted the backboard.

CRAAAAAAAAAAACK.

The backboard split under Jimmy's weight and the bombardment of balls. The hoop buckled and drooped, peeling down a veneer of wood with it and dumping Jimmy to the court on his butt. He backpedaled like a crab while all the others stood, gaping at the mangled basket in horror.

"Now you've done it," squeaked a boy standing in the corner.

Richard recognized him. His name was Eddie. The kid really struggled in school. One of Abigail's friends who ran the PTA had mounted a campaign to get Eddie transferred to an institution set up specifically for students who had trouble keeping up developmentally and academically. The boys were pretty merciless to him. A lot of the girls, too. A few even said their parents believed in sterilization laws to keep the intellectually disabled from having children.

"Shut up, stupid!" Jimmy shouted.

One of his buddies strode over and grabbed Eddie up by the shirt. "You're cruising for a bruising, germ."

"HEY!" The booming voice of the school's head coach reverberated through the gym and silenced all else. "What happened? Who's responsible for this? Get your butts in line. NOW!"

Everyone scrambled, including Richard. But Vladimir sauntered, dribbling.

The gym teacher walked the lineup. "You have to the count of twenty for the meathead who broke the basket to fess up. "One, two, three . . ."

The boys squirmed and frowned.

"Five, six, seven . . ."

They looked down at their feet. Richard bit his lip. It would feel pretty darn good to finally give Jimmy some pain, to arrange some justice for all the times he'd bullied Richard. But ratting on another kid was a guaranteed ticket to social nowheresville. A snitch was a pariah.

"Nine, ten, eleven . . ." The coach paused. "Okay, you jokers, if no one says anything, you all get detention."

A few of the boys elbowed each other, looking toward Eddie. Richard started to feel queasy watching them out of the corner of his eye. He could see an unspoken conspiracy forming to make a kid who wouldn't know how to defend himself the fall guy. Eddie was just different enough, and had had enough scrapes with teachers for breaking rules before, that pointing the finger at him would seem totally plausible. All those guys had to do was keep their story straight among them. And if enough people named Eddie, he'd be convicted for sure.

"Thirteen, fourteen, fifteen . . ." The gym teacher had also noticed the boys' glances toward Eddie. He paced his way there, slowing his counting until he stood toe-to-toe with him. Poor Eddie looked like he was about to pee his pants.

"What do you have to say about this?" The teacher lowered his voice to a nasty snarl. "Retard."

Eddie started shaking his head violently, repeating, "No, no, no, no."

The teacher grabbed Eddie's collar. "Stop acting like an idiot! Fess up. I know you did this. Only a retard would break the basket and ruin the gym for everyone else. I always said you had no business at this school."

Some of the boys starting sniggering. Jimmy grinned outright with relief.

Vladimir stiffened. "What an SOB," he muttered.

The coach gave Eddie a short but jarring shake. "Come on. Out with it."

Eddie burst out crying.

"Leave him alone!" Vladimir exploded. "He didn't do it!"

The coach stopped midshake. Then, in what felt like a second flat, he was standing eye-to-eye with Vladimir. "Then who the heck did?" he thundered.

Richard could sense the line of boys trembling. He sure was.

But Vladimir didn't wince. And he didn't point the finger at anyone. "We were all screwing around. Just too many balls being thrown at the basket at the same time. Sorry, Coach."

What? Was he nuts? thought Richard. He'd get them all thrown in the hoosegow. They might not be able to try out for the team, even. And he and Vladimir hadn't done anything!

The teacher eyed Vladimir. "Okay, wise guy. You're in charge of organizing the fund-raisers to replace the basket. Meanwhile, all of you donkeys will spend the next two weeks staying after school to bang chalk out of erasers and clean the school grounds. I'll ask the janitors what other things need doing. Bet they'd like a break from scrubbing toilets."

The oaths the boys muttered were nothing compared to the hot hatred in the looks they threw toward Vladimir and then Richard.

Richard's heart sank. Even if he did get a chance to try out for the team, these guys would find a way to squeeze him out of play in retribution for being Vladimir's friend. Guilty by association, after all. And God knows what they'd do to Vladimir.

And what about Dottie? He dared to glance over to the sidelines. He couldn't believe his eyes. Dottie looked like she might swoon as she gazed at Vladimir. Richard could almost see little hearts popping over her head like in Looney Tunes cartoons.

Great. In one moment of altruism, Vladimir had fouled Richard out of gaining any respect from boys who'd humiliated him for years, plus he'd made off with the girl of his dreams.

When Richard got home, totally dejected, he could hear another interrogation. Following the agitated voices, he tiptoed down the front hallway and peeked around the dining room door. Ginny was sitting at the kitchen table across from Don and Abigail. Their parents did not look happy. A paper lay on top of the table between them. Richard flattened himself against the wall to eavesdrop.

"Jackie Kennedy told me to," Ginny was saying.

"Mrs. Kennedy told you to start a petition saying the Air Force had accused some Red-leaning pinko lieutenant unfairly?" Don asked, his voice quaking with suppressed anger.

"No, Daddy. Mrs. Kennedy told me that if I wanted to be an inquiring camera girl that I needed to keep up on the news. So I watched *See It Now,* and Mr. Murrow said that . . ."

Abigail broke in. "Honey, you snuck downstairs after bedtime to watch TV?"

"I can't help it, Mom, if CBS changed the show from Sunday at six thirty to Tuesday at ten thirty."

"Listen, missy, bedtime is bedtime. Especially on a school night. Don, do you think we should ground her from the TV for a week?"

Don ignored his wife and instead addressed Ginny with her full name, which said a lot to Richard about how much trouble she was in. "Virginia, do you understand what you are claiming in this petition and why your teacher called us?"

"Of course, I do, Daddy. I wrote the petition myself, you know." Wow, thought Richard, that was pretty sassy. She sounded like . . . like him. He frowned.

"Mr. Murrow was very clear about it," Ginny continued in that adult tone she was so good at mimicking. "He said that Lieutenant Radulovich was dishonorably discharged just because his father read Serbian newspapers and his sister *might* be a pinko. Even the Air Force said the lieutenant hadn't done anything wrong himself. Mr. Murrow said that all the evidence against him was hidden in a sealed envelope."

She cleared her throat. "Mr. Murrow said that wasn't very American because the stuff in the envelope could just be hearsay or gossip or slander, not hard fact. I wrote it down—'hearsay or gossip or slander, not hard fact.' Then his reporters interviewed a nice lady in Lieutenant Radulovich's hometown. She's passing around a petition. She's asking the Air Force to let him back in. It's the fair thing to do, don't you think, Daddy? So I made a petition, too. That's all."

Don and Abigail were silent. Listening, Richard at first felt an odd sense of vindication. The darling of the family was losing her shine a bit. But he knew this wasn't good for his little sister. He could imagine how much Don's hands might be shaking right now. This was exactly the kind of stuff that really set him off.

Abigail was the first to speak. "What if Mr. Hoover finds out? Isn't signing petitions what landed so many Hollywood stars and writers on blacklists?"

But Don clearly wasn't listening to Abigail. Something about Ginny's speech seemed to have rattled Don. Richard could hear it in his voice.

"Ginny," he began, somehow both patient and stern, "President Eisenhower and Mr. Hoover and Congress and a bunch of other smart men know how bad people like Communists can wheedle their way into our government and corrupt us. They . . . we . . . believe that someone serving in our armed forces, or in the State Department, for instance, might become a security risk if he has a family member who's a left-leaning liberal or a radical. Here's how, honey: the man could be blackmailed to act contrary to national security. Commie agents could threaten to expose that man's father or sister if he doesn't help them and their cause.

"Or worse, say that American diplomat or serviceman has a relative he loves still living in a Soviet bloc country— like Czechoslovakia." Don was trying hard to keep a fatherly tone, but his voice was becoming progressively harsher. "Those Red governments could throw that uncle or cousin in prison if our guy doesn't pass on our secrets. See what I'm saying?"

Richard frowned at the mention of Czechoslovakia— technically Vladimir's homeland. He dared to peek around the edge of the door again and watched Don reach across the table to pick up Ginny's petition.

"Sometimes, if we don't act on our suspicions, if we don't investigate things that may seem small or just purely coincidental, really bad things can happen—things that destroy our national security, things that hurt or kill lots of people."

Don shot to his feet. His head was down and his back was toward Richard, but the scared look on Ginny's face told how much anger must be on Don's. What his dad said next sounded like a roar—one of his explosive moments that always seemed to come out of nowhere, like a whiplash of heat lightning in a sky that was only sort of cloudy.

"And if a person is stupid and doesn't follow the orders of superiors who know better, innocent people can die. They die!" Don pounded the table with his fist making Ginny and Abigail jump in their seats. Then he tore Ginny's petition to shreds.

"Daddy!" she wailed.

Don turned abruptly and walked out of the room, slamming the wall hard as he exited.

He ran straight into Richard.

"What are you looking at?" he snarled and stormed on.

Richard felt himself go cold. *God almighty.* Don really was "psycho," just like the article said. He'd never seen Don yell at Ginny like that.

When he heard his sister start to cry, Richard rushed into the kitchen. "What the heck, Mom?"

Abigail was looking past him to where Don had exited. Her blue eyes were spilling over with her own tears.

"Mom!"

She startled.

"What the heck's wrong with Dad?"

"Wrong?"

"Yeah, Mom. Wrong. Why does he get so upset and all twitchy? On the Fourth, he about jumped out of his skin when some kids set off cherry bombs near us. Then he practically bit my head off. And what's with his hands getting all shaky, like when he was worrying over our POWs in Korea? It's one thing to be all crabby with me, but look at Ginny!"

Abigail's surprise changed to horror and then sorrow. "Sit down, Richard," she said shakily. "Ginny, honey, dry your eyes."

Abigail handed Ginny her embroidered handkerchief as Richard put his arm across his sister's small shoulders.

"I am going to explain something so you two can understand your dad a little better. But you can never repeat it or ask him about it. He would hate me for telling you. Do you promise?"

Richard nodded. Snuffling, Ginny crossed her heart and leaned up against Richard the way she used to at story time.

"All right." Abigail took a deep breath. "On Don's last bombing mission over Europe, a Messerschmitt strafed the plane, killing one waist gunner and shooting up the other, your dad's best friend. That boy was in terrible pain. Don disobeyed his captain and left the tail gun to help his friend. Your dad's like that, you know. He has a big heart."

Ginny and Richard nodded again.

"But as he was trying to stop his friend's bleeding, that Messerschmitt circled back and shot at the plane from behind. Your dad wasn't at his post to fire back." She hesitated, looking at them nervously. "Their plane went down because of it. The Nazis caught your dad and the other survivors. Things went really bad at the POW stalag. There were SS officers —Hitler's zealots. They executed your dad's pilot and copilot, claiming they were trying to escape. They weren't. The SS just murdered them to terrorize the other prisoners and break their spirits to keep them in line."

Horrified, Richard choked out, "Did . . . Did Dad try to do anything to stop the execution?"

Abigail sighed. "Yes. And he spent a lot of time starving in solitary confinement as a result. They called it 'the hole.' He won't talk about it."

She let that information sink in for a moment before continuing. "Your dad has had a hard time dealing with the guilt he feels about all of that. He rejoined the FBI to have a purpose, a way to make up for his mistake. He was assigned to a really important case—the Judith Coplon case. But . . . it went all wrong."

She paused. A tear slipped down her face. "What got into that woman to make her do such traitorous things is beyond me. She was a cum laude graduate of Barnard College, for pity's sake. She worked for the Justice Department. I would have loved a job like that." Abigail shook her head. "But Miss Coplon decided to tip off Soviet agents about FBI investigations. She claims she did it for love—that her Russian boyfriend coerced her. Lord, what some women will do for their men."

"Mom, please," Richard interrupted. "Stick to the story."

"What?" Abigail startled out of her thoughts. "Oh, you're right, son. I'm sorry. So, the FBI figured out that Miss Coplon might be a rotten apple and put her under surveillance. Frankly, they had plenty of evidence against her from her telephone conversations. But your dad says they couldn't submit the tapes to a jury. I suppose technically, those wire-taps are top secret. The only way to convict Miss Coplon in a court of law was for the FBI to catch her red-handed, in the act of handing an American document to her Soviet contact."

She stopped. "Is this all making sense so far?"

"Yeah," Richard answered for Ginny. The tough-guy private detectives in his LA noir crime novels constantly railed against the strict requirements for a *legal* arrest. "So what did the FBI do?"

"Mr. Hoover created a fake classified memo about atomic power as bait. Miss Coplon swallowed it hook, line, and sinker. Two dozen FBI agents were assigned to follow her as she went to meet her handler with that cooked-up document. And by the way—can you imagine—that man's cover was working at the Soviet embassy's UN delegation. The United Nations! Isn't the United Nations supposed to be all about peace and cooperation?"

"Mom!" Again, Richard shifted impatiently.

Abigail held up her hand to stop more comment from him. She rubbed her forehead like she had a sudden headache before continuing, "That Miss Coplon was clever. She took precautions. She hid in crowds. She hopped a bus. She changed trains in the subway. The agents lost her for about twenty minutes. When they found her again, she was walking with her Russian beau, side by side, like they were out for a stroll. The agents were afraid that she had already given him the documents while they didn't have eyes on her, and that the Soviet contact would hightail it back to Russia if they didn't arrest them both right then and there.

"So they moved in. But Miss Coplon still had those dang papers in her purse. There were other things in her handbag— FBI reports on spy suspects, for instance, that she had no business carrying around.

"But . . ." Abigail pursed her lips before continuing with uncharacteristic anger, "that woman got off scot-free! Her lawyer claimed there wasn't a proper search warrant issued before her arrest. That she'd been set up. *Entrapment*, he called it. And there was a huge brouhaha about those FBI wiretaps."

Abigail sat back and crossed her arms. "The whole mess was very public and a terrible embarrassment for the agency and Mr. Hoover."

"Soooooooo? What's that got to do with Dad?" Richard asked.

Abigail lowered her voice. "Your dad was one of those agents who lost Miss Coplon for twenty minutes."

She looked at Richard and Ginny intently to make sure they were really listening before continuing. "The suspicion was that Miss Coplon was connected to the Rosenberg ring. You know how your dad feels about all those boys dying in Korea and how the Rosenbergs' treachery may have helped start that war."

She sighed heavily. "Now he carries that guilt, too." Abigail fidgeted with her curls before continuing. "I think what your dad needs is to break a big, important case. For all his chest-beating, Senator McCarthy hasn't unearthed any new *real* Communists like the Rosenbergs. He's just gotten a lot of liberal-leaning teachers and writers and government workers fired. So Mr. Hoover is itching to get him a real Soviet agent, a real spy to prosecute."

She nodded, to herself really, and repeated, "Your dad just needs to break a case to feel redeemed—with Mr. Hoover and with himself. It'll be like getting back up on a horse after being thrown and then crossing the finish line first."

For a long while, Richard stared at their mother, not knowing what to think. He replayed the Coplon information in his head. Was she saying Don was a screwup?

No, he couldn't believe it. He didn't want to believe it. His dad was a G-man hero. Wasn't his dad working undercover for Mr. Hoover? Like Philbrick? He had to be. "What's the deal with the money I saw Mr. Hoover give Dad at Harvey's?" Richard finally asked, hoping to restore some of his idolatry of Don. "Does that have something to do with a case?"

Abigail seemed shocked by the question. She frowned. "Don't ask, honey."

There wasn't any sound of hidden I-know-something-you-don't pride in her voice. Then she left the room.

Chapter 6:

NOVEMBER
1953

During hearings on suspected espionage in the Army Signal Corps, McCarthy blasts witnesses: "What have you got against this country? Do you feel if Rosenberg was properly executed, you deserve the same fate?"

Two people he attacks are New York City teachers who worked with the corps during World War II. Facing such accusatory questions, they "take the Fifth," since many of McCarthy's hearings had proved to be fishing expeditions: calling witnesses with the ulterior goal of unearthing reasons to prosecute them or to cite them for contempt of Congress if they refuse to "name names" of others they think might have hidden Red ideology.

Following their appearance in McCarthy's hearings, New York's board of education fires both teachers. Their fate echoes that of a Columbia University professor, previously called to testify because she belonged to progressive women's clubs and coauthored a pamphlet on race equality. During World War II, the USO had commissioned the work to encourage tolerance among servicemen and women. But now, the anthropologist's research is deemed "subversive" in its tacit support of integration. Columbia announced she would not return the next year.

Educators across the country are subjected to such suspicion. The American Legion's "Americanism Committee" runs ads tarring many colleges as secret hotbeds of Communism, including Sarah Lawrence, which it dubs "the little RED schoolhouse."

HOW RED
IS THE LITTLE RED SCHOOLHOUSE?
ORGANIZED COMMUNIST PROPAGANDA
It's high time American parents knew the facts!

McCarthy subpoenas former president Harry S. Truman, accusing him of having ignored an FBI report that suggested Truman's assistant secretary of the treasury spied for the Soviets. Truman refuses to testify, denouncing what he calls *McCarthyism*—"the rise to power of a demagogue who lives on untruth."

J. Edgar Hoover then publicly criticizes Truman, even though during his administration, Truman had allowed Hoover to double the number of his FBI's agents.

McCarthy demands free radio and TV time to defend himself against what he calls Truman's "completely untruthful attack." He threatens to ask the Federal Communications Commission (FCC) to review the license of any station that fails to carry his rebuttal.

In his address, McCarthy decries "the whining, whimpering appeasement" that he claims characterizes American foreign policy. "Are we going to continue to send perfumed notes?"

(Top) President Harry S. Truman •
(Bottom) FBI Director J. Edgar Hoover

ONE crisp afternoon, Richard came home to the cinnamon and nutmeg smell of pumpkin pie baking.

"Mom?" he called as he dumped his books by the front door. No answer. She must be in the kitchen. Every year she made a dozen Betty Crocker–perfect pies to be sold at the church's Thanksgiving bazaar. And every year she roped Ginny and him into digging the guts out of pumpkins and removing seeds so she could make the puree for those pies. He'd loved fishing around in orange glop as a kid, like playing in a mud puddle, but he just wasn't in the mood to be tied into one of her bright yellow aprons. It'd been such a lousy day at school.

Since he and Vladimir didn't have any classes together, Richard was trying to make a few additional friends. So he'd joined the Classics Club. Actually, he really liked Latin, and the teacher was a cool guy straight out of Princeton. Richard was helping him plan a banquet of the gods, with togas and everything. The teacher had asked him to play Julius Caesar and recite a speech. Richard had been pretty stoked. It was Caesar, after all!

But unfortunately, Jimmy had gotten wind of it. That day, in the cafeteria, in front of everybody—including Dottie—he'd ridiculed the club. "A bunch of four eyes," Jimmy had sneered, "playing dress up in sheets. Figures you'd want to join that, Dickie."

Later, Dottie had given him the cold shoulder in Biology. Since he'd introduced her to Vladimir, he usually got a smile and a real hello in addition to the fifty minutes he got to stare at the back of her beautiful head. But today? Nada.

Vladimir was still his friend, at least, despite his making the basketball team. Richard, as he'd anticipated, did not.

After the incident with Eddie, the broken hoop, and a week of detention, Jimmy spearheaded a campaign to freeze out Vladimir during the tryouts. The bleacher boys fouled him mercilessly as he dribbled in for floaters. But his shots were just too perfect. The coach knew a good thing when he saw it.

When he couldn't take down Vladimir, Jimmy told his flunkies to make Richard look as stupid as possible. He was, after all, Vlad's fellow traveler, his loyal sidekick, the Robin to Vlad's Batman. Of course, it hadn't taken much. Even with Vladimir feeding him the ball, Richard dropped it over and over again. The few shots he tried either missed the board entirely or bounced off the rim with a humiliating *ka-ping*.

Vladimir had also won Dottie's heart. Richard hated to admit his jealousy. He reminded himself that he'd never told Vladimir about his lifelong crush on Dottie, so it wasn't as if Richard could blame him for snaking her. Besides, the songs Richard was secretly writing now were all angsty and tragic in his unrequited love. Good stuff. The pain you have to suffer for art, he figured.

"Richard, is that you, honey?" Abigail called. "We're back here."

Richard dragged his feet on the way to the kitchen. As he rounded the back corner of the center hallway, he could hear Mrs. Emerson's voice. Thank goodness, maybe she would distract his mother. She was sitting at the table sipping tea as

Abigail rolled out the piecrust dough. Flour covered the table and his mother.

"There's my gallant weed puller!" Mrs. Emerson brightened when she saw him. "How are you today?"

"Hey, Mrs. Emerson." Richard smiled halfheartedly. "I'm okay, I guess."

He'd have to come up with a way to get out of the kitchen fast before Mrs. Emerson thought of some other chore around her house that needed doing. He'd been going back every other week for the weeds since July Fourth. She just seemed so pathetic and all, and so grateful. But she was starting to ask Richard to change lightbulbs and the cat litter now that autumn frost had killed off the weeds. She peppered him with so many questions, it took an hour to do a five-minute favor.

He gave his mom a quick kiss on her cheek before heading to the refrigerator. Hiding behind the open door, he tried to conjure up some story to get him out of the house or up to his room.

Ginny was in the sun-drenched kitchen, too, at the ironing board. She threw him a happy "Hi Rich! Want to help me make place mats for Thanksgiving?" She held a roll of wax paper and a bowl full of leaves—orange maple, scarlet dogwood, and golden hickory. Each year she ironed the leaves between wax paper for the holiday dinner.

Closing the icebox's door, Richard picked up a carrot-colored leaf and twirled it by its stem. His little sister had an artistic eye. The montages of autumn hues she made were pretty gorgeous. And a lot less controversial than petitions for Air Force guys in trouble with the government!

But he needed to get out of Mrs. Emerson's line of fire. "Sorry, Gin. I've got a big report due tomorrow I gotta get to. But be careful with that iron."

She eyed him. "You okay?"

Geez, she could see right through him—great for a budding reporter, maybe, lousy for a big brother trying to exit a room. He made himself appear nonchalant and said, "Sure."

"Shoot, I didn't know you had that report, honey," said Abigail. "What's it on?"

"Ahhh . . . ahhh. The Roman Empire."

"Goodness, that's a large topic," chirped Mrs. Emerson. "What aspect? Which emperor? I hope it's not on that Caligula. No teacher should be talking about him! What is your teacher's name?"

"I don't know who Caligula is, Mrs. Emerson," he fibbed. His teacher had shared a little about Caligula's cruelties and eccentricities. But Richard sure didn't want Mrs. Emerson getting the guy in trouble somehow. "No, it's going to be . . . to be . . . on . . . on Caesar's campaign."

"Well . . ." Abigail began, saving him as Mrs. Emerson opened her mouth to ask more questions, "before you start your work, could you run over to Vladimir's house and invite them to come to the bazaar with us tomorrow? Teresa was telling me she was looking for a church for the family. Good way for her to meet some neighbors."

"Oh, my dear," Mrs. Emerson said, "what a sweet, considerate thought. I invited Teresa to my bridge club with the very same purpose."

Abigail continued kneading a ball of dough and rolled her eyes a bit at Richard, knowing a long story was coming.

"She's quite competitive, I have to say. But she still charmed the ladies, despite her . . . ethnicity. She wears it rather well, though, even with some elegance. Something about that Old World allure, don't you think?"

Mrs. Emerson didn't really want an answer from Abigail and kept right on talking. "She had all the ladies fascinated with stories of London during the war. She'd even met Mr. Churchill at a party. She said he was quite the wag. A photographer took his picture—goodness, Mr. Churchill must be close to eighty now—and the cameraman politely said that he hoped he'd be photographing the prime minister on his one hundredth birthday. And Teresa says that Mr. Churchill replied, 'I don't see why not, young man, you look reasonably fit to me.'" Mrs. Emerson tittered in appreciation of her story.

"But, you know . . ." She paused dramatically and leaned forward, toward Abigail. "Teresa is a bit shocking. She told us all about her Jewish relatives being rounded up and hauled off. Not really conversation for a ladies' bridge club." She stopped and pursed her lips. "Oh, and"—her lips slid into a happily scandalized smile—"she even suggested we place small bets, to make it more exciting. Only lollipops and such. But still! We ladies had never done that before."

Abigail laughed lightly. Or was it nervously? Her voice sounded really odd. "Placing a bet isn't so egregious these days, is it? Don told me that Senator McCarthy paid his way through college by betting on his poker games. The most unlikely people seem to be into betting. Horse races, for instance, out in Laurel." She fell silent.

Richard stared at his mother. What had gotten into her? What would she be advocating next? Hanging out at pool halls? Besides, Herbert Philbrick said in *I Led 3 Lives* that a betting man was always a target for coercion—it was a vice Reds could use to blackmail the guy into following commie orders.

Mrs. Emerson frowned, disappointed that she hadn't managed to shock Abigail. "There's more!" Mrs. Emerson lowered her voice to a whisper. "Teresa told us that she has been playing rummy with wives of the Czech delegation. That one was a childhood friend." She made a face at Abigail and sat back against the bench. "Communists, mind you!"

Abigail froze, mid-knead. "Really?"

"Really. She claimed she wanted to keep up her language skills and that the wife had been very dear to her when they were little." Mrs. Emerson crossed her arms. "I like Teresa, but I certainly hope she has her head in the right place. We all better keep an eye on who comes and goes from that house."

"Hmmmm . . ." Abigail picked up her rolling pin and squashed the dough intently. Then she looked over at Richard, as if weighing something. Finally, she said, "Vladimir is Richard's friend. Going to our church bazaar is a good way for Teresa to get to know more Washingtonians. That way she won't have to rely on a friend from childhood. Go on over to their house, honey, and ask if they'd like to come with us. Tell her ten o'clock sharp. We'll pick them up. She can help us carry the pies into the parish hall."

Richard threw his mother a smile of thanks before trotting happily out the front door. He pushed up the collar of his peacoat against the brisk winds that swept waves of fallen red leaves skittering down the street in front of him. When he reached the walk of Vladimir's house, he could hear his friend furiously playing scales on his saxophone, up and down two octaves, one key after another. Richard knocked. Still the saxophone charged up a hill of notes and back down. Vladimir stumbled and started over, faster.

Richard knocked again, harder. Another scale ripped through the house.

He leaned against the door to listen, and could hear orchestral music, too. Teresa must be home. She always had symphonies going on their record player, especially when she was painting. Richard banged on the door. But Vladimir's music inside only seemed to grow more stormy, more intense.

He decided to tap on the side door that led to Teresa's studio. As Richard skirted azaleas to the porch he could see her through its windows. Her easel was up, a canvas half-splashed with color. She held her palette and a brush in one hand, but she was on the telephone. And she looked worried. Richard hesitated. Maybe he should come back at another time.

Her record ended, violin chords fading. Teresa tucked the phone under her chin and turned to pull the needle off the LP. That's when she spotted Richard.

Teresa jumped a little in surprise. Then she put on a mom's oh-look-who's-here smile he'd seen Abigail use a dozen times when she opened the door and someone like Mrs. Emerson was standing there. It definitely wasn't a gosh-I'm-so-glad-to-see-you expression. Not at all. But Teresa put down her palette and motioned for him to come to the door. Stretching the telephone wire as far as it would go, she leaned over and unlocked it for him.

Richard stepped inside as she continued her telephone conversation in a low, careful voice. *"Nemohu mluvit ted . . ."*

Awkwardly Richard looked around, not at her, as she finished the call. His eyes fell on her worktable, covered with rags and paint bottles and—he did a little double take—a big map that had red marks on it.

"Ano . . ." Teresa reached out, putting her arm through his, and turned Richard toward the living room as she finished with *". . . zavolam pristi tyden."* She hung up the receiver. "Vladi is upstairs, Richard. Perhaps you can find out what happened to him at practice today. He will not tell me." She gracefully extended her hand up toward the staircase. "Please." She nodded affirmation. "Go on up." And she walked away before Richard could explain his mom's invitation.

●   ●   ·

Slowly, Richard climbed the steps. Vladimir was plunging along the octaves now chromatically, swimming upstream in half-step notes, then cascading back down. To Richard, the music sounded like his friend was desperate to get away from something or hoping to drown it. The door was shut. Richard knocked.

The saxophone squeaked to a halt. "I told you I don't want to talk about it, Mom!" The scales raced again.

"It's me. Richard!"

Silence.

"Vlad? You okay, man?"

The door jerked open. Richard gasped. Vladimir's right eye was red and bruised and swollen half-shut.

"Geez, what happened?"

Vladimir looked at first like he wanted to take a swing at Richard. Then he forced a who-cares swagger. "Got in a fight." He tapped the keys on his saxophone like he was still playing scales.

"Who with?"

Vladimir snorted. "Everybody."

"What?"

"They've been fouling me constantly at practice. Below-the-belt stuff. Today I just snapped. I gave the guy who did it a knuckle sandwich." He grinned. "You should see his face."

"Whose?"

"Whose do you think?"

Of course, Richard thought. "Jimmy?"

Vladimir smirked and nodded.

"Didn't the coach stop it?"

"Oh, yeah, he broke us up. But not before most of the squad jumped me."

"What? You're joking."

"Wish I were. They're total morons. They do anything that jackass Jimmy tells them to. Why is that? He's such a pissant."

Richard shook his head. "I wish I knew. What happened then?"

"Well, Coach benched Jimmy for our first two games for purposely fouling me so many times."

"But you still get to play, right?"

"Nope. He benched me, too."

"What? But, Vlad, that's not fair. You didn't start it."

Vladimir shrugged. "'Them's the rules,' Coach said. It was my swing that he saw. I don't want to talk about it." He put his saxophone down. "Let's go get a milk shake at that ice-cream counter you like so much."

● ● ·

That night, Richard and Don sat down together to watch *I Led 3 Lives*. Don had finished reading the afternoon paper and leaned back to light his pipe. "I can't wait to see what old Philbrick gets into tonight," he said in between puffs to pull the match flame into the pipe bowl. Richard watched anxiously to see that the pipe worked properly. He'd had a devil of a time getting that one screwed back together straight in his rush to avoid being caught in his father's closet.

Ever since Don had been so brusque with Ginny, and Abigail had described his losing that Coplon spy lady, Richard had been searching for proof that Don really was as good a G-man as he'd always believed his dad to be. Besides unscrewing the pipes, he'd rifled through Don's drawers, hoping to find some 007-style paraphernalia. But all Richard had unearthed were a couple of spare buttons rolling around in a sock drawer and big cuff links on top of the dresser. Richard hoped for a second that they were little microphones. But they weren't.

So now, sitting in front of the television together, Richard watched his dad's face for some sign to gauge Don's state of mind—maybe a hint of satisfaction or confidence that would mean Don was doing well with the FBI. On the other hand, a glimmer of smoldering "psycho" stuff or even a lingering shadow of humiliation—like what Richard saw every day when he looked at himself in the mirror—would signal that

Don was still under Hoover's thumb and struggling to redeem himself.

But the only little flare was Don's pipe catching as he puffed and shook the match out. A plume of sticky-sweet smoke drifted toward Richard, making him sneeze, just as the new episode began with its signature voice-over:

"This is the story—the fantastically true story—of Herbert A. Philbrick, who for nine frightening years did lead three lives. . . ."

The episode opened at a college campus. Philbrick and the band of Communists he faked being part of had broken into a student's dorm room. Told to find something with which they could blackmail the student, they rummaged through drawers and books. Finally, one of the men pulled out a note and said, "Hey, boss, look at this . . ." as the screen faded to black.

The program paused for an Alka-Seltzer commercial: *Plop-plop, fizz, fizz, oh what a relief it is.*

During the jingle, Richard's mind wandered to thinking about Teresa and how oddly she had acted on the phone that afternoon. Did she put her arm through his to distract him from that map? He hadn't thought about it before this moment. But now, watching Philbrick, her behavior seemed kind of fishy or nervous or guilty or . . . something. And what about her being friends with those Czech Embassy commie wives?

The program came back on as the TV Philbrick tailed the college student into a drugstore. The kid ordered an ice-cream float. Philbrick sat down beside him and passed him a note his handler had written. The student dropped his spoon and looked at Philbrick with horror on his face.

The scene faded to a commercial of a woman dancing on Christmas morning with a ribbon-wrapped vacuum and singing, *"She'll be happier with a Hoover, a Hoooooover!"*

His pipe clenched in his teeth, Don clapped his hands and rubbed them together. "This episode is getting good. That's exactly how radicalization happens. Agents hoping to undermine the United States target some innocent, idealistic kid. He will just be sitting there, and boom, they sit down and fill his head with nonsense." Both he and Richard squirmed to the edge of their armchairs as the show came back on.

Now Philbrick sat on a park bench, reporting in with an FBI special agent. The two men ate bagged lunches and pretended not to know each other, looking in opposite directions. "That kid?" the agent asked in surprise when Philbrick told what the student had been convinced to do.

Philbrick answered grimly, "You can't spot a Red by his face."

With that, the show ended, the baritone announcer booming:

"Next week, we'll bring you another story from the files of Herbert A. Philbrick—Citizen . . . Communist . . . Counterspy."

Don applauded, pipe clenched in his teeth. "Woo-eee! That was a good one, wasn't it, son?"

Richard nodded. Then his mind repeated the episode line: *You can't spot a Red by his face.* Just like the Rosenbergs, just like Abigail had said. *Wait!* Richard gasped. Could Teresa be one, too? Maybe?

"Hey Dad, I need to ask you something." His voice shook a little with disbelief, with a strange feeling of excitement.

"What's up?"

"When I went over to Vladimir's house today, Mrs. White was on the phone and talking some foreign language."

"Czech, I'd suppose."

"Yeah, I guess. She also acted kind of weird when she saw me. And there was a map on her table."

"I'm sure she doesn't know her way around DC yet. It's hard getting oriented when you've had to move as much as they have. Maybe Abby needs to give her a little tour." Don stopped puffing and grinned at Richard. "Wait a sec. Thinking like a G-man, I see. What else did you see? What kind of map?"

"I'm not sure. But it didn't look like one of Washington."

"How could you tell?"

"Well . . ." Richard thought a moment. He closed his eyes to pull the map back up in his memory. "There was a grid of streets on the left and what looked like a lot of green to the right . . . and a river going through the middle. Which could be DC. But . . ."

"Analyze what you saw, son. Think."

Richard got up and paced. "I don't know. It just didn't seem the same. And if it were DC, she could have asked me about it, don't you think?"

"There you go! Always dissect a scene by figuring out the meaning or motivations of people's behaviors." Don nodded. "Good man!"

He stood, clapping Richard on the back. "Keep on thinking thataway and you'll give old Philbrick a run for his money someday! But right now? Let's sneak a piece of one of your mom's pumpkin pies." Don put his arm over

Richard's shoulders. "After all," he said with a wink, "we FBI agents gotta stay fortified, if we're going to keep a sharp eye out!"

Richard grinned back at his dad. This was the Don he believed in.

Chapter 7:

DECEMBER

1953

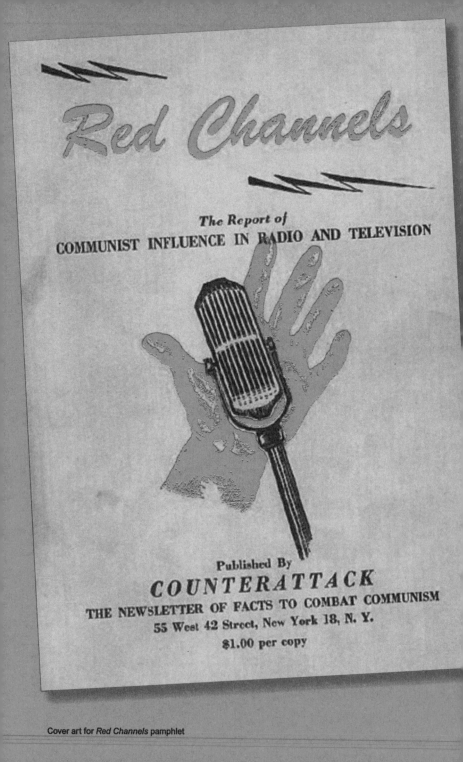

Cover art for *Red Channels* pamphlet

The country remains suspicious of the entertainment industry because of the Hollywood Ten—screenwriters accused of being Reds and of lacing hidden communist ideas into their movie scripts. (The Ten had argued their First Amendment right to freedom of expression but were found to be in contempt of Congress and sentenced to one year in prison each. Now released, they are blacklisted and unable to find work.)

Newspaper ads urge viewers to boycott any TV show or film that seems "subversive." Responding to the public's continued anxiety, which is fueled by McCarthy's hearings and insinuations, the entertainment industry polices itself with blacklists like *Red Channels*. This privately published pamphlet becomes a secret checklist for hiring "safe" creative artists by naming 151 actors, writers, musicians, and journalists its authors believe spread dangerous left-wing political beliefs.

People denounced in *Red Channels* include: writers Dashiell Hammett and Arthur Miller; jazz musicians Lena Horne and Artie Shaw; folk singer Pete Seeger; and Hollywood star Orson Welles. Each name is followed by a list of his or her actions thought to substantiate the pamphlet's accusations.

The *Red Channels* entry for poet Langston Hughes runs four full pages. It points to things like his belonging to the Southern Conference for Human Welfare and the New Theatre League. His poem "Goodbye, Christ" is listed as "a typical example of vicious and blasphemous propaganda Communists use against religion."

Langston Hughes

"VITEJTE!"

Teresa threw open her front door, spilling warm light, Christmas music, and the sweet scent of a blazing fireplace into the cold December night.

"*Veselé Vánoce!*" a bundled-up couple responded cheerily. They were just ahead of Richard and his family, who were coming up the walk with Mrs. Emerson in tow.

"Merry Christmas!" Don shouted, waving his gloved hand after Teresa kissed the cheeks of the couple ahead of them in the doorway.

"Welcome!" Teresa called back. She gestured at them to hurry in. "Please, please come! It is so cold tonight." She smiled brightly.

"*Humph.* No maid to answer the door," Mrs. Emerson murmured and elbowed Abigail. "Odd for a holiday open house, don't you think?"

But before Abigail could reply, Teresa embraced her and pulled their group through the front door. "Do let me help you." Teresa held the shoulders of Abigail's swing coat so she could slip out of the heavy material, static electricity popping. "Natalia will put it upstairs."

Vladimir's sister was already piled to her chin with coats and struggling to keep them from cascading to the ground.

"Goodness, let Richard help! He can carry ours!" Abigail nodded for Richard to extend his arms. She plopped her coat on him, followed by Ginny's, Don's, and Mrs. Emerson's.

As Richard staggered along behind Natalia toward the staircase, he heard Mrs. Emerson say to Teresa, "My dear, I have the names of wonderful help you might like to employ next time. There's a Negro gentleman who butlers at the White House occasionally. He'll be able to guide you in proper protocol. There is a way of doing things here in the nation's capital, you know."

Natalia rolled her eyes dramatically. "Is everyone in Washington such a white snob?" She didn't even bother to whisper.

"What?" Richard startled.

"Come on, really? You don't see it? She's probably one of those bourgeoisie who think anyone who is friends with a Black person or believes Blacks should have equal schooling is a Red. What a bunch of fascists!" She waddled up the steps with her mountain of wraps to unceremoniously dump them on her bed. It was already piled high with bright red-and-green scarves and mink or wool coats glittering with pins of Christmas trees and angels made of jewels. From that jumble wafted up a muddle of perfumes. There would be quite a fishing expedition at the end of the party to sort out individual coats. But following her lead, Richard threw his family's into the mess.

Natalia was assessing him when he turned. "You're Vladi's friend, aren't you?" She extended her hand to shake his. "Glad to meet you. I felt awful deserting him so soon after we moved here. This sure isn't London or New York, so I was glad he had a friend right away." She flopped onto the pile of coats, pulled out a long black straw-like holder from her bedside table, and tucked a cigarette into it.

Richard felt himself gaping at her as she crossed her legs and bobbed her top foot up and down. She wore a tight black sweater and straight black slacks ending above the ankles, wide gold cuff bracelets and gold hoop earrings—like something straight out of Hollywood magazines. Her face really was almost identical to Teresa's—with keen smoke-gray eyes under thick, arched brows. He forcefully snapped himself out of his stare by asking, "You go to UCLA, right?"

"Uh-hmmm." She nodded, chewing lightly on the holder without lighting the cigarette.

"Do you like it?"

"Loooooove it," she sang.

"Home for Christmas?"

"And Hanukkah. It's the only part of her Jewish background Mother celebrates. Seems kind of hypocritical to me, but . . ." She smiled mischievously and shrugged. "It means more presents for me and Vladi!"

Richard had no idea what to say to that, it sounded so cynical. He changed the subject. "Ahhh . . . What are you studying?"

She laughed. "The question to ask a girl when you get to college is 'What is your major?' That's the icebreaker. I need to remember to tell Vladi that." She smiled at him. "I am going to major in art. I am an artist."

"Oh, like your mom?"

She nodded. "But I am actually going to make my living at it. Mother's never been able to do anything other than be a hobbyist. Father has dragged her so many different places. At least she's got a real studio here on the porch. It's nice. She has a lot of her own art hanging down there. You should go look. Someone should." She shrugged, still gnawing on the holder.

"I will, then." Richard nodded. "What do you paint?"

"Everything!" She laughed lightly. "But mainly I want to illustrate children's books. Like these." Natalia swam over the coats to the other side of the bed to haul up a stack of picture books off the floor.

First, she held up *Finders Keepers*, a bright red book with two orangey-red dogs and a bone on its cover. She leafed through its pages to show Richard the drawings. "They are so simple and bold. Like graphic design, almost. Aren't they great?"

Richard thought they looked kind of goofy, like cartoons he could draw, but he nodded. "Yeah, they're swell."

"It just won the Caldecott Medal for illustration. But some librarians in the Midwest are claiming the book is subversive. I mean, really! The dogs are just figuring out how to share a bone between them. But these women claim"—Natalia flipped to a page that had a big black dog trying to take the bone away from the two little red dogs—"that the white spots on the black dog resemble the outlines of the United States, Great Britain, Germany, Taiwan, and Japan. They claim the picture is suggesting imperialism, that we and our capitalist allies are trying to bully Communist-leaning countries." She made a face. "I think those librarians must have been smoking some tea."

Richard squinted at the picture.

When he didn't say anything, Natalia dropped that book and picked up *The Two Reds* by the same author and illustrator. That cover featured a red cat and a redheaded boy in front of a city skyline.

Richard did do a double take on that one. If nothing else, the title seemed pretty questionable. But Natalia didn't seem to notice his expression. "This one won a Caldecott Honor while we were still living in New York. It's such great modern illustration. A clerk at that marvelous FAO Schwarz on Central Park— You know the store?" she interrupted herself.

Richard didn't. He'd only been to New York City a couple of times to visit a great-aunt. She always took him to the Met to see the ancient Greek and Roman statuary—which he loved, actually. He shook his head.

"No?" Natalia seemed stunned. "Well, anyway, he's a friend of ours. He planned a whole window display of the books. But Maurice told us that the store owner nixed his idea because he thought the title was provocative—subversive—and because the illustrator, Nicolas Mordvinoff, is a Russian émigré. And probably Jewish. You'd think after the carnage of World War II that here in the United States we'd have some sense and not be so afraid of people thinking or worshipping differently. But thanks to Senator Low-Blow Joe, the Red Scare has also become about Jews and Blacks." Natalia shook her head. "What a bunch of fascists."

Richard did think the idea that the dog's spots were maps of countries was pretty stupid. But he kind of wondered about a writer who'd name a book *The Two Reds*. Still, he could tell Natalia wouldn't much appreciate his opinion. Talking to her felt like standing on a cliff and surveying an exciting, uncharted wilderness. He didn't want to ruin it. "What else do you have there?" he asked.

"Oh, these illustrations are totally different. Old-school gorgeous." On top of the coats, she laid out *Robinson Crusoe, The Last of the Mohicans*, and *Kidnapped*—all with similarly styled lush, detailed scenes on their covers. "The illustrations are by N. C. Wyeth." Natalia stretched back over the bed and fished out two other books from underneath it. "These two are my favorite: *Treasure Island* and *Robin Hood*."

"*Robin Hood!*" Richard couldn't help exclaiming and reaching for it. He ran his hand lovingly over the cover. He had really wanted to finish reading this story. He remembered some of the illustrations inside—Robin meeting Maid Marian, Robin knocking down a villain with a quarterstaff, Robin's Merry Men hiding behind trees, their arrows drawn along taut bows. All the scenes had set his own imagination flying.

Reluctantly, he handed the book back to Natalia.

"You can borrow it if you want," she said.

Richard shook his head. "Can't. My mom said—" He stopped himself from criticizing Abigail publicly—a big no-no with Don. Besides, he could sense Natalia might make fun of his mom, and he wasn't sure that he'd like that. So he shifted gears. "People are pulling it from libraries because they think it promotes Communist ideals."

"You mean that nutty textbook commissioner in Indiana who's mounted a national campaign against *Robin Hood*?"

Richard shrugged.

Natalia pointed at him with her cigarette holder. "You know what I love most about college?" She didn't wait for an answer. "Learning how to think for myself. And recognizing manure when I smell it." She dipped into the pile of jackets and held up his blue peacoat. "This yours?"

He nodded.

She tucked *Robin Hood* inside it. "Just give it back to Vladi after you're done. Come on!" Natalia jumped off her bed. "Let's go give him some relief. He's manning the record player for the party."

Richard followed, his mind as much a jumble of conflicting thoughts as the tangle of coats in her room. Think like a G-man, he told himself. See and analyze the meaning behind people's behaviors, just like his dad had said. Richard knew McCarthy and Hoover would label a lot of what Natalia said as being subversive. Big-time. They'd probably brand Natalia a Red or a pinko. Heck, they might even be right. Natalia definitely seemed kind of over-fond of that Russian illustrator and his book's themes.

But he liked her. And Richard was really excited about having a copy of *Robin Hood* again. The trick would be smuggling it home.

●   ●   ●

Downstairs was a Babel of conversation. Adults were massed in little groups, laughing, chatting, and debating in snippets of Czech and English, sipping cocktails, glasses clinking, bracelets jangling merrily. Through emerald silks and vermilion satin dresses Natalia passed, the sole black-clad figure, like a defiant exclamation point.

Richard followed, catching small ripples of talk as he wiggled his way through elbows. A conversation between two bow-tied, bespectacled men caught on him like fishhooks.

"I swear, I found steam marks on all my letters. Did you have to take a lie detector test, too?"

"Yeah, I did."

"It is very disturbing. I didn't take the Fifth on any of the questions, but with the ones about my lifestyle, I sort of felt like telling them to go to hell."

"Yeah, I'm with you. I'm sick of all the loyalty oaths. The constant questioning since Ike's beefed-up executive order. I swear I'd resign, except I'd be shackled with that stigma if I did. Anyone who leaves the State Department these days is just assumed to be a closet Red. Or a gossip you can't trust. Or a lush. Or Hoover's pet fear—a homosexual. You can't get a job anywhere."

Letters with steam marks? Lie detector tests? Taking the Fifth? Richard stopped to eavesdrop, pretending to warm his hands by the fireplace.

"Maybe it'll get better with the midterm elections," one of the men said hopefully.

"Unlikely," his friend answered. "Not as long as Nixon is VP. I think you were posted over in Scandinavia when he ran for Senate, but the guy basically won on Red-baiting. He was up against Congresswoman Helen Gahagan Douglas. You know, the old Hollywood actress?"

His companion nodded. "She was a New Dealer, wasn't she?"

"Yes, and a good, gutsy liberal, even if she is a woman. She opposed the Internal Security Act and was against funding HUAC's hearings. So, you can imagine it was pretty easy for Nixon to paint her as 'the Pink Lady.' He actually dared to say that a vote for her was a vote for Stalin. But the most egregious thing"—the man lowered his voice before continuing—"were the penny postcards that his volunteers mailed to every voter right before Election Day, when there wasn't time for the congresswoman to refute the message."

His companion shook his head and asked, "Postcards?"

The man smirked. "They read, 'Vote for Our Helen for Senator. We Are With Her One Hundred Percent.' And they signed it: the Communist League of Negro Women. It was totally fake. No such group existed."

His companion exhaled. "Well, that would do her in on two fronts, wouldn't it? What a dirty trick."

Richard frowned. He was unused to hearing that kind of criticism of elected officials. His dad basically worshipped President Eisenhower because of his Steady Eddie leadership during World War II. And if the congresswoman was against tightening things up for the sake of national security, then maybe she was a pinko. Like everyone said: if it walks like a duck and talks like a duck, then it's gotta be a duck. But Richard had to admit the postcards didn't sound ethical at all.

The conversation gave Richard some of the same weird mishmash of thoughts as his exchange with Natalia had. Is this how people who had been friends with the Rosenbergs had felt? Had they ever had sneaking suspicions that they now wished they'd followed up on? How would Agent Philbrick interpret what Richard had just overheard?

Richard scanned the crowd for Don. His dad would know what to think. He spotted Vladimir instead, wading through the crowd toward him.

"There you are, man. I've been looking for you!" Vladimir punched Richard's shoulder. "Natalia's given me a break from the music. I'm heading to the dining room. I want some of Mom's *vánočka* before it's all gone."

"Her what?" asked Richard.

"Apple strudel."

Then why not just call it by its American name, thought Richard with a little bit of irritation. All this Czech stuff could give people the wrong idea about his friend. Couldn't Vladimir's family see that?

"Come on." Vladimir grinned and grabbed Richard's collar to pull him through the crowd with him. "It's a Czech Christmas tradition. Mom says that when she was a little girl, her family would feed a piece to the cows on Christmas Eve to make sure there'd be lots of milk all year. And if we eat a piece at Christmas, it's supposed to bring us good friends in the New Year."

● ● ·

In the dining room, Richard was happily stuffing himself with the honey-glazed apple bread when Vladimir elbowed him. "Our old men sure seem serious." He nodded toward the corner, where his father and Don were talking.

The dads stood in front of that exhibit poster Richard had noticed the day Vladimir moved in. In the brightly lit, cheerful Christmas decorations, the artwork's thick black outlines and dark purples and blues, the people's downcast looks, seemed even more sorrowful. A strange piece of art to put in a dining room, he thought. But then again, so much of the stuff hanging on the walls of Vladimir's house seemed odd to him—speckles of primary colors or enormous flowers stretched to the edge of the frame. Nothing like the tame pastel landscapes decorating his house.

This was one of the few times Richard had actually seen Vladimir's father. Mr. White was always working late, it seemed. He was tall and willowy, an almost frail man, with unusually long, dark eyelashes and a round, animated face. His hair bobbed in short, dark curls as he talked, gesturing enthusiastically, spilling his martini on himself. Don, on the other hand, seemed to be at attention, straight, broad-shouldered in his typical FBI dark blue suit and starched white shirt. He held a Royal Crown Cola bottle.

"What's with your dad?" Vladimir asked.

"Nothing. He's just listening to yours." But Richard recognized that look on Don's face. He was making mental notes. To outsiders, Don might appear stern in these moments, but really, he was standing post, keeping watch, absorbing information.

"*Humph.*" Vladimir started toward their fathers. "Let's go see what they're talking about."

Don greeted them. "Hi, son. Good to see you, Vladimir. Wonderful party your folks are throwing! Your dad was just telling me about your time in Prague."

"Cut short all too soon, I fear, because of the Communist coup," said Mr. White. "We did love it there, didn't we, son? I was just bragging about your mother and her involvement with this exhibit." He pointed to the poster.

"Did you tell him what an idiot that congressman was?" Vladimir asked.

Don cocked his head in surprise at Vladimir. Richard knew that expression, too. If it had been Richard, Don would have warned him to watch his mouth. Disrespecting people who served the country was pretty verboten in Don's rule book.

Mr. White laughed. "No, no, son. This is Christmas, after all. A time of peace."

"Come on, Dad. You always tell me to call a spade a spade."

Mr. White put his arm over Vladimir's shoulders and gave Don and Richard a diplomat-perfect, inscrutable smile. "It was just a sad set of circumstances. The State Department had gathered the art of many important American artists, like Georgia O'Keeffe and Edward Hopper. We sent the exhibit to Eastern Europe as a way of combating Soviet influence. To show the artistic freedom allowed here in America, in democracy. It was quite a success. Eighteen thousand people came to the show in Prague alone. My wife was very involved in helping to spread the word and then explaining the philosophies and techniques of the exhibited artists to Prague's news reporters. She knows several of the painters personally."

He sighed. "But back home, some conservative radio commentators and congressmen decided that the art was . . . hmmm . . . Well, their words were *dark* and *depressing*. They felt the paintings didn't adequately portray our happy American opportunities, and in that regard actually forwarded Communism. So the exhibit was recalled." He cleared his throat. "Tell me, Don, have you ever traveled to Czechoslovakia? Prague is exquisite, like Paris."

But Teresa had appeared by her husband's side as he talked, and she interrupted before Don could answer. "Such a tragedy. Complete foolishness. The exhibit was working! The Czech people were much impressed, especially by the honest presentation of the common man's struggles. Look at this piece by Gwathmey, for instance." She pointed to the poster. "It's called *Worksong*. The Soviets would never allow such an expressive and moving depiction of sadness and fatigue." She paused, gazing at it. "There is such dignity in these faces. Can you believe that congressman, the one from Michigan—oh, what was his name? Dondero, that's right. Dondero called this beautiful, soulful painting grotesque. He claimed that"—she made little quotation marks in the air—"'Expressionism aims

to destroy by aping the primitive and insane.' *To destroy?*
Aping? Insane? I mean, really." She laughed with derision
and ended, "How . . . provincial."

"Yes, darling, a disappointment, certainly." Mr. White
looked at Don with obvious discomfort and caution. "But that's
in the past. Recalibrating our efforts is the diplomat's job. Now,
Richard, what are you doing over the holidays?"

Startled by the sudden non sequitur shift to him, Richard
stammered slightly. "I . . . I . . . I . . . I'm not sure. See some
movies. Read."

"You should come with us to New York!" Vladimir
exclaimed. "We're going up after New Year's Eve to see that
play I told you about. The one Mom's friend wrote. Ever seen
a play on Broadway?"

Richard shook his head.

"Oh, then come, my dear," Teresa said. "It will be such fun
to have you. Vladimir wants to climb to the crown of the Statue
of Liberty again, and I really am not interested in dealing with
that rickety spiral staircase. It's terrifying! You can go with him
instead and save me. Yes?"

"Can I, Dad?" Richard asked, half expecting Don to defer
to Abigail. She always made the family's holiday plans. But
instead, Don immediately gave permission. "I think that's an
excellent idea."

● ● •

On the way home, Don pulled Richard toward him on the sidewalk as Ginny skipped ahead with Abigail and Mrs. Emerson.
Fortunately for Richard, Don didn't take the arm that braced
the copy of *Robin Hood* tucked inside his coat.

"Hey, Rich, you might have been right to feel your antennae go up about Teresa's phone conversation. For starters, I know all about that art exhibit. There was a pretty big stink about how hungry and oppressed the people depicted in those paintings looked—like they were *victims* of our American way of life. It ruffled a lot of feathers. Half those artists emigrated here from Eastern Europe or Russia or are on our FBI watch lists. Including that guy Gwathmey.

"Do me a favor, son. Keep an eye out when you're up there in New York City. Think like a G-man. If you notice something odd, remember it. Nice family and all. I genuinely like them. But I'm not so sure about some of their friends."

Chapter 8:

JANUARY

1954

In the entertainment world, actress Marilyn Monroe marries baseball star Joe DiMaggio, to the delight of an adoring nation. The Tournament of Roses parade is aired in color for the first time. A newcomer named Elvis Presley pays four dollars to record a ten-minute demo in Memphis.

And the first Black-owned national radio network, the National Negro Network, begins airing on 40 charter member stations across the country. Programming reflects Black life and music to appeal to a Black audience, but the owner, W. Leonard Evans, insists on hiring an "interracial" staff. Broadcasts include live symphonic concerts from Black colleges, DJ-hosted music, and soap operas, including *The Story of Ruby Valentine*, starring Ruby Dee, a Hollywood and Broadway star and activist.

The United States launches its first atomic-powered submarine, the USS *Nautilus*. Nuclear propulsion allows it to travel much farther than any diesel-powered sub and to reach undersea locations previously too far away to explore.

The *Nautilus* submarine

"THAT looks interesting." Richard sat next to Vladimir on a train for New York City. Vladimir was reading a book titled *Fahrenheit 451* by Ray Bradbury.

"It is! Mom gave it to me for Christmas. I'm almost finished. I can lend it to you when I'm done."

Richard squinted at the figure on the cover. The man's head was bowed, his arm was held up to shield his face, and his suit was burning. Maybe the weirdest thing was the guy seemed to be a bunch of newspapers folded and twisted into the figure of a man. "He's made of paper."

"Yeah, good eye, daddy-o." Vladimir's vocabulary had gotten hipper the instant they sat down on the train. "It's like a symbol for the whole book."

"Yeah?"

"It's this dystopia." Vladimir sat up and got increasingly animated as he described the plot. "Books are totally against the law. Firemen don't put out fires, they start them. They burn any books that are found. Four hundred fifty-one is the temperature that paper ignites. The main guy, Montag, is a fireman, a true believer in the government. He goes on raids to destroy any books in the name of public happiness. But he meets this freethinking teenage girl who makes him start questioning his job. He actually starts smuggling away books from the houses he's burning down to read them himself and . . . well . . . I don't want to spoil the ending." He smiled. "I sure would like to meet the author. Do you remember that line in *The Catcher in the Rye*, about authors feeling like friends?"

"Yes!" Richard brightened. "It's one of my favorite quotes." He added without thinking, "I wrote it down." Realizing he'd admitted something he could be teased for by a lot of guys, Richard looked sideways at Vladimir with some trepidation.

"No way! You do that, too?" Vladimir nodded. "I've got scraps of paper all over my room with quotes on them. Half the time, though, I forget which book it came from." He laughed at himself. "But I'm not going to forget Bradbury's stuff. To write a story condemning book burning and weasels turning over friends to the government—right now, with everything McCarthy and his henchmen are doing? He's got a lot of chutzpah."

Richard cocked his head quizzically, and Vladimir immediately translated, "Cheekiness. Sass. You know, in-your-face. To write this when that kook McCarthy has everyone on the run. Wow."

Richard caught his breath and fought the urge to look over his shoulder. If a classic like *Robin Hood* could get him and his father in trouble with Mr. Hoover, what could a book like that cause?

He ran his hand over the Merry Men on his own book. Richard had snuck Natalia's copy of *Robin Hood* into his suitcase, knowing he could finish it safely in Vladimir's company. But he suddenly felt really queasy. He stood up abruptly, dropping his book with a bounce onto his seat.

"Bathroom," he muttered to Vladimir and hurried down the aisle, fighting the lurch and sway of the train rushing north along the tracks.

He doused his face with cold water and took a towel from the porter watching him. He felt a lot better. Motion sickness, he told himself, from reading on a moving train.

But Richard was about to be hit by another wave of nausea. He'd tucked some of his song lyrics into *Robin Hood*, planning to work on them when no one was looking. When he got back to his seat, Vladimir was reading them.

"What the hell, man!" Richard snatched the papers away.

"Whoa, sorry, Rich!" Vladimir held up his hands. "They fell out when you dropped your book. I just picked them up before they slid to the back of the car. I couldn't help reading it when I realized it was poetry."

"Lyrics," Richard blurted. He crossed his arms and spread his feet against the swing of the train in a bring-it attitude, braced for ridicule.

"Lyrics? A closet songwriter. Wow. I didn't know you had it in you! You're like Holden's brother, writing poetry in his baseball mitt." Vladimir lowered his voice. "Seriously, your stuff is killer, Rich. Real troubadour material. Any doll is going to be on cloud nine listening to this. I really like the part when you say that . . . mmm . . . hand that back to me for a sec."

Richard hesitated. That particular song was about Dottie. About dancing with her at McCarthy's wedding. But he hadn't named her. A good thing, since she and Vladimir were practically going steady these days. Well, thankfully, Richard hadn't brought along the heartbroken verses about her loving someone else. Vladimir might figure things out from those.

"Come on." Vladimir gestured impatiently. "Maybe I can write the music for it. We can be like Ira and George Gershwin."

Vladimir started singing, "'*S wonderful! 'S marvelous, you should care for me . . .* Oh, oh, or *Someone to waaaatch over meeeee . . .* Or, or . . . *I got rhythm, I got music, I got my gal, who could ask for anything more.*"

Richard couldn't help but grin.

"Hand it over," Vladimir said again.

Richard held his breath and gave the page to him. Vladimir half sang, half read them:

"*Strawberry blond all in my eyeeees,*
It is youuuu I've got on my minnnnd,
With your red lipstick and sweet perfummme,
You've got this fella all in a swooooon,
Let me hold you in a dance so we're a pair,
Then you can be mine and I can smell your haiiiir. . . ."

Vladimir paused. "Honest, Rich, these are swell." He read again, then looked out the window at warehouses and telephone poles and wires whizzing by. After a few moments, he said, "I'm thinking of Sinatra's recording of 'I've Got a Crush on You.' You know how it's almost a duet between the trumpet player and Frankie? We could do that. I could write the music to your words and play the saxophone, and you could sing."

"I can't sing!"

"Sure you can. I can keep the range narrow so you don't have to work your voice through too much. And think about it. Frankie isn't that stellar a singer."

Richard blanched. Not that good of a singer? Old Blue Eyes? The Sultan of Swoon? Sacrilege! But . . . maybe? Was it possible Richard could be a singer, a Sinatra-style crooner?

Richard plopped back down into his seat as Vladimir started singing again, this time the Sinatra tune: *"I've got a crush on youuuu, sweetie piiiiiiieee."* Then he hummed, pretending to play an invisible saxophone. When he started singing again, Richard joined in: *"Could you coo, could you care, for a cunning cottage we could share."*

They'd only just passed Baltimore, but Richard already felt a world away from home.

● ● ·

"I miss all this," Vladimir said quietly. "Look at that skyline. See over there? That needle sticking up higher than any of the other buildings? That's the Chrysler Building. And to the left of it"—he pointed—"that's the Empire State Building." He sighed. "Look how the Brooklyn Bridge gleams in the moonlight—a big ol' steel-and-cable spiderweb. Can you imagine building that thing back in the 1880s? We should walk across it tomorrow. In winds like this, it hums."

Shivering, Richard tightened his hold on the fire escape railing. They were staying across the East River from Manhattan in Brooklyn Heights, where Teresa's friends lived. Vladimir had pulled them out onto the rickety, see-through catwalk of connecting ladders and landings. They were sitting, dangling their feet, five stories up, like it was a balcony or something. The darn thing swayed whenever one of them moved. But Richard wasn't about to admit he was scared. And the view was worth the terror. If he didn't freeze his butt off.

A long lonely call of a foghorn drifted up to them, followed by an answering *honk-hooooonnk*. "Tugboats coming back in from getting tankers out," Vlad explained. "You'll see a bunch of them tomorrow when we go to the Statue of Liberty. They are shrimps, but they shove around the huge ships. Talk about a can-do attitude. There's some kind of metaphor in them. Old Bradbury would come up with one for sure."

The boys stared at the inky waters.

"Oh, man. Maybe I can get you down to the docks before we go back to DC. It's so hip. You never heard so many languages. And there are guys from Senegal with tattoos all over, and Russians in pajama-like getups and Indonesians in sarungs. A bunch of them wear earrings, like Blackbeard." Vladimir pushed his coat collar up around his ears. "I wish it weren't so cold. We could go roller-skating on the esplanade along the river if it wasn't for the wind. It gives you a great view of the city."

Teeth chattering, Richard managed to answer, "So m-m-much to s-see."

"That ain't the half of it, buddy boy! There's Birdland, the jazz club. And Rockefeller Center. Those Rockettes . . ." He whistled. "But we'll cover as much as we can. Hey!" He punched Richard. "We'll be like Frankie and Gene Kelly in that movie *On the Town*. Remember?" He started singing, *"New York, New York, a helluva town. The people ride in a hole in the groun'."*

He threw his arms out for the verse's finale and was basically shouting, *"New York, New Yorrrrrk. It's a hell-uv-a towwwwwwwnnnn!"* just as his mother knocked loudly on the window.

"Vladi! Get inside!"

"Busted!" Vladimir grinned. "It really bugs her when I climb out onto these things. But I should remember what

Dad told me: Nazis threw people she loved off fire escapes in Czechoslovakia."

As he crawled back in, he apologized. "Sorry, Mom."

"You should really be sorry for singing that song for anyone in the street below to hear, young man," joked one of their hosts, the husband of Jane Bowles, whose play they'd come to see. He wagged his finger at Vladimir and winked.

Vladimir had told Richard earlier that Paul Bowles was a composer, a protégé of Aaron Copland. He'd come back to New York from Morocco to write the play's instrumental music and watch over rehearsals. He'd done the same for a guy named Tennessee Williams and a play called *The Glass Menagerie*.

Richard didn't know any of those names, but he didn't let on. Vladimir had seemed so proud to know the guy.

"I'm already under enough suspicion being friends with Maestro Copland," Mr. Bowles continued, still with mirth in his voice. But he grew more serious when he looked at Teresa and said, "Can you believe they canceled his performing the *Lincoln Portrait* for Eisenhower's inaugural just because that one moronic congressman asked if he was a commie? Could it be because he is friends with Russia's Shostakovich? Don't they realize artists connect over borders without politics? God Almighty! Things are only getting worse with McCarthy."

He turned back to Vladimir. "You see, Leonard Bernstein wrote the music you were singing, Vladi. And now he's supposedly a pinko, too." He ruffled Vladimir's hair. "That little serenade of yours could bring the FBI jumping out of trash trucks and straight in here, waving their notebooks."

Richard frowned. The man was kidding around, yeah, but he was still ridiculing the bureau. Richard pressed his lips together to keep from saying something rude. He was these people's guest. But he sure didn't like the composer's attitude. And he knew Don wouldn't either. In fact, it was the kind of thing that might spark one of his dad's alarming outbursts of anger.

Richard glanced over at Vladimir, who opened his mouth—probably to tell Mr. Bowles that Don was a G-man—but his wife spoke up too quickly for that.

"Don't be silly, darling. If they come, it'll be for me. After all, in Hoover's and McCarthy's eyes I check many subversive boxes." She held up a finger with each label she named. "I'm Jewish, alcoholic, a Communist—and I write about lesbians." She laughed sarcastically. She leaned toward a table lamp and in a stage whisper said into the light's shade, "Isn't that right? You getting all that?"

Quickly, Teresa put her arm through her friend's. "Richard's father is an FBI agent, you know. He is quite a lovely man. You'd like him, *miláčku*."

The playwright eyed Richard. "No, I don't believe I would." Even though she said it with a smile, Richard bristled and felt all the freckles on his face burn. Well, this short, snotty woman was someone to tell Don about, for sure.

She picked up her cane. "Time to go, players. The curtain rises in a few hours."

The two women headed for the door arm in arm, slowly to allow for the playwright's limp. She kept chattering all the way down the hall and into the see-through cage elevator. "Tennessee was so helpful in reading the different draft versions of my final scene. I had such a hard time deciding which ending I preferred. Casting was an ordeal, too. I'm still not sure we got that right. There was this young man who auditioned for the lover, Lionel. I remember his name because he was quite beautiful—James Dean. But he was too normal, not sufficiently anguished for the part. Still, I'm not sure the boy we picked captures the role either. . . ."

The playwright didn't stop talking in the cab. Richard would have given anything for a notebook. But in his mind he repeated the names she brought up to burn the list in his memory: composer Benjamin Britten and a bunch of writers named Arthur Miller, Norman Mailer, Truman Capote, W. H. Auden. Some old guy advocating civil rights named W. E. B. Du Bois. They all seemed to live nearby.

Sitting in the theater, watching the production of *In the Summer House*, Richard felt a weird mixture of guilt and smugness when one of her characters said, "I have the strangest feeling about you. . . . I feel that you are plotting something."

● ● ·

"So, what did you think of her?"

Richard had a mouthful of warm roasted chestnuts he was eating from a bag. After climbing up and down the twenty-two-story-high Statue of Liberty, they'd come back across the waters on a ferry. As soon as they landed at Battery Park, they'd purchased the sweet nuts from a street vendor, his truck a wonderful warm caldron of steam. Richard had wanted to crawl into it. He felt frozen solid. Winds had hit Bedloe's Island so brutally that the statue shivered as they stood inside her.

"Amazing," he mumbled, as he finished chewing. "I didn't realize that she's completely hollow, like a big huge bell."

"Yup. The statue's hull is only the thickness of two pennies. Can you believe? Maybe I should become a sculptor."

Richard laughed. He'd come to realize that Vladimir just kind of wanted to be anything that was awesome and hip.

"And the doll ahead of us on those stairs wasn't so bad either, was she?"

Richard blushed, remembering how Vladimir had caught him glancing up the skirts of the pretty girl ahead of them. He didn't mean to, honest. The spiral stairs were just so narrow and steep, everyone climbing them was on top of one another. When she stepped up, his head was basically at her ankles. He switched the subject to the swirling steps. "That staircase was unbelievable."

"You know, they were thinking they'd have to fill her with sand to keep her from falling over until someone got the bright idea to ask Gustave Eiffel to figure out something different. She's balanced and braced like the Eiffel Tower. You should see that someday, too, Rich. It's . . . it's . . . *extraordinaire*, as Parisians would say—how something that delicate-looking could stand so strong."

"Wait. You've seen the Eiffel Tower, too?" Vladimir had told him a lot about London and Prague. All Richard had been able to educate him about were the Delaware beaches, Monticello, the Smithsonian Castle, and Luray Caverns. "Is there any place you haven't seen?"

"Are you joking me? The world! I want to go to Istanbul and Cairo and Hong Kong. And Copenhagen. Oh, and Saint Petersburg—I mean Leningrad."

"Russia? For real?"

"Sure! Saint Petersburg, anyway. The Winter Palace is supposed to be as great as Versailles. Hopefully, someday, Dad will have a diplomatic mission there, and I can tag along."

They sat down on a wrought iron bench, looking back across the churned-gray waters toward the statue, the Brooklyn Bridge to their left. Richard finished his last chestnut. They'd been surprisingly delicious. But he was ready to get back inside a building now. "When are we supposed to meet your mom?"

"She said she'd be here at three o'clock." Vladimir pulled his glove back to check his wristwatch, and then wound it. "About twenty minutes. We got here faster than I thought we would. Mom's always late, too."

They both hunched down and crossed their arms, tucking their hands under their armpits for extra warmth.

"This is stupid," Vladimir grumbled within a few minutes. "I could have walked us back across the bridge to the Heights. We don't need a keeper to hold our hands to cross the street!"

Richard shrugged. "Yeah. Moms. Whatcha gonna do?" Frankly, though, he'd been stunned at what Teresa had allowed. Abigail never would have put the two fourteen-year-olds on a ferry to cross a harbor alone. Especially not when all those boisterous, pushy people crowded the dock. But the whole trip had been like that—new liberties and new sights. The three days had been a blast. He slowly scanned the vista ahead of him, taking a mental snapshot.

That's when he noticed a man and woman walking slowly along the promenade's railing, arguing. She was getting kind of riled. She shook her fist at the guy. Richard focused on them. *Wait a second*. The woman looked a lot like Teresa.

"Hey, Vlad?" He elbowed his friend. But Vladimir was already sitting up and staring in that direction. His oddly silent alertness kept Richard quiet, too. The boys just watched as the man talked and Teresa seemed to calm. Then the man pulled an envelope out of his breast pocket and handed it to her. She put it in her purse. He tugged on the brim of his fedora in good-bye and walked away.

Teresa remained, looking out at the bay, the silk floral scarf she'd tied over her hair flapping in the wind. She pulled a handkerchief from her coat pocket and dabbed at her eyes.

Without a word, Vladimir stood and walked quickly toward his mother. Richard followed.

"Mom?" Vladimir called.

Teresa turned, startled, surprise and worry on her face. But when she spotted them, her expression morphed as quickly as a seasoned actress's. She flashed a big beauty-queen smile, dazzling enough for everyone in the park to see.

"*Drahoušek*," she called dramatically, "how was Lady Liberty?"

She tucked one arm through Vladimir's and then reached for Richard with the other, so the three of them walked side-by-side-by-side. "I hope Vladi didn't talk your ear off, Richard. He knows so much trivia about her. The nose is three feet long . . ."

"Four and a half feet," interrupted Vladimir.

". . . with two hundred steps to her crown . . ."

"Three hundred fifty-four, Mom."

"Ah, you see?" She squeezed Richard's arm. "Vladi knows everything! It is a marvel, though, isn't it, that statue? Like being inside a giant dressmaker's dummy. We see her ribs that hold her copper skin."

Richard couldn't believe Vladimir wasn't asking about the man. Or the envelope he had given her that Teresa now carried in her purse. Richard's own curiosity was choking him. But Teresa was chitchatting so fast and with such animation, there wasn't room for questions. Perhaps that was her point.

"Now, on the way back we need to stop by Mr. Miller's house. He lives just a few blocks away from Jane on Willow Street. A fantastic playwright, Richard." She turned to him. "Do you know *The Crucible*?" But she didn't wait for a reply. "It opened last spring. It is about the Salem witch trials, and, of course, a metaphor for other things. Fear, conformity, mob-mentality politics." She was panting a little as she spoke, both from the cold and the velocity of her chatter. "Anyway, poor Arthur is having terrible trouble getting a passport from the State Department to go to Brussels for a Belgian premiere of his play. He is hoping Vladi's father can help convince the New York office to grant him the necessary visa."

"Why would Dad have to help with that?" Vladimir asked.

She lowered her voice. "There are new regulations that deny passports to people believed to be supporting the Communist movement. It seems some people think a play about a witch hunt is a slap at McCarthy and a danger to his crusade against the Reds. Such terrible power for a mere play." She smiled. Or was it a smirk?

Could whatever she carried in that envelope from the mystery man have something to do with that? But she'd probably have said so if it did. Wouldn't she? Richard had to fight an itch to grab the purse and rummage through it to find out.

When they reached Willow Street, there was such a crowd on the front stoops that they stopped before reaching Miller's house.

"What's the scoop?" Vladimir asked a boy their age.

"They found another hollow nickel!"

"No kidding!" Vladimir whistled long. "With the same old ladies?"

"Nah," the kid answered. "At a pharmacy."

"Oh, goodness, there'll be all sorts of goings-on again." Teresa kept them walking. "Don't let me forget to tell our hosts. That way they won't be jumpy if a police officer knocks on the door."

"Policemen?" Wow, this was getting good, thought Richard.

Vladimir laughed. Richard must have looked like he was drooling or something. "Yeah, you'll love this, Rich. This is 007 stuff. Right before we moved to Washington last summer, a kid who delivered newspapers got a hollow nickel from some customer. He didn't realize it until it dropped to the floor and split open. And the craziest thing? It had a tiny square of paper in it with a bunch of Lilliputian-size numbers.

"G-men and cops went all over Brooklyn trying to find out who had given the kid that nickel, like it was the key to some big conspiracy. It ended up just being a pair of ladies who pulled out a handful of coins from a cookie jar to change a dollar for him. That was a dead end, so then the agents went to every five-and-dime store around to see if they sold toy coins that split open like that."

"It is sure to be nothing, just some magic-trick novelty item," said Teresa. "Like hats with hidden compartments for rabbits. Such fuss over nothing."

"I don't know, Mom. Sounds kind of cloak-and-dagger to me."

Richard nodded. His detective books and spy thrillers were filled with things like hollowed-out shoe heels with tiny radio transmitters or cuff links that hid thumbnail-size coded messages.

"Man, I wish I didn't have to go home," complained Vladimir. "We're going to miss all the fun!"

But Richard suddenly couldn't wait for the train to get moving. He might have a heart attack holding onto all this info for the four hours it would take them to get to Union Station! He was bursting to describe everything he'd seen and heard to his dad. Maybe Richard had discovered things that would turn into the case Abigail believed would set things right for Don.

Chapter 9:

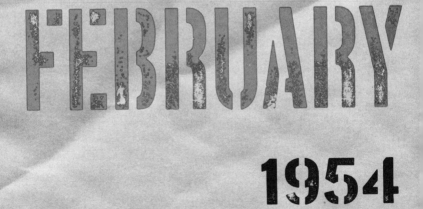

FEBRUARY

1954

IKE *and* DICK

All-American Partners

McCarthy begins hearings on "a pinko Army dentist." Despite being "red-flagged" by the First Army Intelligence for "sufficient evidence of disloyal and subversive tendencies," Major Irving Peress had been promoted. The son of Russian immigrants, Peress had attended the City College of New York with executed spy Julius Rosenberg, and had invoked "federal constitutional privilege" when filling in his personnel questionnaire.

The new camp commander, General Ralph Zwicker, called for Peress's immediate removal. An honorable discharge was quickest, decided the Army Personnel Board, since Peress "had done nothing during his military service which was offensive against military law."

McCarthy jumps on the Peress case as proof the Army is soft on Communism. Long enraged by McCarthy, President Eisenhower finally speaks out when the Senator attacks the integrity of Zwicker, a decorated World War II veteran. Eisenhower holds a rare news conference to praise his military friend's gallantry in combat. Following that, Vice President Richard Nixon—a well-known "Red-hunter"—makes a televised rebuttal of McCarthy's claims:

"Men who have in the past done effective work exposing Communists in this country have, by reckless talk and questionable methods, made themselves the issue rather than the cause they believe in so deeply." Nixon doesn't name McCarthy, but adds: "When you go out and shoot rats, you have to shoot straight, because when you shoot wildly, it not only means that the rats get away more easily, but you might hit someone else who is trying to shoot rats, too."

Dr. Jonas Salk administers the first mass human test of his polio vaccine to elementary school children in Pittsburgh in his quest to stop a disease that attacks nearly 60,000 people a year, leaving a third of its victims paralyzed.

(Top) Salk with medicine bottles
• (Left) Nurse helping two children with polio

"DON! Over here!" Abigail waved to Richard's dad as he stood in the door of the holding room of WTOP's brand-new broadcast house. Don took off his fedora and clambered through two dozen other parents, all there to watch their children appear on the *Pick Temple's Giant Ranch* show.

"Excuse me. So sorry. Thanks." He wedged himself between Abigail and a rather round lady awash in gardenia perfume and a billowing lime-colored skirt. Her stiff white petticoat ballooned her skirt out even farther.

"Thank you, ma'am," Don drawled and nodded at the woman, who had moved aside an inch, maybe, to make room for him. "That's right neighborly of you, as our singing cowboy friend Pick might say."

The lady was not charmed. With obvious irritation at being crowded, she tried to smooth down her skirt to just one yard diameter of pouf.

Don turned to Abigail and grinned in an oops, gosh, teacher-doesn't-like-me way. "I was afraid I'd miss the beginning. Where's the sugarplum?"

Abigail pointed. "There, dead center. Doesn't she look cute?"

Don squinted at the line of televisions in front of the parents containing a grainy, black-and-white picture of thirty excited children. They were all corralled behind bales of hay and in front of a big sign with the show's name written in lasso-looking letters. "Where?" he asked.

"Between the two boys in cowboy hats and fringed vests."

"Abby, honey, all the boys are wearing cowboy hats."

"Right in the center, dear. Oh, oh, look at her smile. She's a natural on camera. I think I might cry." She put her white-gloved hands to her face.

Don frowned, squinting at the small TV monitors. "Why can't we just be next door in the studio with the kids?"

"They're afraid parents might talk during the airing. Or try to prompt their kids. You know how some parents are, dear, trying to direct from the sidelines."

"*Sssssshhhhh*," the voluminous lady next to him shushed. "It's about to begin."

Vladimir leaned forward to point over Don's shoulder. He and Richard were sitting together directly behind. He spoke quietly into Don's ear. "See the kid who's got his hands on top of his head and is wiggling his elbows, Mr. Bradley? Probably so he can find himself in the camera monitor? Right under the *h* in the word *ranch*."

Don nodded.

"Ginny is down and to . . ."

"Aha! I see her! Aaaaahhhh, ain't she purty."

"*Sssssssshhhhhh!*" the lime-green lady hissed.

Don looked back at Vladimir and winked. He mouthed the word *thanks* and then faced forward.

Richard squirmed a little, both inside and on the bleachers. His dad being all casual-friendly with Vladimir felt so . . . so . . . He wasn't sure of the right word. . . . So . . . fake? He was pretty sure he'd noticed Don flinch when Vladimir touched his shoulder to point out Ginny.

Of course, Richard was feeling a little like a fraud himself these days. He'd been double-dealing with Vladimir ever since getting back from New York. Vladimir was his best friend, and yet Richard had sung out to his dad all the strange stuff he'd seen up in Brooklyn Heights, just like a stool pigeon, as soon as he got home.

Don had been real interested, too, and asked him to repeat the story of Teresa and the man a couple of times. No, Richard hadn't gotten a good look at him. The man's hat was tugged down, covering a lot of his face. No, he hadn't seen what she put in her purse. No, he hadn't heard the guy's voice. But he was of medium height, medium build. And Don looked like his eyes were going to pop when Richard told him about the hollow nickel.

He'd ruffled Richard's hair, saying, "Fine work, Junior Agent Bradley." It was half joke, half serious. But the next thing out of Don's mouth was all gravy. "I'm proud of you, son. Those kinds of observation skills are real important to a man out in the world. You might even make a fine under-cover agent."

Richard was dying to ask, "Like you, Dad?" But Don left the room abruptly, and then the house.

A man. Out in the world. Undercover agent. This is swell, Richard thought.

Still, for a while after that, Richard had a hard time look-ing Vladimir in the eye, especially as Vladimir worked on different saxophone tunes for Richard's lyrics. He'd named the Dottie song "Strawberry Blond Perfume." Richard kept reminding himself of something Philbrick had said about leading a double life. He'd written the quote down in his notebook. *"Sometimes . . . in fighting to preserve what is worthwhile, you are forced to do things which are not in accordance with the very principles to which you are dedicated."*

Like telling the truth. Friendship. But which was more important? Being loyal to his friend or to his dad? Plus, sharing stuff about Vladimir was definitely getting Don's attention. Conversations that were guy-to-guy. Talks Richard had longed to have. And maybe they'd be helpful to Don, too. Get Mr. Hoover's attention.

Finally, Richard made himself feel better by realizing he hadn't said anything *bad* about Vladimir. He'd simply passed on some interesting things he'd observed about people in Brooklyn Heights and Teresa's oddball friends. Don was the G-man. He'd know what to do with that information and whether any of it indicated a danger to national security. Richard's job was done. He could relax.

Now Vladimir was spending a couple of nights at Richard's house because both his parents had gone back up to New York. His dad had business with the State Department's United Nations office, and Teresa, well, she hadn't really said why she needed to return to the city. Although Richard had his suspicions. Don's eyebrow had shot up, big-time, when Abigail had described Teresa's request. She was all excited about Vladimir coming, saying it would be a nice favor to pay them back for inviting Richard to New York City.

At first, Vladimir had been pretty darn annoyed about his mother lining up babysitters for him, saying he was perfectly capable of taking care of himself. But then he had Abigail's crab cakes and decided three dinners at the Bradley house was good news. That's why Vladimir was at the *Pick Temple's Giant Ranch* show. Don made a big deal of inviting him during that first supper, joking it was Ginny's TV debut and Vladimir would be able to say years from now that he had witnessed it.

Richard had been totally baffled by Don's buddy-buddy attitude with Vladimir at dinner that night, given all the questions he'd asked Richard about the Whites and their New York friends. Plus, *Pick Temple* was for little kids. Richard was mortified to be sitting in those bleachers, surrounded by parents, watching a bunch of children dressed up like cowboys and cowgirls with toy six-shooters, each one hoping to be chosen to shoot at balloons on a hay bale target range. Vladimir should be as well. If the basketball team heard about his being there, he'd be toast. Jimmy would have a field day with it.

Well, maybe that was why it seemed so important to Don that Vladimir go with them. Maybe his dad was just looking out for him, making sure Richard had protection in numbers. He could hope that, but who knew for sure? Richard was often confused by Don's and Abigail's reactions to stuff Ginny did.

Take Ginny's selection for the *Pick Temple* show. She'd been sending in postcards to WTOP for months, hoping hers would be drawn out of a drum—which was how the studio audience of kid guests was selected. Totally random. But Don had been bragging on her show appearance like she'd been personally *invited* to be on a celebrity interview program like *Person to Person* or something.

Richard craned his neck a little to see her. Weirdly, Ginny didn't seem that happy about it. He watched her for a moment and had a revelation. As gregarious as she was with adults, she wasn't talking to any of the kids around her. He shifted in his seat, suddenly worried rather than peeved. A little girl being so all-fired smart might be as bad as a teenage boy loving books. He hated how their parents were always so impressed by her, but he'd hate it even more if his little sister had to endure some of the persecution he had.

● ● ·

Twangy guitar music filled the studio. In jogged Pick, waving his arms in hello, his faithful collie named Lady dancing behind at his heels. "Heidi, pardners!" he called.

The children went wild, bouncing in their seats and clapping furiously, with seeing-Santa-Claus exuberance. Except for Ginny. She smiled brightly, but kept a ladylike cool as Pick greeted them. "Thanks for coming to Giant Ranch. Are you ready to have some fun, Rangers?"

"Yes!!!" the children squealed, clapping again and wriggling with joy, cued by two men who held clipboards and stood on the side out of camera view.

"Okay, then. Let's play Pass the Spinach!"

While the children passed a box of frozen spinach between them as fast as possible so they weren't caught holding it when the music stopped, Pick was handed his guitar. After the hot-potato game, he strummed the tune of "On Top of Old Smokey." Practiced from hours of watching the show at home, the children sang along: *So let's all eat Heidi's, and before very long, all Giant Rangers will grow big and strong.*

"Heidi's?" Vladimir asked.

"It's a local bakery. It and Giant Foods sponsor the show. Pick goes to all the store openings. Hundreds of kids go to see him, like he's Frank Sinatra or something. Ginny will get a big bag of Heidi's cookies at the end of the show. "

"*Shhhhhhhhh*," the lime-poufed lady hissed again.

Next up, a little boy was chosen to shoot at the balloons. The child was completely tongue-tied when Pick asked if he was a good target shooter. He couldn't even say what his name was. He just stared—like a deer in headlights—at the monitor in which he could see himself.

Richard noticed Ginny cross her arms and look down, shaking her head. He knew she was thinking the kid was a dope. Vladimir chuckled beside him. "Your little sister kills me, Rich. She's way too sophisticated for this. She should go on *Dr. I.Q.* instead!"

"*Shhhhhhhhhhhh!*"

Finally, Pick helped the boy by asking which balloon he planned to hit. The boy pointed to the far right and aimed. *Pop-pop-pop* went his cap gun. The balloon exploded.

"Hey, did you see that long needle come up and pop that balloon?" Richard whispered. "There must be some guy hiding behind the haystack. If Ginny spots that, she'll be furious. She always hates it when she catches us letting her win at Monopoly."

"*Shhhhhhhhhhhh!*"

The shooting boy was jumping up and down now, shouting, "I did it, I did it, I did it!" Pick had to gently herd him back to the bleachers.

At that point, Ginny stood up.

Abigail gasped and grabbed Don's hand. "What is she doing?"

The lime lady was so taken aback, she didn't bother to *shhhhhhhhhhhhh*.

The two men on the side waved their clipboards frantically at Ginny to sit down. But she ignored them.

"Well, Heidi there, young lady." Pick smiled at her kindly.

"Hello, Mr. Temple. My name is Virginia Bradley."

Pick grinned. A child standing up and taking control of the show was new, and its cameras were rolling, live, filling thousands of TVs in living rooms all across the East Coast. He played along. "Would you like to say hello to your family and friends, Virginia?"

"Watch this," Richard whispered. "Any kid who takes too long in her hellos gets mooed."

Vladimir looked at him sideways. "What?"

"They play a loud cow moo to interrupt the kid, and then Pick helps the kid end with, 'Hi, everybody else.'"

"Oh, is that where that comes from? I've heard a bunch of kids at school say that and then laugh, like it was a tremendous witticism."

But Ginny was quick and precise. "Yes, sir. Hi, Mom. Hi, Dad. Hi, Richard and Vladimir. Hi, Mrs. Emerson." She stopped there. "What I would really like, Mr. Temple, is to say hi to Piccolo. May I ride him, please? It's time for a Ranger to ride Piccolo, isn't it?"

Sure enough, the Shetland pony one lucky child rode during the show, led around by Pick, was standing saddled and ready, nipping irritably at the guy holding him.

"You are absolutely right, little lady! Come on down." In an instant, Ginny stood beside Pick as Piccolo was led up. "Have you ridden a pony before, Virginia?"

"No, sir. That's why I want to. I plan to write a story about this. Brand-new experiences are good things to write about. I want to be an inquiring camera girl for newspapers when I grow up. Like Jackie Kennedy was. Maybe even a reporter for

Edward R. Murrow. And then after that, when I get married, I want to own a radio station like Mrs. Lady Bird Johnson does, even though she is married to the senator. Not many people know that about her. Senator Johnson gets all the attention."

The children and the parents sitting next door were all silent, stunned at Ginny's little speech. But Vladimir laughed outright. "I'm serious. Your sister kills me, Rich. She's like Phoebe."

"Who?"

"You know, the little sister in *The Catcher in the Rye*."

Richard looked at Vladimir with surprise and then back to Ginny. Holden Caulfield had adored his little sister. He'd loved all her crazy quirks and how smart she was. "Chewing the fat" and "horsing around" with her was the one thing Holden could name that made him happy. And Phoebe was completely loyal to him. Even willing to run away with him.

Suddenly, as Ginny was led in a circle around the studio on Piccolo, Richard felt ashamed of how jealous he could be sometimes about her. He'd never have the guts to speak up like she just did. And her persistence was actually something he wished he had. Maybe that was what made him feel envious sometimes—wanting to have her chutzpah, as Vladimir would call it.

When Pick handed Ginny his microphone and let her end the show, Richard felt kind of big-brother proud as she led the other Rangers in Pick's Pledge:

"I will live up to the creed of a Pick Temple Ranger—to carry on the principles of good citizenship; to help the needy, the aged, and the sick; to respect my parents and teachers; to love my neighbors, city, and country. . . ."

● ● •

On the drive home, Ginny doled out Heidi's treats from her Pick Temple bag. "Thank you for coming, Vladi." She smiled at him as she turned around to hand him a packet of mini cupcakes. Don was at the wheel, Ginny between him and Abigail on the long bench-like seat.

They were passing Fort Reno, the highest ground in DC, where the Union Army had built a fort during the Civil War. The moon was rising, fat and glowing, spilling white-silver light onto the old stone observation towers. Richard used to love playing there, rolling down the green grass hills or sledding the slopes. But recently there'd been a lot of construction and fences put up around the nineteenth-century battlements.

"Hey, Rich." Vladimir elbowed him and talked through a mouthful of cupcake. "We should go poke around up there Saturday. My dad heard rumors that the government is thinking of building some secret bunker in case the Soviets nuke us. I guess the whole White House or Congress could end up squirreled away up there, like Hitler hiding at the end of World War II. Wouldn't that be something? Hey, Ginny, you should come along. It'd be a great breaking story for an inquiring camera girl!"

"Oh my gosh! I'd love that. I could—"

"Nobody in this car is going anywhere near the fort. *Kapish?*" Don's voice was brusque. Abigail looked at him with some alarm—Richard knew the expression well. His mom's face was such an open book. She'd never make it as a secret agent.

Don glanced over at her and then back to the road, his grip on the steering wheel tightening. Richard also recognized Don's way of steadying his hands if they were shaking.

Clearing his throat, Don composed an easygoing voice. "A construction site is dangerous, that's all." He glanced at Vladimir in the rearview mirror. "You've got a vivid imagination, Vladimir. No wonder you and Rich are buddies. I bet your dad was pulling your leg. He'd know better than to talk at the dinner table about top secret things he might have picked up at the State Department *if* they were going on." He put on one of those grown-up, thin-lipped, give-me-a-yes-sir kind of smiles. "Wouldn't he?"

Vladimir caught the rebuke—it was hard to miss. He was uncharacteristically slow and careful in his response. "Of course, Mr. Bradley." But Richard could tell his friend was biting his lip to keep from saying more.

Don gazed in the mirror for a few more moments at Vladimir before speaking again. "Here's what's up. You know how the old towers were converted into water tanks at the turn of the century? Well, they don't hold enough reserve water anymore. The city's grown that much. So they're thinking of digging another water reserve, and they might add a tower for radio antennae and civil defense warning sirens. That's all. There are guys taking measurements and ground tests.

"Nothing to look at, sugarplum." He smiled down at Ginny. "Just some holes you could fall into. So going there is verboten."

He flipped on his turn signal as an uncomfortable hush filled the car, pierced only by the mechanism's *click-click-click-click.*

Vladimir frowned, his face a little red.

Abigail broke the silence, in that let's-save-the-situation way of hers. "Soooooooo, Ginny, honey. I didn't know Mrs. Johnson ran a radio station."

"Yeah, that's swell, Gin," Vladimir chimed in, trying to please. "What's the scoop there?"

Ginny twisted around to kneel facing backward. "Mrs. Johnson is so interesting! One morning when I was over there, I saw her taking dictation from the senator as he ate breakfast. Fast scribbles. She told me she'd learned to do that when she studied journalism at the University of Texas. I didn't know you could go to college for journalism!"

Ginny got more and more animated as she talked. "Did you know that she bankrolled the senator's first election campaign with a little inheritance she got from her mom? Then she purchased a rundown old radio station in Austin. She hired a new staff, and pretty soon she was making a profit. Eighteen whole dollars that first month. And now she says it makes thousands! Mrs. Johnson's really smart. And she's got gumption. That's her word. She says I have it, too. And that I have brains. She also says people who do stuff without thinking are 'the type to charge hell with a bucket of water.'"

They all laughed. She was killing everybody, as Vladimir would say. *"Everybody with any sense, anyway"*—Holden Caulfield's line suddenly rang in Richard's ear. As Ginny gushed on, prompted by Vladimir's questions and completely in the spotlight, they passed the Whites' house.

Teresa's studio was all lit up.

That's weird, thought Richard. He turned backward in his seat to look again. *Whoa, wait a minute!* Two men in plain button-up raincoats were walking briskly down the sidewalk, away from Vladimir's house. But that wasn't what caught his eye so much. It was the fact that they both carried matching briefcase-size black bags. The guys looked exactly like the FBI agents who broke into the college student's dorm room on *I Led 3 Lives*. Exactly! Down to the black bags that—on the TV show, anyway—carried tiny cameras and bugging devices!

Richard sat up taller to look again through the back window. The men were gone. Vanished. Like they'd jumped into bushes or trash cans.

With some excitement, Richard shifted back to face forward. He started to elbow Vladimir and tell him he should look out the window. But his friend was engrossed in Ginny's story about the Johnsons' barbecue recipe.

"Senator Johnson says a good side of beef can convince a man to do most anything," Ginny was saying. "He's won a bevy of votes because of his wife's secret recipe."

Abigail laughed. "Goodness! I'll have to ask Lady Bird for her recipe, then."

"Maybe she should give it to the State Department," joked Vladimir. "They could use some magically persuasive recipes!"

Frustrated that he couldn't get Vladimir's attention, Richard looked forward toward Don to report what he'd spotted. But his "Hey, Dad" stuck in his throat when he realized his father was watching him carefully in the rearview mirror. Richard stared back into his father's eyes in the narrow reflection. Did he imagine it, or did his father shake his head ever so slightly and speed up the car?

"So, what's for dinner, Abby?" Don asked suddenly, interrupting Ginny. "I'm hungry enough to eat a horse."

"Steak! I thought we'd celebrate."

"Oh, you're in for a treat, Vlad. The missus cooks a mean steak!" Don put on his good-humored joking voice. "Did you wrassle it up on the range like a cowboy wife, honey?"

Richard's mind raced as his dad described the first steak she'd tried to fix Don, which burnt to a crisp—but he ate it anyway. "For love," he said. "Pure love."

What was the meaning of what Richard had just seen? Who were those guys? And what did Don's look mean? Did his father know something about them?

Richard sucked in a sharp breath. Was that why it had been so important to Don that Vladimir and Richard both went to the *Pick Temple's Giant Ranch* show? To guarantee Vladimir wouldn't suddenly show up at his house when . . . When what? Did the FBI just search Teresa's studio? Did they wiretap Vladimir's house?

On what Richard had told Don?

Richard had just figured that the bureau would go after Teresa's radical friends and that mystery guy up in New York. But maybe they'd detected something really covert going on from the intelligence he'd given them! A big-deal case, maybe. A real winner for his dad, even!

Still . . . Richard glanced over at Vladimir. He hadn't meant for them to be rummaging through his best friend's life. His face flushed, thinking of all his hidden songs and book notes and the things he muttered to himself in aggravation in the safe privacy of his own room. Angsty stuff he wrote in the heat of disappointment or hurt. Snipes he'd said when angry. New thoughts he tried on and then discarded later. Things that would really hurt Ginny's and his mom's feelings. Things that might land him in hot water with authority figures. Stuff he'd never want other people to hear or read.

Richard scrunched down in his seat, feeling great and awful at the same time.

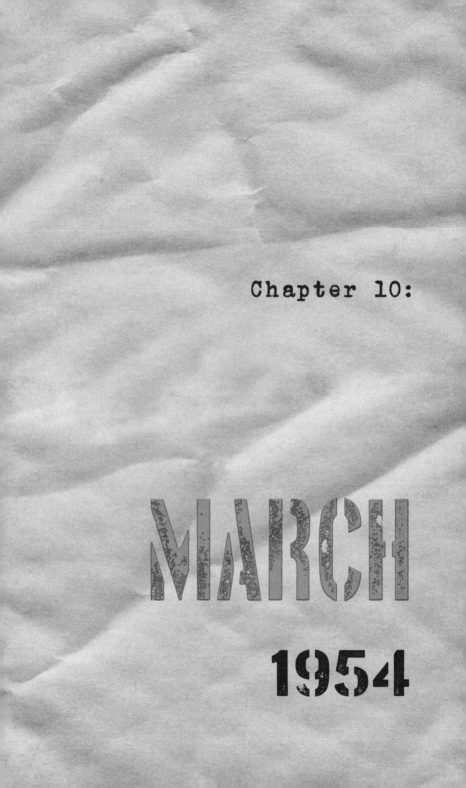

Chapter 10:

MARCH
1954

Edward R. Murrow broadcasts a *See It Now* report on Pentagon Teletype operator and widowed mother of four, Annie Lee Moss. Moss had been called before McCarthy's committee when her name appeared on membership lists of a local communist party. The Army had suspended Moss as a result.

In her Sunday-best hat and overcoat, Moss whispers into the hearing-room microphone as McCarthy's right-hand man and the subcommittee's chief counsel, Roy Cohn, peppers her with questions. It becomes clear that hers might be a case of mistaken identity.

Senator Stuart Symington interrupts to ask Moss to read aloud her suspension order. She stumbles over its large words. "Did you read that the very best you could?" he asks.

"Yes, sir, I did."

The senator asks if she has heard of Karl Marx.

"Who is that?" she replies.

The hearing room rumbles with laughter.

"Do you think you are a good American?" he asks.

"Yes."

"Would you ever do anything to hurt your country?"

"No, sir."

Pausing, the senator shakes his head. "Do you need work?"

"Sure I do."

"If you don't get work pretty soon, what are you going to do?"

"I am going down to the welfare," she replies.

"I may be sticking my neck out," says Symington, "[but] . . . I think you are telling the truth. If you are not taken back into the Army, come . . . see me."

Playwright **Arthur Miller is refused a travel** visa for an opening of his play *The Crucible* in Brussels. He is rejected "under regulations denying passports to persons believed to be supporting the Communist movement, whether or not they are members of the Communist party."

Roman Holiday, starring Audrey Hepburn and Gregory Peck, wins Oscars for best lead actress and costume design. It also, secretly, wins an Oscar for one of the blacklisted Hollywood Ten—Dalton Trumbo—who ghostwrote the screenplay for the man who accepts the golden statue.

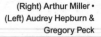

(Right) Arthur Miller •
(Left) Audrey Hepburn &
Gregory Peck

"THIS knocks me out." Resting his elbows on the balcony of the visitors' gallery, Vladimir gazed down into the chamber of the United States House of Representatives. "This is the room where it happens!"

Richard scanned the enormous space, its cool, palatial marble, and the wide fan of gleaming mahogany desks. Below them, members of Congress were gathering. Many clustered in conversation, animated gaggles of navy-blue–suited men. Voices drifted up to the boys, who sat directly above and to the left of the podium. Vladimir had positioned them there so he could hear everything the Speaker of the House said. They also sat only a few feet away from other adolescent boys in coats and ties, perched on stools, taking notes on the proceedings. Serving as errand boys for the nation's legislators, these congressional pages were the go-betweens for congressmen and their staff during sessions. They carried notes across the aisle to build coalitions or political coups and kept records on what the representatives said and did.

Once upon a time, pages had been as young as eight years old. But now they were high schoolers. Vladimir was hoping to join the select corps of teenagers who helped grease the wheels of lawmaking.

"Ginny's comment about having her first pony ride on *Pick Temple* so she could write about it made me figure that I should experience a session firsthand before writing my application essay. That way it's more authentic," he'd told Richard's parents. He'd been so earnest about Ginny's example, he'd easily convinced Don and Abigail to let Richard play hooky, too, in order to accompany Vladimir on his personal field trip to Capitol Hill.

"Apply with me, Rich!" Vladimir said now. "Imagine working here every day. The world leaders you'd get to meet. You'd witness history being made!"

Richard stared at his friend, surprised at how idealistic, even patriotic, Vladimir sounded, given how radical his opinions on books and music could be. Being a page would actually be way cool. But what if Vlad made it and he didn't? Just like basketball. What would happen to their friendship then?

"But what about school?" Richard asked, embarrassed to say what was really worrying him.

"They've got a special school for pages, on the top floor of the Library of Congress. Georgetown University professors teach some of the courses. That'd beat the heck out of some of the idiot wardens at our high school. I swear I could teach Civics a lot better than Mrs. Russell does. She doesn't know diddly-squat about Europe. She had to think hard about where Czechoslovakia was on the map." Vladimir paused. "I have to be honest, though, the schedule is kind of brutal. They start classes at six A.M. so pages can get to work on the House floor at ten thirty. But I think it'd be worth it."

"But . . . but what about basketball? You're the best shooter the team's got."

"Yeah, well, ain't that the truth?" Vladimir pretended to preen. "They'll just have to do without me. They're a bunch of crumb-bums anyway."

"But won't you miss playing?"

"Believe it or not, Rich, the one sport the page school has is basketball." He punched Richard's shoulder. "Hey, I bet you could make that basketball team." He nodded toward the pages sitting to their right. "Look at those guys." They were gawky and bespectacled. "They wouldn't last a minute in a full-court press."

"Gee, thanks."

"No, seriously, buddy boy, I didn't mean it that way. I just mean these guys are brains—like you—so you'd fit in better. That's all."

Sure, that's what you meant, thought Richard. He knew Vlad was too nice to say he stunk at basketball. But all Richard replied was "Very diplomatic. Maybe you should join the Foreign Service instead, like your dad."

"No way. The State Department's crocked. McCarthy's suspicions of it have everybody running scared. I'd rather be here and show up jackasses like McCarthy for the a-holes they are. This is where that game is played."

Richard couldn't help looking over his shoulder, afraid of some McCarthy informer sitting right behind them.

"And the best part, I swear, is I'd get a salary. About two thousand dollars a year. So I can keep on with my music. I'll compose when Congress is on recess and use the money to go to all kinds of jazz clubs. I've got it all figured out."

"Two thousand dollars?" Richard's mind began to race. What would James Bond do with two thousand dollars? How much did an Aston Martin cost?

WHACK, WHACK, WHACK. The Speaker of the House thumped his gavel and called the session to order.

"*Shh-sh-sh!*" Vladimir hushed Richard and wriggled to the edge of his seat to rest his chin on his hands atop the railing like a little kid watching TV.

With the thump of the gavel, members took their seats. The Speaker called for a vote to permit debate on whether to consider a bill that would allow Mexican migrant workers to pick crops in border states.

"You mean they have to vote to decide whether they are going to allow discussion of whether or not they want to hold a vote?"

"*Shhhhhhh,*" Vladimir quieted him. He was enthralled.

As congressmen voted yay to hold a debate on the merits of House Resolution 450, Richard's attention wandered to the other spectators in the gallery. He'd been surprised to see a sign calling it the Ladies' Gallery, but the guard had explained that after the Civil War, lonely widows would spend entire afternoons watching Congress. Several elderly ladies sat there now, one of them knitting. Anyone could come in to observe, whenever. That was the way the founding fathers had wanted it—a totally open process. No admission ticket or special permission needed.

Vladimir had whistled softly when they crossed the threshold. "This is amazing. You know, in Czechoslovakia, no way could people watch government at work. People are hauled off for saying anything that sounds the least bit critical. Even making some dumb joke. A couple of Mom's friends have just vaporized. She worries they're in prison somewhere." He paused. "Or worse."

Really? Richard would have sworn that if anything, Teresa would have been pro-commie. She was so obviously subversive in her art and friends. He had wanted to ask more, but as soon as they sat down, Vladimir was all about the Congress members and pages. Now he was totally wrapped up in what the legislators had to say about Mexican citizens crossing the border temporarily to pick harvest crops in the United States.

While the debate dragged on, Richard noticed a very different-looking woman enter the gallery directly behind them. He'd bet a thousand dollars that she wouldn't start knitting. She was strikingly pretty, even kind of glamorous, wearing a close-fitting, light-colored suit. Her black hair was perfectly styled at shoulder length, and her mouth was bright with Hollywood-red lipstick. Three men with pencil mustaches accompanied her.

"Mr. Speaker," began another congressman, as he rose from his seat to express his opinion, "I believe for my constituents it is vitally important to consider . . ."

Half listening, Richard kept looking over his shoulder, eyeing the new spectators as they sat down in the balcony's back row. Something about them seemed out of place. And the men seemed itchy. Really itchy.

Down below, a representative from Colorado moved that the House vote on the resolution. A man from North Carolina seconded. The 243 legislators settled into their seats to await the final tally.

Meanwhile, the woman Richard was watching whispered to her companions. They nodded and bowed their heads. Almost like they were praying. Richard craned his neck to watch them more closely. His skin kind of prickled. *Weird.*

"One hundred sixty-eight ayes," the Speaker of the House announced. "And the nay votes come to . . ."

The woman opened her purse. She looked back and forth, wild-eyed, before pulling something out. She stood. Her companions lurched up with her. They reached into their coat pockets.

Oh my God. Richard grabbed Vladimir's elbow and shook it just as the woman shrieked: *"Viva Puerto Rico libre!"*

She held a pistol up toward the ceiling.

Bang! Bang! Bang-bang-bang-bang!

The members of Congress looked up in shock.

Throwing her gun to the floor, the women pulled out a flag. *"Viva Puerto Rico libre!"* she cried again as she waved the island's banner.

That's when her three male companions began shooting. But they aimed their guns downward—right into the House chamber!

Bang! Bang-bang!

Phht-dut, phht-dut.

Richard had heard that sound before—at a rock quarry near Quantico when his dad had taken him target shooting. It was the sound of bullets glancing off rock!

"Look out!" He yanked Vladimir's arm and pulled both of them out of their seats and to the floor.

Bang-bang-bang! Bang!

Phht-dut, phht-dut.

Marble dust sprayed Richard's hair.

People began shrieking and scattering all around them, climbing over seats, crawling underneath them.

From below came shouts of panic from the lawmakers: "This way!"

"Run!"

"Hurry!"

And then cries of pain:

"I'm hit!"

"Oh God!"

"Help me. Please!"

Bang! Bang-bang-bang!

The pages! thought Richard. They were right in the line of fire! He lifted his face up from the floor to find them. The teens crouched under their long desk. One had managed to crawl to a telephone in the wall under it and was frantically calling for help.

Bang-bang.

Phht-dut, phht-dut.

"Keep your head down, Rich!" Vladimir reached up and flattened Richard's face against the floor. He kept his hand on Richard's head. Crammed together between the balcony wall and the legs of their seats, Richard could feel Vladimir trembling. His own teeth were almost chattering. They had no place to go. No way to crawl out from underneath the spew of bullets.

Bang-bang.

Phht-dut, phht-dut.

Suddenly, the shooting stopped. Richard twisted around and could see one gunman trying to unjam his pistol. The others were reloading.

Within that fraction of a pause, a male spectator threw himself over the bank of seats at one of the attackers. He managed to grab that gunman and shove him out the door into the hall. Then he turned and pinned the arms of a second shooter as Capitol police rushed in. Together they wrestled the male assailants to the ground and nabbed the woman as she tried to run.

Guards hustled her out the door as she yelled in English: "I did not come to kill anyone. I came to die for Puerto Rico!"

Now the House filled with groans and cries for help from below. Richard and Vladimir sat up onto their knees in time to see the pages yank open a small door and race down a tiny staircase to the chamber, shouting for doctors and stretchers.

"Man, those guys are brave," murmured Vladimir. "Come on!" He jumped to his feet.

Richard staggered up, his knees aching from hitting the floor so fast and hard. Now that everything was over, he thought he might throw up.

People around them in the visitors' gallery were crying and cursing and checking each other.

"Are you all right?"

"Are you hurt?"

"What happened?"

"Who were those people?"

"Is it safe now? Are we safe?"

The boys looked over the railing.

Directly beneath them lay a congressman, his back turning red through his white starched shirt as his colleagues pulled off his jacket and tried to stanch the bleeding. Aides and secretaries and pages swarmed the floor, dodging through the maze of desks, looking for more wounded. "Over here!" one teenager shouted and began waving frantically. From the back of the chamber, other pages dashed in with stretchers. Guards secured the doors. Above it all rose the eerie, high-pitched whine of dozens of police cars and ambulances racing to the Capitol.

"Everybody out! We're clearing the Hill," a security officer shouted from the gallery doorway. "Walk this way. Let's go!

Right now, folks! Look lively." The man's school-yard, fire-drill voice sounded so bizarrely calm and normal.

Vladimir and Richard pulled their gaze away from the chaos below and started for the door. "I hope that congressman makes it," Vladimir said. "That much blood coming from his chest can't be good." He shook his head. "God, those pages sure were brave," he repeated, more to himself than to Richard.

Guards herded the spectators outside but kept them corralled by the Capitol's sweeping marble staircase, asking them to wait so the police could ask what they had witnessed.

"This is where they hold the inaugural swearing-in ceremony, isn't it?" Vladimir asked absentmindedly as he sat down on the cool white steps. Richard noticed his friend's hands were still shaking a little. He sat down beside him.

"You know, Rich, my earliest memories are of the Luftwaffe dropping bombs on London. Walking past craters and mounds of rubble on my way to nursery school. We were lucky. My family was never right in the middle of a bomb blast. But we knew a lot of people who . . ." He trailed off with a slight shudder. He looked up at the sky for a long while before speaking again. "Hey, Rich?"

"Yeah?"

"I think you might have saved my life. I guess I was so surprised by the gunfire that I wasn't processing what was happening. Not until you threw me to the ground—right before those bullets hit the marble wall next to us." He put his hand on Richard's shoulder. "It's stupid because I heard ack-ack guns and buzz bombs all the time in London. But never gunfire like that. Not that close. Not firsthand. I . . . I just froze. So . . . thank you. Seriously. They might have been taking me out on a stretcher if it hadn't been for you."

Richard hadn't really thought about it at the time. He'd just reacted with gut instinct. But now that Vladimir put it that way, the deadliness of the shooting really hit home.

"You're a hero, man."

Slowly, Richard smiled. Being the leader of the two of them for once felt pretty darn good.

The two friends stared at each other until Vladimir regathered his more typical swagger and punched Richard's shoulder. "We're like war buddies now. Brothers."

● ● ·

"You sure you're up for this, son?" Don hadn't taken his protective hand off Richard's shoulder since he'd gotten home from the shooting. They stood at the front door of the FBI director, Mr. J. Edgar Hoover himself.

Richard nodded, even though his heart knocked loudly in his chest.

"Mr. Hoover just wants to ask what you saw, son. We're on the hunt for anyone who might have abetted the shooters. Even just giving them a stick of gum, I swear. Those guys sent five congressmen to the hospital. The SOBs." Don shook his head angrily. "And nobody gets to take a potshot at my kid."

He cleared his throat and squeezed Richard's shoulder. "You were so smart to recognize something was up with those jokers before most anybody else did. Mr. Hoover thinks you might have seen other clues without realizing it."

Richard nodded again, although he really felt like throwing up now. He'd gotten pretty darn shaky when he described to Abigail what had happened. She'd cried and nearly squashed him with hugs. Having to relive it all over again, under Hoover's legendary cross-examinations, was making him queasy.

Richard kicked himself. Hadn't he just survived a shooting? Talking to Mr. Hoover was easy. Just giving a report, like any G-man. Besides, he saw Hoover all the time, passing by the house in his chauffeured car. It was so heavy with bulletproofing it needed a truck engine, and made so much noise it might as well have been the presidential motorcade. The neighborhood never missed his comings and goings.

Of course, it hadn't helped when Abigail made a big-time fuss over his remembering to be polite to his dad's boss. And then to get to Hoover's door, they waded through a dozen armed FBI agents guarding the lawn—as if an invading army was on its way.

"Wow, everyone's out in force," said Don. "It's possible today's shooting might be a coordinated attack. Puerto Rican nationalists tried to assassinate Truman a couple years back. Evidently that woman from today—Lolita Lebrón—had been in contact with Truman's would-be assassin in prison. We're also wondering if these four jokers are just Communist dupes. Puerto Rico certainly doesn't benefit from this kind of craziness.

"So, until we know the whole story, agents brought Vice President Nixon and his family here. We can protect them both better in one place. Besides, they're big buddies, Nixon and Hoover. They talk on the phone every morning."

The door opened and an agent ushered them into the living room. It was all neatly arranged, with carefully pressed cream slipcovers on the armchairs and sofa, the floors brightly polished and covered with boldly geometric Oriental rugs. Richard tried not to gape at the endless gallery of photographs of Hoover with famous people that covered the walls almost ceiling to floor.

Don noticed his gaze and murmured, "The director keeps a diagram of what picture goes where so we can put them back up in the right spot after we've painted rooms for him."

"You've painted his house for him?" Richard whispered.

Don grimaced. "Yeaaah." He drew the word out like a sigh. He obviously regretted having let that slip.

There was a lot of hubbub and laughter in the next room. Then in lumbered Hoover.

He was a thick, stolid, brooding man. Richard felt himself recoil inside, even though Hoover smiled at him in what most people would describe as a friendly manner. In bad weather, Hoover often had his driver stop to pick up children shivering at their neighborhood bus stop and dropped them off at school on his way into the bureau's offices. Richard himself had ridden to school that way a couple of times. So Hoover obviously had some kindness in him. And yet, something about the man made Richard want to take a giant step backward.

"So, Richard, I hear you were at the House shooting today." Hoover did not ask him and his father to sit. The director was a formal man, and somehow standing in the living room felt more man-to-man anyway. Don stood at semiattention, so Richard squared his shoulders and planted his feet slightly apart, like his dad always did in that you-can't-knock-me-over kind of stance.

"Yes, sir," he answered.

"Can you describe what happened?"

Richard recited the events of the afternoon, trying not to be distracted by the stuffed buck's head above Hoover, or the very anatomically correct ebony statue of a naked man to the director's right.

"Tell me what the shooters looked like."

He did, including details that proved he'd seen them first-hand. Hoover nodded, analyzing him as he spoke.

"Excellent observations, Richard. Your dad said you had a keen eye. When you get a little older, I hope to see you apply to the bureau."

Richard flushed hot with pride. He knew Hoover was a tough man to impress, so this praise was thrilling.

Hoover leaned his elbow on the mantelpiece, friendlier. "Now, think, Richard. Did you see any other wetbacks in the gallery?"

Richard frowned. His parents never used that derogatory word, although a lot of politicians and jerks at school did. "No, sir. I didn't notice any other Puerto Ricans."

Hoover studied Richard a moment before asking, "Any Negroes?"

"No, sir." Why did Hoover ask that?

"You sure?"

Richard frowned again. "Yes, sir."

Hoover eyed him. "Positive?"

"Yes, sir."

"Remind me why you were there and who you were with."

"I went with my friend Vladimir White. He's thinking of applying for the congressional page program. He wanted to watch a session, so he could write a better essay for the application. But he was looking down onto the floor of the House when it happened, sir. He wouldn't have noticed anything in the gallery."

"I see." Hoover glanced at Don. They seemed to nod at each other.

"All right, boy. Go into the kitchen and have some cake. The cook just made one fresh." He turned to Don. "I'd like a word with you."

Boy? Richard was pretty crestfallen at being dismissed from the conversation so abruptly and suddenly reduced once again to being a kid. But he found his way to the kitchen, through all Hoover's pictures, glancing over his shoulder to watch Hoover talking with his dad.

● ● ·

On their way home, Richard couldn't keep from asking, "What did Mr. Hoover want to talk to you about, Dad?"

"A case."

"Are you going to be working on the shooting?"

"No, it's one I started on a while back."

In the light spilling from the houses onto the street as they passed, Richard could see that Don was smiling. That was rare after an encounter with his boss. So Richard dared to ask in a low voice, "Dad, does it have to do with that money I saw Mr. Hoover give you back in July? At Harvey's?"

Don stopped short. "What?" His voice was sharp. "How do you know about that?"

"I—I—I saw him give it to you." Richard was kicking himself for bringing it up.

"Damn," Don muttered.

"Was it . . . Is it . . . Were you doing undercover stuff?"

"What? No. Don't ever ask me about that damn wad of money again, Richard, you understand?" His voice was a verbal slap. There it was—that "psycho" stuff again. Don took off walking in big, fast strides.

Richard had to jog to keep up.

Then his dad stopped dead once more. Richard nearly crashed into him from behind. Don rubbed his jaw for a moment, thinking. Richard could hear the scratch of evening beard stubble against his dad's hand. Then he clasped his hands together for a good long moment. Steadying them, Richard figured.

Finally, Don spoke with careful fatherly control. "Do me a favor, Rich. Forget what you saw in July. That's over with. Things are looking up for me now." He put his arm over Richard's shoulder. "Thanks to you." He started them forward, their steps now in sync. "Let's go tell your beautiful mom that everything is A-OK."

Richard was no dummy. He could put pieces together. If his dad's case wasn't about the shooting, and he had it thanks to Richard, then it had to be about Teresa and the mystery man in New York City. That probably meant Richard had been right about those guys in raincoats that he'd spotted coming away from Vladimir's house the night of the *Pick Temple* show. They'd probably been FBI agents on a bag job, maybe even bugging Vladimir's home. His best friend. A kid who now thought of Richard as a war buddy. As a brother.

Richard looked up at Don's face. For once it seemed proud, clear of conflict. Could Abigail be right that a good case could be the cure for all Don's ills? His shakes, his regrets, his guilt, his mistakes? And for Richard's? Here they were walking together, in one step, man-to-man. It was what Richard had been longing for with his dad. And yet, that arm across his shoulder felt very heavy.

Chapter 11:

1954

A Herblock cartoon of Senator Joseph McCarthy and his hearings

Televised hearings begin on McCarthy's accusations that the Army "coddled Communists" and the Army's countercharge that the senator's allegations are retaliation for the Army refusing to grant preferential treatment to a recently drafted member of McCarthy's subcommittee staff. The nation is riveted by the explosive testimony.

McCarthy's special counsel holds up an enlarged photograph of the Secretary of the Army, smiling and standing next to the former McCarthy aide. "Isn't it a fact," he asks, "that you were being especially nice and considerate and tender of this boy . . . for the purpose of . . . pacifying [McCarthy and his right-hand man, Roy Cohn]. To get [them] to suspend the investigation?"

Ironically, Cohn had repeatedly badgered the Army to excuse the aide from boot-camp training, even threatening "to wreck the Army" if it didn't comply.

The Army Secretary is flustered, not remembering ever being in a situation like the photo depicts. Because he never was. Not exactly.

The Army's lawyer, Joseph Welch, produces the *original* snapshot. Unedited, the complete photograph included a third man. The secretary's smile was clearly directed at *that* man, not McCarthy's aide. Someone on McCarthy's committee had cropped the photo to create an out-of-context image to incriminate the secretary.

Next, McCarthy's counsel submits a carbon copy of a letter reportedly written by a young intelligence officer who felt "deeply disturbed" by the Army ignoring FBI warnings of espionage within its ranks. But McCarthy's committee cannot produce the original. McCarthy won't (or can't) name the sender, raising speculation that it was made up or altered, too.

Walt Disney announces plans for the first Disneyland theme park, in what had been a 244-acre orange grove. He also announces a weekly television show premiering in the fall. Its biggest hit will be *Davy Crockett*, sparking the sale of 10 million raccoon-skin hats.

Says the animator-turned–movie mogul, "There is more treasure in books than in all the pirate's loot on Treasure Island."

"GOOOOOOD morning."

Richard turned in his chair, recognizing Natalia's oddly insolent yet charming voice. He and Dottie were at Vladimir's house prepping for a debate competition. Vladimir had formed a debate team at the high school and recruited them. The Whites' kitchen table was covered with encyclopedias and newspaper articles on Indochina. The debate question had to do with France's colonial rule and whether the United States should aid the French Vietnamese fight against the Communist rebels. It was pretty obvious Dottie needed all the help she could get to hold her own in a give-and-take that required knowing a lot of facts. Richard was thrilled since it meant she was sitting next to him and actually talking to him!

"Good afternoon," Vladimir countered his sister, who stumbled sleepy-eyed into the kitchen.

"Is it?" Natalia laughed. "Oh well! They may call them sleeper trains, but no one can really sleep on those things for three whole days and nights. I can't wait for the airlines to make their new transcontinental flights affordable for us peons. Supposedly they are starting an economy class—just no champagne for us!" She rubbed her eyes and yawned. "What a bunch of fascists! Anyway, this is normal for college. No one gets up before noon on Saturday."

"It's Thursday!"

"Yes, but I am on my spring break. Even if I am here to help Mother paint all her *kraslice*. Every day will be Saturday for me for the next two weeks!"

Natalia stretched dramatically. She wore a UCLA T-shirt and sweatpants, and her dark, short-cropped curls stood up in pillow-squished tufts. Dottie, in her perfectly crisp blouse and skirt, looked her up and down with disapproval.

But even without makeup and with uncombed hair, there was something California-glamorous about Natalia. "Please tell me there is coffee," she said.

"Nope." Vladimir grinned. "But I bet Mom would fix you some. MOM!" he bellowed.

"*Shhhhhhh!* You'll wake Maurice! Besides, I know how to make coffee now. Instant, anyway." She put on the teakettle and pulled a jar of Nescafé from a cabinet. She turned and looked at Vladimir. "You haven't seen him up yet?"

"Nope. Mom commandeered the couch in the living room for him and gave me strict instructions this morning not to disturb the guy. So we've been tiptoeing around. Sorry I couldn't stay up to meet him last night. But you know Mom's midnight-curfew rule."

Natalia nodded, stretched again, and then plopped down into a chair next to Richard. "Oh, look." She smiled at him. "It's the closet subversive."

Richard's face flamed red. "Wh-what?"

She turned to Vladimir, pointing her thumb at Richard as she said, "I have high hopes for this one. He isn't afraid to read."

"Read what?" Dottie finally spoke up.

Natalia eyed Dottie. "Read what? Books!" Natalia answered emphatically. "And what book is on your bedside table at the moment?"

"Oh my gosh, it's *The Clue of the Velvet Mask*. It's fantastic! Nancy goes to a masquerade ball, where really important works of art are stolen. I've just gotten to the part where a pair of thieves wrap her up in bedcovers and try to suffocate her. But she gets away!"

"Nancy Drew?"

"Yes, do you read the series, too?

Natalia forced a smile. "I used to when I was, like . . ." Vladimir cleared his throat loudly. Natalia paused and forced a smile. "I used to." She looked over at her brother with a raised eyebrow that screamed, *Really*?

Now it was Vladimir's turn to redden. But before his sister could say anything else, Vladimir hastened to make introductions: "Dottie, this is my sister, Natalia. Natalia, this is my friend, Dottie."

"*This* is Dottie?" Natalia repeated the name with a tone of voice that made clear she knew all about their puppy love romance.

Richard was aware that Vladimir and Natalia wrote each other weekly—a sibling friendship that amazed him. Clearly Vladimir had bared his heart to his big sister. Richard wondered fleetingly if Ginny would ever write him at college one day to ask his advice on her first crush. They had been that close once. But age seemed such a rubber band—right now the four-year difference between them was pulled out taut, almost to the snapping point. Maybe once Ginny was a teenager, she'd stop annoying him so much. Or—Richard had a sudden and uncomfortable self-revelation—maybe when he was in college and *less* of a teenager, he'd be less annoyed by everything.

He squirmed a bit in his chair and was glad that Natalia's voice pulled him out of his thoughts. "How very nice to finally meet you," she was saying to her brother's girlfriend.

Dottie giggled.

"So, how is Mother taking all this?" Natalia continued, her voice mischievous. "Her baby having a love interest?"

Dottie twisted a tendril of her strawberry blond hair. She might as well have been twirling Richard's sad heart as well.

"Your mother is taking it just fine." Teresa entered the kitchen. She wrapped her arms around Natalia's shoulders and kissed her head. "Leave your brother be." She straightened up and gently stroked her daughter's hair into place. "Eggs?" Teresa moved toward the stove.

Natalia groaned. "Can't I just drink some coffee before we start working on your Easter eggs, Mother? Good grief."

Richard tensed, expecting Teresa to reprimand her daughter's back talk. But she merely smiled. "Eggs to eat, *miláčku*. We will paint later. Scrambled?"

"I don't really eat breakfast at college, Mother."

"But now you are home."

As Teresa cracked eggs and whisked them, Natalia turned back to Richard. "I've been meaning to include some news for you in my letters to Vladi. You're going to love this. College students have finally had enough of McCarthy's witch hunt. We are starting to rise up! And you can thank Robin Hood for it!"

"What?" Richard asked with some confusion.

Teresa handed Natalia a cup of coffee. She swallowed half of it before starting to talk again. Like she needed the caffeine fortification to give a speech.

"Last month, Indiana University started a movement against that idiot librarian who wanted to ban *Robin Hood*. Five students went to a chicken farm and stuffed burlap sacks with every feather they could find. Then they dyed them green. Like Robin Hood's green cap and feather. So poetic, right? They spread them all over campus to protest censorship. It was incredibly gutsy—I mean, this is Indiana! The university still requires its male students to do ROTC. Fascists."

She finished her coffee and held up the cup for more. "The local press totally tore them apart. Now the word is, the FBI is all over those students."

Again, Richard squirmed in his seat.

Teresa filled Natalia's cup, smiling at her with obvious pride. At that moment, Natalia reminded Richard a lot of Teresa—actually, of Teresa's speech about art the night of the Whites' Christmas party.

Natalia sipped and started talking again, with growing fervor. "But their message is spreading anyway! Harvard is making green feather pins. And a bunch of us are organizing a march at UCLA. We're going to dress up like the Merry Men! It'll make a great visual. Who in their right minds can think the Merry Men should be censored!"

She put her cup down and tapped the table impatiently with her pointer finger as she spoke. "Adults may go to the McCarthy slaughterhouse like sheep. But we're not going to. Even if the fascists in the Senate vote down giving us eighteen-year-olds the vote! Student activism like the Green Feather

Movement is going to blow away McCarthyism. We'll break open the floodgates of free speech. We'll wash away all this oppression. You wait and see!"

Vladimir started clapping. "You kill me, sis. You're becoming a regular Emma Goldman."

She grinned.

"Oh dear, not like that poor woman," Teresa said as she handed Natalia her breakfast. "We don't want you deported, *miláčku!*"

"Hoover was able to deport Emma Goldman, Mother, because she had been born in Russia and was a true anarchist." Natalia rolled her eyes. "I'm simply a U.S. citizen arguing for my First Amendment rights."

"Ahhh. Like the Hollywood Ten? How long were they in prison?"

Vladimir laughed. "Mom's right, sis. You radical! If the FBI had bugged our house, you might be on your way to the hoosegow, right now! Hey, Rich, this is like an episode of *I Led 3 Lives*, don't you think?"

Richard's heart started beating wildly. If their house was bugged. His pulse kicked into a violent throbbing as his mind repeated it. *If their house was bugged!*

He could tell Vladimir was saying something to him, but his heartbeat was knocking in his ears so loudly he could barely make it out.

"Right, Rich?"

"Wh-wh-what?"

"You read all those detective stories. And your dad's a G-man." Vladimir punched Richard's shoulder. "That was exactly the kind of speech that might set the FBI scurrying to set up surveillance on my feather-toting, left-wing sister. Look at her. She's gotta be dangerous! She could take down our government with Robin Hood green feathers!"

Natalia made a goofy face at him.

"But you could help me break Natalia out of jail if she gets caught. You know all that clandestine spy stuff. How'd we do it?"

"I—I—I . . ." Richard's face felt hot and sweaty.

"Goodness, my dear. You look ill." Teresa put her hand on his forehead. "Are you all right, Richard?"

It was Dottie who unknowingly saved him.

"Excuse me, Mrs. White? Are you going to dye Easter eggs? I just love making them. I can give an egg four different colors the way I dip and hold them in the bowls. Mom says I'm very clever that way. Can I help? The Easter bunny is my favorite holiday character. Does anybody read Beatrix Potter? Or *The Velveteen Rabbit*?"

Everyone in the kitchen stared at Dottie. Even Vladimir seemed to shake his head at the non sequitur. But Richard wanted to kiss her—her questions gave Richard a chance to recover himself a little.

"It isn't just *dyeing* eggs," Natalia answered sharply, barely disguising her disdain. "We paint them with flowers and geometric figures. Mother makes and sells dozens to raise money for Czech refugees who fled the communist coup. Have you never seen Russian Easter eggs? They are works of art."

"Oh, yes, I have. Oh, goody." Dottie clasped her hands and bounced a little in her seat. "Can I try making some? Please?"

Natalia glanced over at Dottie with a profound are-you-kidding-me expression.

But Teresa caught Vladimir's pleading look. "Of course, Dottie. I will show you. We can make some right now. That is, of course, if Richard feels up to it." Her hand was still on his forehead, and she leaned over a little to look into Richard's eyes. "You feel cool now. Are you better?"

"Oh, yes, ma'am." He nodded so forcefully that it knocked her hand away. "I'd love to paint some eggs."

• • ·

The four teens cleared the table of books and afternoon breakfast while Teresa mixed her special dyes. She explained to Dottie what they would do.

"*Kraslice* means 'embellished egg,' and we give them as special gifts at Easter because of a story about Mary Magdalene. She traveled to Rome to preach and had to bring the emperor a gift. Just like diplomats must do today.

"Wealthy visitors gave the emperor jewels, but country people gave crops or game they'd caught. Mary presented Tiberius all she had—a humble white egg—and said, 'Christ has risen.' He responded, 'Nobody could rise from the dead. It is as impossible as that egg turning red.' And within that moment, the egg she held in her hand turned a rich crimson."

She put down bowls of red, green, and gold dye.

"No blue? That's my favorite color." Dottie pointed to her eyes and batted her eyelashes.

Natalia rolled hers.

Vladimir turned red.

Seeing her son's mortification, Teresa hastened to answer. "No, no blue, dear."

Natalia added wickedly, "In the old country, blue represents death and suffering."

"What?" Dottie looked insulted.

Teresa frowned at her daughter and then smiled broadly at Dottie. "Just Old World superstitions. These are the traditional *kraslice* colors: red is thought to ward off evil, gold is the color of harvest grains, and green reminds us of the rebirth of trees each spring."

She started melting a pot of beeswax. As Teresa stirred, she kept talking to Dottie, perhaps as a way of silencing her daughter from brewing trouble. "When we start painting, we don't just dip eggs into those dyes. We divide each egg into sections and then draw designs in each field with melted beeswax. Eight-pointed stars, for instance."

"Oh, that sounds awfully hard to draw."

Natalia sighed heavily. But when Teresa shot her daughter yet another disapproving look, Natalia grudgingly said, "It's not that hard. I'll show you how."

Dottie beamed.

Teresa lifted the pot from the stove. "Ready! Vladi, please get the hot plate from the dining room, so we can keep the beeswax warm and liquid. Richard, may I ask you go to my studio, please? On my drafting table there are half a dozen styluses I laid out already. We need those needle points to draw the designs."

Richard got up, happy to have a moment to breathe after his panic. As he left the room he could hear Dottie's *eeeeeewww* as Teresa explained that they didn't boil the eggs. They would prick each end and blow out the yolk and white so the unbroken shell could last for years.

He tiptoed past the sleeping mound on the living room couch. All the curtains were drawn shut in the room, as well as in the adjacent enclosed porch, so Natalia's friend could sleep. But even in the dim light Richard spotted the silvery, needle-tipped metal pencils. As he reached for them, his eyes fell on a pile of newspapers—Czech newspapers!

Wait a second.

Richard glanced over his shoulder before moving the newspapers a little to see them better. Underneath was a stack of letters addressed to Terezka Jacobowitz. Jacobowitz? Was that her maiden name?

The letters lay next to an empty envelope, plus that map Richard had spotted months before. Now he could see that it was of Prague and its surroundings. It was bloodied with red circles and arrows. There was also a map of France, and a bunch of *New York Times* clips about the United Nations with the dates of the articles circled in red, plus a *Life* magazine.

"Whoa," Richard breathed. The magazine was opened and Teresa had drawn red horns and a beard and tail on a photo of a guy named Oatis.

Richard recognized the name from news reports. He was that AP bureau chief in Prague who'd been accused by Communist Czechoslovakia of spying for the United States, and imprisoned for two years. He'd just been released. The headline: WHY I CONFESSED: "I AM NOT A SPY," SAYS U.S. REPORTER BUT TELLS HOW REDS FORCED HIM TO SAY HE WAS.

Teresa had also highlighted parts of the article—about his arrest by secret police, about the two days of sleep deprivation and the questions fired at him by "the Boss" about his bureau employees—three Czech reporters who'd been hauled off the month before. A quote attributed to the Boss's interpreter, "Your boys are here today for interrogation," was circled and circled and circled in red. The next paragraph was about the Boss grilling Oatis on articles written by the three Czech reporters and their source—a refugee living in Paris who returned to Czechoslovakia on "mysterious errands." That, too, had been highlighted furiously.

Richard leaned over to turn the page, reaching up to the lamp beside Teresa's desk to switch light onto this obvious collection of evidence of . . . of . . . of what, he didn't know.

His gaze glued on the article, he groped his way to the lamp pull. When he felt what he thought was its cord, he tugged. But it caught and snagged. No light came on. With impatience, Richard glanced over at the lamp. Hanging down from the bulbs was the usual chain pull with a bell-like knob at its end, but right above it, dangling from the shade, was a dime-size disc suspended on a thin wire. His fingers had caught on that wire.

Richard did a double take, squinting. But he already knew what the little black disc was. He'd seen a dozen of them on *I Led 3 Lives*.

It was a tiny microphone.

It was true. He'd been right. Those guys had planted bugs. They were listening in to every word the White family said. They were probably eavesdropping on his own movements at that very moment, wondering who was rustling around at Teresa's desk. Involuntarily, he looked over his shoulder.

Hands shaking, Richard reached up into the lamp and gently stuffed the bug back into a slight cut he detected in a seam of the shade's lining. Vladimir's joking warning to Natalia rang in his ears: *"If the FBI had bugged our house, you might be on your way to the hoosegow, right now!"*

Richard swallowed hard, fighting off vomit. He was weirdly elated and riddled with a horrible sense of responsibility at the same time. He knew there was something suspect about Teresa. But he liked her. And what had he done potentially to Natalia? To the brother who loved her so much, his best friend?

Not knowing what else to do, he hurried back into the kitchen, clutching the beeswax styluses—his ticket back into friendship and a simple afternoon of Easter holiday fun with his best friend's family and the girl he still adored from afar. Richard was so rattled by what he'd seen, so shot full with guilt, he didn't notice that the living room sofa was now vacant.

But as he entered the kitchen, he stopped dead, halted by an awkward silence where once there had been animated conversation. Had someone seen him spying? Richard looked anxiously around the room, his eyes stopping on Dottie's face. Her mouth was hanging open. He followed Dottie's gaze.

Natalia's friend was now awake, taking a cup of coffee from Teresa. He was Black.

"Richard!" Dottie's voice was way too excited when she spotted him. She stood. "I am so sorry, Mrs. White, but I have to go. I forgot. My mother and Richard's mother wanted us to . . . to . . . you know, do that thing, right, Richard? That Easter party thingie. At the church. We need to go. Right now."

Before Richard could protest, Dottie was beside him, tugging on his arm. "Come on, Richard, we have to go." Richard managed to hand Vladimir the beeswax needles and to thank Teresa before Dottie dragged him away. As she yanked the front door open to shove Richard outside with her, he could hear Natalia say, "I told you, Vladi. She's one of those."

Outside, the cherry trees lining the street shivered in a cool, about-to-rain April wind. The changing weather was ruining the blossoms. The trees shimmied and snowed pink petals down on them as Dottie hurried along the sidewalk.

Finally, Richard could ask, "What gives, Dot?"

She looked at him like he was a total idiot. "That man was a *Negro*." She paused. "Good grief! You don't think Natalia is dating him, do you?" She frowned, her pretty face puckering into nasty-looking disapproval, and Richard couldn't help being taken aback by it and her words.

"You know, it's one thing to be from Europe and kind of radical. To like weird books and jazz and to know a lot about old stuff. It makes Vladi kind of . . . sexy. But I bet that sister of his is one of those people Daddy calls an *agitator*. I mean, there are people fighting to get schools integrated. Black and white kids together in class! Can you imagine? Daddy says the Supreme Court is about to rule on some case allowing it. He says anyone supporting it is a Red, for sure."

She shook her head. "This goes just a little too far. It's been fun to aggravate Daddy with a jazz-loving beau. But a *real* Red? From a family that marches and protests and thinks integration is a good idea? He'd pack me off to an all-girls boarding school in a heartbeat." She paused to think. "I have to break things off with Vladi. Immediately."

Dottie slipped her arm through Richard's. "My sister is making her debut in a couple weeks. And I have to have an escort." She smiled up at him in a way that made his knees go to jelly. His misgivings about her obvious racism vaporized as she crooned, "Will you take me, Richard? Pretty please?"

Chapter 12:

1954

The U.S. Supreme Court rules school segregation is unconstitutional. The justices' unanimous decision in *Brown v. Board of Education of Topeka* strikes down the country's long-standing concept of "separate but equal."

President Eisenhower expresses his support of the decision. Many jurisdictions begin plans to integrate schools within the year. But other Deep South states, such as Georgia and South Carolina, had already passed standby legislation to abolish public schools before integrating them if the Supreme Court outlawed segregation. Political and racial lines are quickly drawn that will take years to erase before total integration of U.S. schools is accomplished.

Voice of America broadcasts the Supreme Court decision across the world as an example of the triumph of American equality. But in that very same month, the Mississippi Supreme Court awards a white woman $5,000 in damages, ruling that a newspaper had libeled her by erroneously identifying her as "a Negro."

(Opposite top) Integrated classroom, Barnard School, Washington, DC, a year after the Supreme Court ban on segregation • (Opposite bottom) Protesters

Dien Bien Phu, France's last military stronghold in Indochina (Vietnam), falls to Communist rebels led by Ho Chi Minh. Ten thousand Vietnamese die in the bloody 57-day siege, as do 3,000 French soldiers. French colonial influence in Southeast Asia comes to an end. North Vietnam becomes Communist. As was done in Korea, a demilitarized zone is established between the Communist north and the Republic of Vietnam in the south.

Only the month before, Eisenhower had warned of a "domino effect," saying that if Vietnam fell to communism, eventually Laos, Thailand, Cambodia, and Indonesia would, too—one after another. The events lay the foundation for the United States eventually sending troops in an ill-fated attempt to stop the spread of communism in Asia.

(Opposite) Soldiers in trench during battle at Dien Bien Phu

Bill Haley & His Comets release the 45 single "Rock Around the Clock." The track becomes a theme song for rebellious youth and helps launch a national craze for rock-and-roll music.

Bill Haley and His Comets

"**WOW!** That tanker is going to sail right under us!" Vladimir rolled down the car window and stuck his head out to peer down into the waters of the Chesapeake Bay and the top deck of an enormous freighter.

Richard didn't look. He hated crossing the Chesapeake Bay Bridge. They used to take a ferry to get to Maryland's Eastern Shore and the Delaware beaches, but the bridge had opened two summers ago and now everyone used it instead. The bridge was four and a half miles long and nearly twenty stories high at its midpoint to allow big ships to pass under. It gave Richard the willies to look over the edge from that high up.

"Ooooo, I wanna see!" Ginny was sitting between the boys and clambered over Vladimir to poke her head out, too.

"All heads inside!" Don called from the driver's seat. But he laughed as he said it. The family was on its way to Rehoboth Beach for Memorial Day weekend, and he was in a jovial mood. Abigail's aunt had a summer cottage there and always lent it to them for the three-day weekend. It was the first time Don had been able to join them in years. Usually, Hoover had him doing some undisclosed task on those days.

Reluctantly, Ginny crawled back to the middle seat. "You know, Daddy, this is the third largest bridge in the world. The whole wide world! It's just too exciting not to look."

Vladimir chuckled. "You kill me, Gin."

"Thanks, Vlad!" Ginny smiled up at him, charmed, like everyone seemed to be by him.

At this point, Richard had learned to squash whatever sudden pangs of jealousy he felt about Vladimir, given the double life he was leading with him. Vladimir had also been way cool when Richard fessed up to escorting Dottie to her sister's debutante ball.

"No sweat, buddy boy," he'd said. "She's old news. We didn't have anything in common, anyway. It wasn't meant to be."

Nor were Richard and Dottie.

Yes, the country-club ball had been as incredible a date as all his daydreams had promised. Dottie was beautiful, wearing another fancy sky-blue dress that accentuated her eyes and her increasingly womanly figure. The band was great. Richard stole his first sip of champagne. And he'd looked pretty darn swell in his rented tuxedo. His mom must have taken a gazillion photographs.

But Richard hadn't really talked with Dottie since. She even managed to dart out of Biology class so fast when it was over that he couldn't catch up to her. She was always surrounded by giggling girls, who suddenly turned serious and whispered behind their hands when they spotted him in the hallway. Right around the time the Supreme Court banned school segregation as unconstitutional, he was shocked to overhear one of the girls say something about his being best friends "with one of those n——lovers."

So Richard wrote a song. About lost love. About insensitivity, humiliation, broken hearts. About love making a guy do things he knew were stupid. About popular girls stepping all over outsider boys' souls.

I'm on the outside looking innnn,
Left broken and lonely from a heart made of tinnn.

Why she did it I'll never knowwww,
But Lord knows she left me feeling lowwwww,
so lowwwww. . . .

Vladimir was almost done composing a saxophone melody for it. What he played so far ached with hurt and longing, bitterness and hope, and a sense of resignation. The song would be a total tearjerker. Like that Billie Holiday song "Fine and Mellow."

Richard had never heard of Billie Holiday before meeting Vladimir and Natalia. Now he was listening to her all the time, too.

Interrupting Richard's thoughts, Vladimir said, "Hey, Mr. Bradley, thanks again for asking me to come this weekend. I really appreciate it. I haven't been to a real beach for a while."

"Sure, son. I know how tight you and Rich are. Besides, your being with us fleshes out the brotherhood, gives us a majority over the ladies."

Everyone laughed.

Boy, Dad is in a good mood, thought Richard. He tried to assess Don's expression from what he could see of his profile as Don glanced over his shoulder to talk to Vladimir. Was there a twinge of guilt in his face, too? Maybe inviting Vladimir was a way of making up for spying on his family. Or was it just Richard ladling his own discomfort onto his dad?

• • •

That night, they all went to the boardwalk. After hours of riding bumper cars, shooting water guns into the mouths of cardboard clowns, laughing at their distorted images in wacky mirrors, and eating weird-colored cotton candy and saltwater taffy, Ginny announced she'd had enough. She wanted to go home.

She was reading *The Lion, the Witch and the Wardrobe* and had just gotten to the part where Edmund agrees to spy on his siblings for the White Witch in exchange for some Turkish Delight candy. "I've got to see what happens next. Can you believe? Agreeing to rat on his own brother and sisters and Mr. and Mrs. Beaver. For candy!"

Vladimir laughed. "Have you ever tasted Turkish Delight, Ginny? It's a British favorite, with dates and nuts and jellies. It's brilliant, it is, as my English mates would say. I can see it seriously tempting a guy's soul. Legend says it is so delicious, it stopped a sultan's wives from squabbling and brought peace to the palace!"

"Humph. Well, I wouldn't spy on my friends and family for the enemy," Ginny said steadfastly. "No matter what."

Richard winced.

Abigail took Ginny's hand. "Come on, sugarplum." As they walked away swinging their clasped hands, Richard could hear his mother begin to explain that C. S. Lewis wrote Edmund's temptation as a metaphor for the disciple Judas, who betrayed Christ for money.

"Ooooooooohhhhhhh." Ginny's voice trailed off into the shadows of the dimly lit boardwalk.

Was it the cotton candy that made Richard want to vomit or his suddenly feeling a parallel to Judas?

"Okay, men." Don clapped his hands together. "That's a signal for us to take a walk on the beach and patrol for enemy subs!" He laughed at himself. "Seriously, let's walk off that cotton candy glop. If we head toward the old World War II watchtowers, we'll be away from all the surface light and have a great view of the stars."

So Don, Richard, and Vladimir strolled to the boardwalk's end. "It's hard to imagine today," he said as they walked, "but Nazi U-boats trolled along here, unchecked. Right out there. In fact, in the first months of 1942, right after Pearl Harbor, Nazi subs sank nearly four hundred American freighters and tankers off our Atlantic Coast, most between here and North Carolina's Outer Banks. None of those old tubs were armed. The Nazis called it the Great American Turkey Shoot, the SOBs. Thousands of our guys died."

They stepped onto the cool sand, and Don gazed out onto the dark waters.

"My uncle rejoined the Merchant Marine during the war to keep supplies going to England. Trucks. Guns. Food. Medicines. A lot of old geezers re-upped. Percentage-wise, the Merchant Marine suffered the highest casualty rate of any of the Armed Forces. And people never think about them." Don stopped and did a salute toward the sea. "Thanks, Uncle Jack."

They kept walking. For a long while, the only sound was the boom and fizz of waves slamming the beach, creating sudden shallow pools bubbling and sliding forward, then hissing sadly as they were sucked back into the ocean, making way for the next crash of surf.

When they were illuminated only by moonlight, Don announced, "This is perfect." They flopped onto a dune. Don pointed toward the Atlantic: "There's Sagittarius, the archer. See? That arc of stars that looks like a bow? Low on the horizon, just above the ocean."

The boys nodded.

"Above us, that lopsided *W*, that's Cassiopeia's chair. And over there," he said, pointing slightly inland, "is Cygnus. Look for a cross of stars that makes a stick body. Can you see what looks like a swan's outstretched wings?"

Hushed, Vladimir and Richard looked to where he pointed. Gazing at the heavens was quieting the guilt Ginny had unwittingly poured on Richard. He barely breathed, worrying about distracting Don.

"Now sit real still and focus, boys. Stay on Cygnus. See that very faint swath of gray white around it?" Don held up his hand and swept it from left to right.

"Oh, yeah! I see it!" Vlad said quietly. He nudged Richard and pointed, and soon Richard found it, too.

"That's the Milky Way. Keep an eye out. Don't move and you'll eventually see something bright skip across it. That'll be a shooting star."

Amazed by the unmistakable reverence in his dad's voice, Richard glanced over and saw a quiet, peaceful smile on Don's face.

"I didn't know you knew so much about stars, Dad."

"What?" Don frowned a little. "Yeah, I guess we haven't had enough time for sitting and talking about stuff like this. That's going to change, Rich." He reached over and ruffled Richard's hair without taking his eyes off the sky.

All three kept their gaze heavenward, chins up.

"Did you study astronomy in college, Mr. Bradley?"

"Nope. Political science and frat parties. Wish I'd been more of a reader, like you two."

Vladimir elbowed Richard and gave him a wink that said *Hear that?*

Don laughed, noticing the gesture. "No, I learned about the stars during the war. On the way home from missions. The

Brits flew night raids. We went in daylight. But sometimes, on our runs into Germany, we didn't get back to our base in England until the sun was long set. After all that exploding flak, planes rupturing and going down, the cannon fire of the Messerschmitts chasing us, the flash-bang of ack-ack guns from below . . ." He trailed off for a moment and then almost whispered, "If we were lucky enough to make it back to it, there was a blessed darkness over the English Channel."

He paused. In the gloom, Richard could see his father lift his hand as if brushing away a mosquito. But Richard wondered if it was a tear, if Don was thinking about his own plane rupturing and his capture and . . .

"Up front," Don almost whispered, "the pilots could spot those bright white cliffs of Dover shining through the gloom. That's what they flew toward like starved, thirsty men. For me, back in the tail, it was seeing the stars suddenly pop out, one after another, like angels showing up to tell me I was going to survive. I learned to pick out the constellations that took me closer and closer to base, to going home to Abby."

Richard had never heard his dad talk like that before. He seemed so different.

"AHA!" Don pointed. "There! Did you see it?"

A razor-thin streak of golden fire.

"I did!" Richard cried.

"I did, too!" called Vladimir.

Don laughed. "Make a wish, boys."

Richard's was that the night would never end.

But, of course, it had to.

● ● ·

On the walk back, Vladimir darted away from Don and Richard, waving his arms wildly, to chase the zigzagging eddies rushing up the beach and then back toward their mother ocean. They laughed at his antics. Vladimir rarely acted so silly. Richard shook off the thought of how his friend's unabashed glee would vanish if he knew that Don was spying on him. And that the surveillance was prompted by Richard's ratting on Vlad's family.

Richard didn't want to think about it. The night was too wonderful for that. Instead, he said, "This is great, Dad."

"That it is, Rich. Sure beats the heck out of what I've usually been doing over Memorial Day."

At that moment, when his dad seemed so open, so at peace with himself, Richard dared ask, "What *were* you doing, Dad?"

Don drew in a sharp, deep breath. But he answered quietly: "Placing bets for Mr. Hoover at the horse races."

"What?" Richard exclaimed, before he could edit himself.

Don looked over at Richard and smiled sheepishly. "He and the FBI's number two man, Clyde Tolson, vacation in San Diego every year, enjoying box seats at its famous Del Mar racetrack. For free, I might add.

"But the director doesn't want people knowing that he likes to wager on horses on a regular basis. Hell, betting is something McCarthy uses as evidence against people—claiming it makes them vulnerable to being blackmailed by commies into doing traitor's work. Some federal workers lost their jobs because they like to lay down a few bucks on a race."

Richard was stunned, listening. That was so . . . so . . . Dare he think it? So hypocritical.

Don seemed to read his mind. "There's a lot of hooey in our government these days."

He paused a moment and then continued, "But here's the thing, Rich. There are people out there in the world who do hate America. Hate the way we live. Hate our freedoms, our individualism. A lot of Communists want to destroy democracy because they don't understand it. They've been told it's corrupt. They've been fed a lot of propaganda about capitalism and our supposed greed and evils. They *have* set up spies among us, and seduced or coerced some of our fellow Americans to betray us."

Richard nodded to keep his dad talking. Thinking about Vladimir and what he may have done to his best friend's family, he needed to hear this truth, this rationale, as much as Don seemed to need to say it.

"The Cold War is real," Don continued. "The Soviets have the bomb. Communism is spreading. Now China is Red. North Korea. North Vietnam. The Cubans almost turned into a satellite for the Russkies a few months back—just one hundred miles from Key West! Communism is bad mojo. Look how viciously the Soviets put down the East Berliners who simply wanted to reunite with their neighbors.

"So I'm like those old merchant mariners. I know there are some serious holes in the boat, but there's a job that needs doing against bad guys. Right now, it ain't perfect, but the FBI is my best ship. Does that make sense?"

Richard couldn't tell if Don's question was really for him or not. But he answered anyway. "Yes, sir. That makes sense."

Don studied Richard's face for a moment, then shrugged off whatever he was thinking. "Anyway, going back to my placing bets for the director. The deal at the bureau is this: if you screw up a case, you're on the outs with Mr. Hoover. You have to work your way back into his graces with stuff like placing bets for him. Running errands. Painting his house.

"But looks like there'll be no more of that for me. That's finally changed."

Don put his arm over Richard's shoulder, and the two of them stopped to watch Vladimir run up and back, up and back, laughing with the waves.

This, this kind of connection, this kind of conversation, seeing his dad calm, his sense of purpose restored, this was Richard's Turkish Delight. He looked to the heavens for another falling star to sanctify his new wish—that it would all be worth selling out his best friend's family.

●　●　·

The next day, Vladimir and Richard were lying on the beach as Ginny frolicked in the waves. Don had taken Abby out for lunch, saying he wanted a date with his sweetheart, and the boys were in charge of keeping watch over Ginny.

"I really like how much your dad still goes weak in the knees over your mom," Vladimir said.

Richard laughed. "Yeah, but sometimes it's embarrassing how gooey they get."

"Better than the alternative, trust me."

Richard looked at Vladimir with surprise. "Your parents get along."

"Oh, sure. But it's not the same. My dad is all about his job. And Mom—you wouldn't notice it—she hides it well. But

Mom is pretty haunted. I don't think Dad gets it, and that kind of puts a distance between them."

Richard propped himself up on his elbows. "Gee, I'm sorry, man. I had no idea. It doesn't show at all."

Vladimir's answering smile was rueful. "Yeah, well, I see it on her face when she thinks no one's looking. Like when she's painting. Or when she listens to music by Dvořák or Janáček. Horrible things happened all around her when she was not that much older than we are. She lost a lot of friends and family to the Nazis. That kind of thing has to wreck your heart."

Vladimir grabbed a handful of sand and let it drain like an hourglass. Richard had no idea what was appropriate for him to say. So he stayed silent, to let Vladimir speak again or to change the subject.

"To tell you the truth," Vladimir went on, his voice low and serious, "I think sometimes she feels really weird about being the wife of a U.S. diplomat. First off, the Allies basically sold out her country in the Munich Pact and handed it over to Hitler. All to appease the SOB and avoid another fight. But the war happened anyway."

Richard shifted uncomfortably. What Vladimir said was totally true. The Allies had betrayed the Czechs. His History teacher had talked about it.

"Mom has a lot of guilt about being able to escape Czechoslovakia as the Nazis marched in. She could get out because she was a U.S. diplomat's wife. But she couldn't take anyone else with her, other than me and Natalia. I think she feels like a traitor. To her family, anyway. Most everyone else she loved was trapped. One side of her family completely disappeared in concentration camps. Others died fighting in resistance groups."

Richard cleared his throat. It was dry with discomfort. Americans didn't talk about this kind of stuff. They might joke about how hard it was to get gasoline and shoes and sugar that were rationed during the war, but nothing about losing their entire family.

"Then"—Vladimir drew out the word before continuing—"in the final days of the war we let the Soviets 'liberate' Czechoslovakia and Eastern Europe. The Soviet occupation was just swapping one form of slavery for another. We just stood by with our hands in our pockets and let the commies take over. What little bit of family Mom has left is in terrible danger. Anybody who is pro-democracy or has some relative living in the West is."

He sighed heavily. "That's why she's working so hard to find her cousin."

"Who?"

"You know that guy she was arguing with up in New York?"

Richard sat up abruptly. "Yeah."

"Remember the AP bureau chief the Czechs arrested a few years back and just released recently?"

Richard's heart started beating loudly. He itched to tell his best friend about seeing the magazine article—that's the kind of thing best friends shared and noodled out the riddles of together. Unless, of course, one friend was spying on the other. So he asked as nonchalantly as he could: "You mean the journalist who says he was tortured by the commies into confessing he was spying on them for us, when he really wasn't?"

"That's the one."

Richard nodded. "Yeah, I remember. Dad told me Voice of America called him the first American martyr for freedom of the press behind the Iron Curtain."

"Yup. That's true." Vladimir hesitated. "Maybe I shouldn't talk about this. Mom's got no love for that guy." He looked over at Richard. "You won't tell anybody?"

Richard felt his face flush. "No."

"Swear?"

Richard swallowed hard. "Sure." What a liar he had become.

"Well," Vladimir began, "the journalist had three Czechs working for him—finding him sources and stories. Like one article about a coal mine strike in a small town about twenty miles outside Prague. A Communist government doesn't want information like that getting out. All its workers are supposed to be happy!" Vladimir snorted in disgust.

"What's this got to do with the guy your mom was yelling at in New York?"

Vladimir startled. "I shouldn't be talking about this."

Richard kicked himself. He needed to be patient, that's how confessions worked in his detective novels. Just let Vladimir tell the story how he wanted to. Don't ask questions, or he'd spook.

"Seriously, man"—Richard tried to soothe him—"I'm sorry for interrupting. I'm just really interested, that's all."

"Well, you should be. It's real 007 stuff." Vladimir fell silent, staring at the ocean. But after a long pause, he spoke again, obviously worried about Teresa and proud of her, too. "Mom's cousin was one of the Czechs helping the American journalist report stories. Right before the AP bureau chief was arrested, her cousin was dragged off by the *Státní bezpečnost*, the StB, the Czech secret police."

Richard nodded. He'd gotten that man's arrest story from snooping into the article on Teresa's desk.

"The journalist's trial was anti-Western propaganda all the way." Vladimir grew agitated as he talked. "The charges against him were totally trumped up to convince Czechs to hate the United States, to make it seem like we're sending saboteurs in to undermine their country. And to scare the bejeebees out of anyone thinking of leaking information to American reporters.

"During his trial, the journalist confirmed that Mom's cousin worked for AP. My dad and I think the journalist just didn't realize what his confession would allow the commies to do to his Czech employees. Mom's cousin was sentenced to twenty years. Twenty! He didn't even get a chance to defend himself."

"Geez Louise," Richard murmured. It wasn't fair to blame the AP chief, but he could see why Teresa had drawn horns on his photo, given her perspective.

"I only met her cousin a couple of times when we were in Prague after the war and before the Communist coup six years ago. But I remember his playing charades one Christmas. He gave me that hand-carved marionette that's hanging in my bedroom." He shook his head. "He was a real nice man, very idealistic. I remember that."

"So, what will happen to him?" Richard was beginning to feel queasy. This story wasn't matching his interpretation of the stuff on Teresa's desk at all.

"No one can survive twenty years in a Czech prison. Mom's found out that he's being held in Ruzyně, a hellhole just outside Prague. She's trying to get him out. Find some official or guard she can bribe. She has a childhood friend who fled Czechoslovakia during the coup and made it to Paris. But he still manages to slip back and forth, smuggling people out. He's even got the chutzpah to carry radio transmitters in so Czechoslovakians can hear Voice of America broadcasts. He's trying to get whatever information he can about her cousin."

The refugee doing "mysterious errands" in the article. It had to be. Richard felt himself begin to tremble with misgivings.

"And if that doesn't work," Vladimir continued, "her backup plan is to try to sweet-talk the wives of the Czech Embassy here into asking their husbands to help. Those guys are all big-time operators in Czechoslovakia's Communist Party or they wouldn't be trusted enough to be sent to Washington. That's why Mom plays cards with those women. I swear I hear her vomiting in the bathroom every time she comes back from seeing them."

Richard's head was spinning. Suddenly, all those maps and clips and letters on Teresa's drawing table made sense. She wasn't a Red. She wasn't a pinko. Even with all her artsy, crazy, left-wing ideas. She was the exact opposite!

Oh God. What have I done?

"Hey, Rich?"

"Yeah?"

"Where's Gin?"

● ● ·

Richard looked toward the ocean. For the last half hour, Ginny had been right in front of them, jumping up and down, splashing, up to her knees in calmer water, a few yards inland from the breaking surf. He'd checked that she was still there a few minutes before. But now she wasn't.

He scanned the beach to the right, to the left, looking for her red, white, and blue polka-dot swimsuit and the conical Japanese straw hat she'd gotten at the cherry blossom festival. Children digging, mothers scolding, teenagers roasting. No Ginny.

Richard stood, feeling the slightest shadow of panic. He looked back toward the house. Maybe she needed the bathroom? No. No recent wet footprints heading that way, either.

Shading his eyes, Richard looked more closely at the water. A couple of people were floating, treading water just beyond the cresting waves.

"Would she have gone out beyond the break line?" Vladimir asked.

"Maybe. She's pretty gutsy." But she sure shouldn't be. Ginny wasn't that strong of a swimmer yet.

He jogged toward the water, watching the floaters. The sun was so bright, the water glinted and glimmered, blinding him. He couldn't make out their faces. One of them had to be Ginny, though.

But just as Richard waded in up to his thighs and cupped his hands to shout for her, a woman several yards down cried out and fell up to her neck, sliding several feet toward the crashing waves until her husband grabbed her.

"Oh, my," she spluttered, as he righted her. "That undertow is horrible today. It just yanked me off my feet."

Undertow! Richard's heart sank. "Ginny!" he shouted. "GIN-NY!!"

He watched for a response from the floaters as he scrambled into the cold water. Nothing. He dove in and started swimming out to them, holding his head above water so he could see, when he heard Vladimir calling.

"Rich!"

He turned, kicking to keep himself afloat. Vladimir was pointing frantically past Richard. "She's behind you!"

Richard turned around just as a wave crested and crashed down on blond curls and flailing arms.

"GIN-NY!"

Dark swirling water surged over him, crushing all the air out of his chest. Richard came up coughing. "GIN-NY!"

He lunged through the water to where she had been. He whipped himself around, searching. There! Just above blue-ink waters—her upturned face. Thank God, her eyes were open. He could see her gasping for breath.

"GINNY! Swim to me."

He almost cried when he saw how frightened she was. "Rich!" she squeaked.

He pulled himself toward her, kicking and stroking the cold water as hard as he could. Almost there. Almost. Just a few more feet.

Another wave was coming. It would beat him to her.

"GINNY! HOLD YOUR BREATH! GO UNDERNEATH THE BREAKERS!"

How enormous the wave seemed. It crashed and pushed Richard below the angry surface where the competing currents—in, out—tumbled him over and over. He forced his eyes open against the sting of salt to look for gray water, the surface illuminated. He crawled his way up, to the sun, and bobbed up to air, gulping it in desperately like a dying fish.

But no Ginny.

"GIN-NY!!!"

The ocean whipped his legs backward and forward as the tide shoved in and the undertow rushed out, suspending him in a watery push-pull argument. He felt a slap of warmer water streaming out to sea and then what felt like a fish slide along his leg.

Richard would never know what made him do it. He reached down and grabbed it. It was Ginny. Ginny's arm.

He dragged her up, coughing, vomiting water. But alive.

Richard didn't fight the next wave. He just clung to his little sister to hold her up and let it crash and carry them like leaves skimming along a stream to the shore. Vladimir met them in neck-high water and half carried them both out.

Shivering, crying in relief, Richard and Ginny sat on the sand, gasping for air. Richard wouldn't let go of Ginny's hand. Her legs were all scraped up from being dragged by the undertow along crushed shells and pebbles, her lips were blue from the cold waters, and her hair was matted with sand. But she was alive.

Vladimir quickly wrapped her in their beach towels, as Ginny leaned her head against Richard's shoulder. She smiled weakly. "Well, that will make a great first story for an inquiring camera girl." She looked up into his face. "Don't you think?"

The boys gaped at her.

Finally, Richard choked out, "You kill me, Ginny."

"Almost literally," Vladimir added.

The three half laughed, half sobbed, baking back to life in the sunshine.

• • ·

On the drive home from the beach, Ginny stayed tucked up against Richard's side. She dozed most of the three hours and was peacefully sound asleep when they pulled into Vladimir's driveway.

Don whispered to Abigail, "I'm going to walk Vladimir in. I want to tell his parents how grateful we are for his part in saving Ginny."

She nodded.

Vladimir and Richard grinned and waved a silent good-bye to each other.

Don stayed at their front door for a long time, talking to Vladimir's father. When he came back to the car, his jovial weekend attitude, the gratitude for his daughter's life that had lit up his face all day, was gone. He looked ashen.

"What's wrong?" Abigail whispered.

"The State Department has suspended Vladimir's father, pending a Loyalty Review Board hearing. He's been identified as a possible security risk." Don rubbed his hand along his forehead. "It's because of Teresa. She's friends with people on FBI watch lists, with radical writers and artists. She communicates with Communists in Prague and socializes with Communists here at the Czech Embassy.

"It's possible he could be called in by McCarthy to testify, as well. He'll lose his job for sure if that happens."

In the backseat, Richard felt like he was drowning all over again. He couldn't breathe. This was his fault.

"Dad," he gasped. "They've got it all wrong."

"I don't think so, son. They . . . We've got a lot . . ." He paused and looked at Richard in the rearview mirror. "A lot of . . . evidence."

"We?" Abigail asked.

"The FBI. We've had surveillance on her for a while." He and Richard locked eyes in the mirror. "We received a solid tip-off that she might be Red."

"Oh dear," Abigail murmured.

"But, Dad, it's . . . it's all a mistake." As quickly as he could, Richard spilled out what Vladimir had told him.

Don winced, looked down, and shook his head slowly, over and over. When he finally lifted his face again and looked up at Richard in the mirror, his eyes were full of rage. Like he'd just figured out that he'd been duped or something. And his hands were shaking so badly, Abigail had to turn the key in the ignition for him.

Chapter 13:

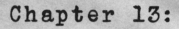

JUNE

1954

The Army's attorney, Joseph Welch (left), listens to McCarthy during hearings

The Army-McCarthy hearings run for nine weeks. On June 9, perhaps recognizing that the Army is succeeding in discrediting him, McCarthy tries to smear its attorney, Joseph Welch. Out of the blue, McCarthy charges that one of the junior attorneys in Welch's private practice had once belonged to the liberal National Lawyers Guild "after it had been exposed as the legal arm of the Communist party." Therefore, Welch was guilty of being a Red by association.

Welch is stunned. He knew all about his junior associate's past work with a progressive group that advocated for the labor movement, civil rights, and members of the American Communist Party. Welch hadn't used him for researching the case against McCarthy, knowing it could put the fledgling attorney in jeopardy of being targeted by McCarthy and the senator's character assassination attacks.

Welch rises to defend his young employee: "Until this moment, Senator, I think I never really gauged your cruelty. . . . Little did I dream you could be so reckless and so cruel as to do an injury to that lad."

McCarthy continues to press his point.

"Let us not assassinate this lad further, Senator," Welch interrupts, continuing in a retort that will be replayed over and over on the news: "You have done enough. Have you no sense of decency, sir?"

Welch's televised and heartfelt dismay and disgust with McCarthy's smear tactics is the final straw that breaks the hold of McCarthyism on American attitudes.

The United States runs its first nationwide civil defense drill. The death of 12 million Americans is simulated in a mock nuclear attack. Children are taught to "duck and cover," crawling underneath their desks and wrapping their arms around their heads.

Children under their desks during a "duck and cover" drill

DON stood, arms crossed, feet spread and planted in a boxing-ready pose, scowling, clenching his unlit pipe in his mouth. He was watching the evening news. Richard crept up behind him. He hadn't been able to really talk with his dad since they'd returned from the beach the week before. Don had been out of the house, working all the time, it seemed. Or maybe he was avoiding Richard?

But Richard was desperate to talk with him. To know what to do, what to say to Vladimir. And what were they going to do to make things right now that they knew what Teresa had really been doing? Vladimir's dad was being investigated on stuff that looked suspect, but in the end, wasn't. Maybe a little left-wing radical, maybe a little pinko-sympathetic, but not a Red.

And it was Richard's fault, for misinterpreting things, for making assumptions based on the bombast of powerful guys like McCarthy, for spreading gossip. For—how had Natalia put it?—for not thinking for himself.

"Dad?"

Don held his hand up, signaling he wanted silence. The ABC broadcast was reporting on the day's Army-McCarthy hearings. It was replaying a heated exchange between the senator and the Army's lawyer, Joseph Welch, about a young lawyer in his firm. McCarthy was trying to undermine Welch and weaken his credibility by painting his young associate as a pinko.

Stunned, Welch replied, "Let us not assassinate this lad any further, Senator."

McCarthy fiddled with his glasses, focusing on his notes. The senator would not look the attorney in the eye as he vehemently defended his young employee. Finally, Welch exploded, "Have you no sense of decency, sir?"

The broadcast then played comments Welch made about McCarthy during a recess:

"Here's a young kid with one mistake—just one mistake—and he tries to crucify him. I don't see how in the name of God you can fight anybody like that. I never saw such cruelty . . . such arrogance."

"Humph." Don snapped the TV off, dropping his pipe on top of it. "It's about time," he growled. "Someone, besides Murrow, needed to expose McCarthy for the blowhard he is. Most of us veterans knew it all along. McCarthy likes to call himself 'Tail Gunner Joe.' The jerk was an intelligence officer in the Pacific. That's an important job, don't get me wrong. But he *debriefed* combat pilots. He just badgered crews to take him up on calm days so he could shoot at coconut trees."

Don was getting more and more agitated as he spoke. "Old Tail Gunner Liar used to walk with a limp, claiming he crash-landed and carried ten pounds of shrapnel in his leg. You know how McCarthy really got hurt? During an initiation ritual. He had an iron bucket strapped to one foot and had to run the gauntlet of sailors armed with paddles."

"What?" Richard finally spoke. "Are you kidding?"

"Yeah, I know, son. That stuff's total idiocy. Anyway, McCarthy fell and broke his foot. Did he get hurt on duty? Yeah. Technically. But it wasn't combat. That's the way he manipulates half-truths to his purposes.

"He's been making the FBI and Mr. Hoover look ridiculous, with his bully tactics, his hate rhetoric, his unsubstantiated accusations. Always waving papers he claims came from the FBI and are irrefutable evidence. Maybe now that the nation's witnessed firsthand what a mean SOB and master manipulator he's been, we can get back to real investigations."

Richard saw his in. He swallowed and said, "Dad, about that. About *real* investigations."

Don glanced over his shoulder. His eyes were sharp with aggravation and disgust.

Richard flinched at the squall of his expression. But he realized the emotions were for McCarthy, not him, as Don's face calmed.

"Yeah, I know, son," he began quietly. "I've been trying to figure what to do about Vladimir's dad, without . . ." Don stopped. "Without . . ."

"Without getting me in trouble, Dad?"

"You?" Don drew in a sharp breath. "Not you, son. Me. And rightly so. I landed on those scraps of information like a starved duck on a june bug. I was just so hungry for . . . for . . ."

"A good case?"

Don smiled. "Well, you sure are grown-up all of a sudden."

Richard smiled. The year had done that for him. Plus his friendship with a kid like Vladimir—a kid whose ideas and background were so different from his. "What are you going to do, Dad?"

Don gestured toward the TV. "The decent thing. Just like Welch did. I'm just not sure exactly how yet. Even with Teresa trying to get her cousin out of Czechoslovakia, she still has friends and opinions McCarthy damns." He rubbed his hand over his jawline, making the scratchy-beard sound that always meant he was thinking hard.

"I'll explain what she's really doing to put the evidence against her in context. But to completely clear Vladimir's dad with the Loyalty Review Board, I will also need some counterweight, something to balance out her leftist politics and friends."

"What do you mean, Dad?"

"I need to find something she's done that's weighty enough to make the board ignore her pretty darn unconventional attitudes and radical friends. To tip the scale in the Whites' favor with the Red-hunters. The bigger problem is the State Department can dismiss him purely for being *vulnerable* to 'coercion, influence, or pressure' according to Eisenhower's executive order. The review board could definitely claim that her cousin being in Red hands could make her State Department husband susceptible to blackmail from the wrong type of folks. That, and they have leftist artist friends on our watch list."

Don paused. "Got any ideas from those books of yours? Something from *The Count of Monte Cristo*, maybe?"

Richard shook his head sadly.

"Just kidding, son." Don clapped him on the back. "I've got this. First order—to admit my overeagerness in suggesting the investigation. Sometimes a man just has to fly straight to the bomb target, full throttle, no matter what flak he might hit. After that, I'll explain her actions. And maybe, just maybe," he said, gesturing at the TV, "the worm has turned."

Don left the room, and then the house. Richard hadn't seen his dad's hands shaking at all as they talked.

Richard didn't see Don that night or the next morning before he headed to the bus stop in the soft morning light of a June dawn. Mockingbirds were out, warbling symphonies. Late-blooming peonies and roses painted the street. He was feeling a lot less tortured about everything now that he and Don had talked. He knew Don would fix things. After a week of being racked with guilt, Richard felt the gentle air's promise and walked with a much lighter, hopeful step.

Plus, in just three days, the school year would be over! That was the best. He had already collected a stack of books to read over the summer. He was starting with Raymond Chandler's latest LA hard-boiled detective novel, *The Long Goodbye.* Then he was going to try a book Vladimir had given him, *Go Tell It on the Mountain* by James Baldwin. He'd had to keep that one in his room. It was a coming-of-age story about the fourteen-year-old stepson of a Harlem preacher. Vladimir had loved it, but Richard knew the novel might fall into the category of dangerous reading material for some people, since the author was Black, his subject matter rooted in the Black American experience. Well, given Don's comments the day before about the Senate hearings, maybe things would loosen up now, book-wise, anyway. Thank goodness!

Richard saw Vladimir turn the corner and walk along the sidewalk toward him. "Hey, Vlad," he called, and greeted him with a countdown song the kids had been singing at school for a week: *"Hark, the herald angels shout, THREE more days until we're out. Three more days of miseryyyy, in that penitentiary."*

"Ha-ha-ha, aren't you the clever one?" Vladimir sniped.

Richard froze. He'd never heard Vladimir be sarcastic like that before.

Vladimir took the last strides to Richard's side quickly, repeating, "Oh . . . so . . . clever."

"What gives, V—?"

But before Richard could get his friend's name out, Vladimir shoved him.

Richard staggered backward.

"So clever!" Vladimir shoved him again.

Richard stumbled, tripping on tree roots.

"What are you talking about?" But he knew.

"This, you SOB!" Vladimir held up a long wire with a tiny black microphone on the end.

"Wh-wh-what's that?"

"Are you joking me? Don't insult me more by lying about it. This is because of you, isn't it? Or your precious G-man Dad."

Richard could feel his freckles flame and burn and then turn pale.

Be honest. Fly straight to the bomb target. Just like Don had said. Richard took a deep breath and nodded. "Yes. I'm sorry, Vlad. Honest. So very sorry."

"Honest? I don't think you can use that word again, ever. And you're sorry? Oh, wait, *very* sorry. So everything's okay then. Doesn't matter that my dad might get fired. That my mom may never be able to get a visa to visit her homeland again."

"Listen, I told Dad what you told me at the beach and . . ."

"What? You swore you wouldn't."

"I know. But I had to. To help you. It's all a big mistake."

"Mistake? The mistake is my trusting you!" Vladimir balled up his hand, pulled back his arm, and slammed

Richard's face with his fist, throwing his whole body into the punch.

Richard fell back, hitting the ground, blood spurting from his nose.

Vladimir threw the wiretap at him. "Go hang yourself with that. Liar! Fascist!"

At that very moment, the FBI director's car pulled up beside the bus stop and paused, the motor still running. Hoover's driver stepped out.

"Everything all right, boys?" he asked as he helped Richard to his feet. "Pretty bad bloody nose, son." The driver looked toward the car as its back tinted window rolled down a few inches—enough for Hoover to hear what was said, but not enough that they could see him. "Want me to drive you home? That needs ice."

"No . . . thank you," Richard muttered. "I live just up the street."

"The director knows that. You're Don Bradley's boy."

"Yes, sir," Richard answered.

Vladimir stood silently, his stance defiant, but his face afraid.

"Does the director need to speak to this boy?" The driver gestured toward Vladimir.

Vladimir bit his lip.

Richard knew it could only make things worse for Vladimir and his family if Hoover thought he was some kind of thug. "No. No, sir."

The driver eyed them both, looked back to the car, and then to the boys. "Didn't this boy strike you, son?"

Richard hesitated. This was one of those moments, like in a book, where everything could turn on a dime, for good or for bad. Hoover was sure to tattle to Don about his son fighting. But more importantly, this might make things even worse for his dad when he tried to explain Teresa to the FBI. Richard knew that Hoover demanded starched shirts and formality, respectful and proper manners from all his agents. A hooligan son, brawling on street corners, made Don look pretty darn bad.

But if Richard told the truth—that Vladimir started the fight—it'd just harden Hoover's suspicions of Vladimir's family. He looked at his friend. He thought of his own dad. What to do? Suddenly, he remembered how Vladimir had protected the disabled kid in the gym, by claiming responsibility for others' actions.

Richard wiggled his foot a bit to cover up the bug that lay on the ground beside him. Then he said, "I started it, sir. I threw the first punch. My buddy was only defending himself."

The driver checked the window once more. After a moment, he asked, "What was the fight over?"

"A girl." Richard answered so quickly and easily, he startled himself. "And she's not even worth it."

The driver grinned at him, then forced it away. "Well, go home and put some ice on that. If you get in trouble for being late to school, Mr. Hoover will send a note explaining."

The driver got in the car and drove off.

Once the car turned the corner and was out of sight, Vladimir turned on his heel and walked away, without a word.

● ● ·

Richard was lucky when he got home—Abigail wasn't there. She would have cried and worried and asked a billion questions.

She was out, driving Ginny to school because his sister was taking in a big display she'd built to show water currents and riptides at the beach. She was giving a report about ocean safety to her classmates. She had even convinced the fire department to come in and teach CPR.

"It's important information," Ginny had told Richard proudly, "especially right before everyone goes on beach vacations. This is the kind of reporting a good news girl does!"

When he'd laughed, she'd added, "And the lede of the story— that's the hook, the first and most important part of a story, in reporter talk—is that my big brother saved my life. Not everyone will be lucky enough to have a big brother to help. So they need to know how to save themselves."

Things were really swell these days with Ginny. He probably owed that to Vladimir's influence, too.

Richard sighed heavily. How did he let everything get so screwed up? He reached into the freezer and pulled out a steak, putting the block of meat-ice on his nose like guys did in the movies.

No way he was going to school. He didn't want to explain his nose, and he didn't know what to say to Vladimir if he saw him in the halls. Who'd care this late in the school year anyway? All their exams were already done. Richard would hide out in his room and wait until his dad came home. He needed Don's advice, bad. If he was real quiet and didn't flush the toilet or anything, Abigail wouldn't know he was there. He'd eat the lunch she'd already packed him and read a book until it was time for dinner.

His plan actually worked. But Don wasn't home in time for supper. At that point, Richard had to come downstairs and face his mom. She gasped when she saw his swollen red nose. He explained it away by saying he'd been hit in the face in dodgeball.

"Oh, my goodness! Honestly, why do they play that game? It's so violent. I have a good mind to call the gym teacher and . . ."

"For Pete's sake, Mom, don't! You wouldn't believe the garbage I'd get from the other guys if you did that."

She bought his story.

Ginny didn't. He could tell by the way she looked at him. But he prevented her from asking questions by asking one of his own. "So, how did the presentation go, Gin?"

As she burbled on about how nice the firemen had been, and how mouth-to-mouth resuscitation worked, Richard's mind wandered onto worrying about how quickly he could come up with such convincing fibs. A great skill for a spy or a G-man, but not appropriate to use on his family . . . or his friends. He'd have to work on knowing the difference.

● ● ·

Don still wasn't home at 10:00 P.M. Richard dawdled brushing his teeth, waiting up. But by eleven, Abigail ordered him to get into bed. He opened his window so he would hear his dad's car when he drove up. Even so, Richard tried to keep himself awake, reading by flashlight. He checked his alarm clock at midnight. Don still wasn't home. Somewhere around one o'clock, he drifted off.

A little past 3:00 A.M., a car door slammed shut in the driveway. Richard bolted up and fell out of his bed. He stumbled downstairs.

Don was in the kitchen, illuminated only by the refrigerator light as he held the door open and drank from a milk bottle.

Richard caught his breath. Don was dressed in a garbageman's overalls.

"Dad?"

Don startled and dribbled milk down his chin. "Darn it!" He wiped his mouth. "You caught me! Don't tell your mom I was drinking from the bottle." He brushed milk off his front. "Hey, what are you doing up, anyway?"

"Waiting for you, Dad." Richard stepped in closer, into the refrigerator's spotlight.

"Whoa, Rich! Where'd you get that nose?" Don slammed the refrigerator closed.

"Vladimir punched me."

Don grimaced. "I'm sorry, son."

"Why are you dressed like that?" Richard felt sick to his stomach. Was this punishment? "Mr. Hoover isn't making you pick up garbage now, is he?"

Don looked puzzled and then glanced down at his clothes. He chuckled. "No, son. The opposite. Come here, let me look at that nose." He flipped the light on over the sink and tilted Richard's face up. "Hmmmm. That must have been a heck of a punch. Not broken, though, thank goodness." He let go and stepped back, leaning up against the counter. "You okay?"

Richard shook his head. "Vlad hates me now."

"I think he'll be all right in a day or two."

"No, he won't, Dad. He said his father will probably get fired."

"That won't happen. Not now."

"How do you know?"

"I just do. I talked to a lot of people yesterday." He put his hand on Richard's shoulder. "Believe it or not, Vladimir's dad is getting called into the Loyalty Review Board on a complaint sent in by someone who works for him. Not because of you."

"What?"

"Yeah." Don nodded. "It happens sometimes. A young go-getter type who wants to move up. He realized Mr. White was prime for investigation, given his wife being born in Eastern Europe and a 'modern' artist, to boot. When he heard Vladimir's dad mention that Teresa had been visiting friends at the Czech Embassy—socializing with the Communist delegation's wives—he shot off a pretty vicious letter to the review board.

"He even brought up that controversial State Department art show she'd been involved with in Prague and how Congress had decided it made us look bad overseas. And he threw in Truman's comment about modern art being 'the vaporings of half-baked lazy people.' The guy's a total jerk. He probably was hoping for Mr. White's job."

"But what about the . . ."

"The board didn't even know about our FBI surveillance. And I was able to close that file tonight. Got the okay for it from Mr. Hoover because of something Vladimir's mom told me."

"You went to see her?"

"Yes."

Richard felt himself turn red. "She must hate me now, too."

"Well, she doesn't like me very much, that's for sure. But we talked for a long time. And she let me in on something she'd heard one of the Czech Embassy wives let slip. And that allowed us to do some good tonight."

"Really? What's that, Dad?"

Don rubbed his chin. "I . . . I can't tell you, Rich. What little I'm going to say, I need to trust you to keep top secret, like a G-man would. Got it?"

Richard nodded solemnly.

"Let's just say she told me about something that could help us decode chatter among some bad guys. And embassies don't seem to pay no never mind to garbage trucks." He grinned.

Garbage truck. Garbageman overalls. His dad had gone undercover that night. He must have planted something or taken something. *All right!* "So does that mean everything is okay now, Dad?"

"Mostly. For the time being."

Richard sighed in relief. "Dad, the other thing Vlad said is that his mom wouldn't be able to go back to Czechoslovakia now. Did you fix that, too?"

Don frowned. "No. It won't be safe for her to visit Czechoslovakia now."

Richard caught his breath, thinking about all her Christmas traditions, her *kraslice*, her grandmother's mezuzah. He knew how important her homeland and heritage were to Teresa. That would be a terrible loss for her. And that was his fault.

"What . . . what about her cousin?" He choked out the question.

"That's up to people other than me. It'll depend on the State Department, and maybe even the United Nations. But I think people are motivated to try interceding now." Don straightened up. "To bed with you, young man. And I need to take a shower, bad. See you in the morning."

Vladimir didn't show up at school. Richard didn't see him around the neighborhood that weekend, either. But the next Saturday, he knocked on Richard's front door.

Heart pounding, Richard opened it. Vladimir held a big box.

"Hey!" Richard said.

"Hey," answered Vladimir.

There was a long, awkward pause.

"How's your nose?"

"Fine."

Pause.

"Want to come in?"

"Can't. Gotta catch a train."

"Where are you going?" Richard asked.

"New York."

"Oh."

"Yeah."

"When are you coming back?"

"Don't know," Vladimir answered.

Richard nodded, pressing his lips together to keep them from trembling in nervousness. "Going to see a show?"

"Nope. Looking for a house."

"What?" Richard's heart sank. "You're . . . you're moving back to New York City?"

"Yup." Vladimir nodded. "Dad's decided to go back to the UN office. He thinks he can do more good up there."

"Is this because . . . because . . ."

"Yeah, it is," Vladimir answered bluntly. "But you know what, buddy boy? We didn't like it much here. Except for you."

"Vlad, I'm so sorry."

"I know you are." He paused. "Mom said to tell you that everybody makes mistakes. What matters most is what you do after them." He shrugged. "Mom's like that. Forgiving. She kills me."

Richard didn't know what to say. He was losing his best friend. And it was his own stupid fault. "I . . . I . . ." Better to fly straight to the target. "I'll miss you, Vlad."

Vladimir nodded. After a few beats of silence, he replied, "I'll miss your old crumb-bum self, too." He looked squarely into Richard's eyes and waited until Richard returned the honest gaze. "You saved my life at that shooting, Rich. We're even-steven."

Richard blinked back tears of guilt, of sorrow, of relief, and of gratitude for Vladimir's largesse. Then he gasped. "Oh no. Wait. Will you still be able to apply for the page program?"

Vladimir snorted. "I'm not sure what I think about working for the U.S. government now. Maybe I can do more good as a musician. Natalia's been telling me there's a lot of important protest stuff coming out of Beat poets and folk musicians." He paused. "I don't know. I can always apply. Most pages come from around the country and find a place to live in DC."

"You could stay here!"

Vladimir smiled wryly. "Not sure how Mom would feel about that, given all that's happened."

Of course. That boat had sailed. Richard squirmed inside and changed the subject. "What's in the box?"

"Sheet music for your latest lyrics. The one about the girl we fought over for Hoover." Vladimir grinned. "We can still keep writing songs, you know. By mail."

Richard smiled back. "Promise?"

"Yeah, sure!"

"What else is in there?"

"Some books you lent me. Like that Philbrick thing." Vladimir put the box down on the stoop and pulled out *I Led 3 Lives*. "I have to be honest, I didn't like it much. But I marked something I thought you should read again. Especially now." He opened the book to the end, to a page pinned with a paper clip. It was an appendix titled "The Communist and the Liberal."

"Philbrick lists sixteen differences between the two, and he starts out saying, 'Unfortunately, some people confuse Communists and liberals when, in truth, they are worlds apart.'"

Vladimir looked up meaningfully at Richard before reading more: "'Number one: a Communist believes the individual must be sacrificed for the good of the masses; a liberal has high regard for the value and integrity of the individual.'" He turned the page. "I especially like number nine." Vladimir cleared his throat before continuing, "'A Communist, although he pretends to be independent, always takes his orders from above; a liberal makes up his own mind.'"

Vladimir closed the book. "It doesn't matter if you're liberal or conservative, man, just make your own decisions about what you believe." He dropped it back in the box. "Oh, I almost forgot." He reached into the back pocket of his jeans. "Natalia mailed this to me right before . . . before . . . you know. Anyway, she asked me to give it to you. I almost threw it away, I've been so mad at you. But then I figured you needed it."

He handed over a small round pin. It was white with a green feather in its middle. "She said to remind you that Robin Hood was his own man, with his own beliefs. Of course, he did make some pretty questionable wardrobe choices." Vladimir laughed.

Richard stared down at the pin in his palm, not wanting to meet Vladimir's gaze, knowing that would bring his friend's good-bye.

"Hey, Rich?"

Slowly, Richard looked up.

Vladimir smiled at him. "If I spot any hollow nickels up there in the Big Apple, you'll be the first to know." He punched Richard's shoulder. "See ya." He backed down the stairs. "Tell Gin to write our story someday. It'd be a heck of a scoop for an inquiring camera girl."

Afterword

JOSEPH McCarthy rose to national celebrity in February 1950, during a speech to the Republican Women's Club of Wheeling, West Virginia. The senator held up a piece of paper and brayed, "I have here in my hand a list of two hundred five—a list of names that were made known to the Secretary of State as being members of the Communist Party, and who, nevertheless, are still working and shaping policy in the State Department."

McCarthy's accusation that our diplomatic corps was riddled with Communists came fast on the heels of the sensationalized trial of a former State Department official, Alger Hiss. He had been convicted of perjuring himself when he denied passing top secret reports to a Soviet spy ring during World War II. Hiss had first been identified by Elizabeth Bentley, a double agent who had named approximately 150 Americans as spying for the Soviets, including 37 federal employees.

Elements of the Hiss trial read like pulp fiction. For instance, a *Time* magazine editor and confessed courier for the Soviets testified that Hiss had hidden strips of microfilm containing State Department documents stuffed inside pumpkins for him to pick up. The documents were linked to Hiss because of a quirk in type that would only occur from a malfunctioning key—like one found on his personal typewriter.

In the same month, physicist Klaus Fuchs confessed to spying for the Soviets while he worked on the Manhattan Project developing the U.S. atom bomb. And by early summer, the Rosenbergs would be arrested—eventually convicted of handing the Soviets our nuclear technology and executed.

Understandably, the country was jittery.

After all, World War II and its horrors had ended only five years earlier. Since then, the Soviets had drawn an "iron curtain" across Europe, taking over Poland, arresting thousands in Hungary, and blockading East Germany and East Berlin. A Soviet-backed Communist coup had won Czechoslovakia. Reports of Russian dissidents being sent to Siberian gulags to labor and freeze to death were growing. And the Soviet Union had successfully detonated its first atomic bomb.

Instead of postwar peace, the United States and the USSR were in a terrifying "Cold War" and atomic-weapons standoff.

Also, in Asia, China had fallen to Communism. French-controlled Vietnam was desperately fighting Communist rebels. By summer, the Korean War's carnage would start.

The piece of paper McCarthy waved in front of that West Virginia audience was hooey, to use a 1950s term. Within days, he himself would backtrack, first claiming he'd left the list of 205 names in his other suitcase when journalists asked for clarification. Under scrutiny by the press, he reduced the number to 81, then to 57, and finally only specifically targeted four people. A Senate committee formed to investigate McCarthy's claims also exonerated the State Department.

But recent events had primed the United States for hysteria. *McCarthyism*—a term we still use today for unsubstantiated accusations used to attack people's character and to suppress political opposition—was born.

● ● ●

Across the nation and across professions, rules were adopted to require employees to sign loyalty oaths. Review boards investigated employees' opinions, behaviors, and friendships.

Civilian watchdog groups mushroomed and coordinated letter-writing campaigns against "un-American" influences. Books were scrutinized and taken off shelves if they contained "subversive" themes—ideas that seemed to advocate the overthrow of American laws or simply challenged our traditions and status quo attitudes. Key members of McCarthy's Senate committee traveled to U.S. embassy libraries to purge suspect books—including an edition of Thomas Paine's writings that had helped spark our own American Revolution in 1776.

Meanwhile, McCarthy called hundreds of people before his Senate subcommittee. Often his accusations were nothing more than "guilt by association," e.g., knowing Communists or attending social events sponsored by groups his staff suspected to be "Red" or "pinko"—leaning sympathetically toward "Red." Typically, the only way for a witness to save his or her reputation was to "name names," to identify others who might have dabbled in Communist or left-wing politics.

The total effects of McCarthyism in terms of breeding fear and suspicion, ruining careers and friendships, are hard to tangibly measure. But historians estimate 12,000 people lost their jobs. The loyalty oaths and security reviews that ensued would harm a wide range of Americans—from the 300 screenwriters, directors, and actors blacklisted by Hollywood to the 3,000 sailors and longshoremen fired from cargo ships and docks. The damage lingered for years. An anthropology professor who lost her university post after McCarthy smeared her was unable to find another teaching job for eight years.

● ● •

How did McCarthy hold such sway over the nation's thinking? A former marine from Wisconsin, full of bluster and backroom poker-game charisma, McCarthy somehow came across as an underdog "skunk-hunter," the guy next door who would run the Red Menace out of town.

He was a compulsive braggart, referring to himself, for instance, as "Tail Gunner Joe." It was self-made legend. The reality my character Don Bradley explains to Richard was true—the shrapnel McCarthy claimed to carry in his leg from a mission was actually the result of falling during a hazing ritual.

Journalists exposed the lie. Yet the American public didn't seem to care. People were captivated by McCarthy's rhetoric. They had grown angry and resentful of the East Coast establishment that had surrounded FDR. They delighted in McCarthy dismissing Ivy League–educated, New Deal liberals as "eggheads." Americans loved his unsophisticated Midwestern bluntness and bad-boy image.

McCarthy was also helped by FBI Director J. Edgar Hoover. Hoover had been "hunting Reds" for decades, starting in World War I, when he served in the alien enemy branch of the War Emergency Bureau. He was soon head of the FBI's Radical Division, a counterterrorism office. A 25-year-old Hoover oversaw the deportation of dozens of radical Socialists following Russia's Bolshevik revolution and a series of coordinated bombings in the United States during 1919. One night's attack targeted several cabinet members, a Supreme Court justice, industrialist J. P. Morgan, five congressmen, the attorney general, and an FBI agent investigating a group of Italian anarchists.

While this terrorist threat was very real, Hoover also arrested many who were simply labor union workers, or pacifists who had protested American troops going to fight in World War I. He started a watch list. His devotion to rooting out Communists steeled when a horse-drawn carriage filled with dynamite was detonated at the corner of Wall and Broad Streets in New York City in September 1920. Thirty-eight people died and 300 were injured. The American Anarchist Fighters claimed responsibility.

Under Hoover, the FBI solved many crimes, hobbled mob bootlegging and violence, and caught a number of Nazi agents. But Hoover was also a rigid moralist and detested progressive lifestyles and ideology. He distrusted foreigners in general and did all he could to discredit Martin Luther King, Jr. and the civil rights movement. He hated First Lady Eleanor Roosevelt and her outspoken support of African Americans' push for equality. Once asked why he never married, Hoover reportedly quipped, "Because God made a woman like Eleanor Roosevelt."

Much of Hoover's power came from damaging files and tapes he amassed on members of Congress and White House staff, with which he essentially blackmailed them. Besides being a grotesque abuse of power, it was a stunning irony since Soviet agents used that tactic to turn Americans. Truman was one of the few presidents Hoover couldn't find dirt on. Yet he was able to pressure Truman into creating the Federal Employee Loyalty Program that required background checks on federal workers, which under McCarthyism devolved into America's "hunt for the disloyal."

By the time McCarthy rose to fame, Hoover had perfected his bureau's surveillance techniques. Hopeful that the news spotlight McCarthy was generating would help the FBI destroy spy rings it had been investigating for years, Hoover instructed his agents to feed names and incriminating information about those individuals to McCarthy's committee.

Hoover praised McCarthy as earnest, an amateur boxer, "a vigorous individual who is not going to be pushed around." The two became friends. They often spent afternoons together at nearby Maryland racetracks—despite federal workers losing their jobs for the same pastime.

Some historians also question Hoover's close friendship with the FBI's number two man, Clyde Tolson, given the fact that any hint of homosexuality became reason for dismissal as well. The *lavender scare* is a term many use for the persecution of gays by McCarthy-era loyalty review boards. Hoover and Tolson vacationed together, rode to work together, and dined together daily (at Harvey's or the Mayflower Hotel). Tolson inherited Hoover's property upon his death and is buried within a few feet of the director in Congressional Cemetery.

Eventually, Hoover distanced himself from McCarthy when the senator recklessly attacked the army and a decorated World War II veteran general. In December 1954, McCarthy was denounced in a formal censure by the Senate for conduct "contrary to senatorial traditions." He died three years later from cirrhosis of the liver. His belligerent right-hand man, the chief counsel on McCarthy's Permanent Subcommittee on Investigations, lawyer Roy Cohn, was disbarred for ethical violations in the 1980s. Before that, he remained a much-feared attorney, helped elect President Richard Nixon, and befriended and advised young would-be leaders such as Donald Trump.

Hoover retained his influence and stature. When he died in 1972, his body lay in state in the Capitol building—an honor afforded to no other civil servant before or since.

●　●　•

My two families—Richard's and Vladimir's—are fictional. They are imagined amalgamations gleaned from careful research into the time period. As such, they are symbolic of people caught up in the firestorm and pressures of the McCarthy era.

The news items opening each chapter and framing the events of that month, however, are historical fact.

While writing *Suspect Red*, I was struck by the relentless power of rumor and our human tendency to assume someone is guilty of something if his friends or family are, or if someone we like and admire says so. The inherent conflict between our desire to succeed, to be popular, and to be safe versus what we know to be ethically right is an age-old challenge. It requires courage. The novel's themes of real dangers versus perceived ones; national security versus individual rights/privacy; racial profiling and labeling; book censoring; and fearmongering, hate-speech, hyperbole, or outright lying for political gain all seem startlingly relevant today.

I was also reminded of what a fascinating and contradictory decade the 1950s was. World War II veterans came home, desperate for normalcy and a sense of personal success. That seemed defined in simple, homogeneous terms—a man owning his own home, preferably with a backyard, and a car; marriage to a wife who kept a neat, tranquil home and who was thrilled to see him walk through the door at night after work. According to magazine and TV ads, her greatest dream was to marry, have polished, polite children, an electric vacuum cleaner, and a refrigerator/freezer. Rarely did a woman have her own career, and if she had strong opinions on political causes, she risked the kind of ridicule about her femininity that many heaped on Eleanor Roosevelt.

What we now call post-traumatic stress disorder was little understood in the 1950s. Dismissive terms like *fright-burned*, *flak-happy*, or *psycho* were applied to very real and disabling symptoms. In Chapter 2, I quote directly an article titled "They Called Him a 'Psycho'" in the *Saturday Evening Post*. I thought it important to use Don to remind readers of how World War II veterans had to push themselves to function in the face of callous characterizations and misdiagnosis of their combat traumas.

It is important to remember these men and women sincerely believed they fought the Axis to make the world safe for democracy. Confronted with Stalin's crimes against humanity, the Iron Curtain, the possibility of nuclear holocaust, and the Korean War—all coming so fast on the heels of World War II—it makes sense they would be swept up in a patriotism and national protectiveness that allowed McCarthyism to grab hold and flourish.

The 1950s were also a time of lingering, beneath-the-surface anti-Semitism and overt prejudice against African Americans, when those agitating for civil rights or labor reform could be dubbed *subversive*, and when progressive social ideas were suspected of having Red underpinnings. Sadly, offensive racial and ethnic slurs, and insensitive labels for people with disabilities were used freely. Occasionally, my characters' dialogue reflects those harsh realities to "show rather than tell" those shocking attitudes.

In reaction to such prejudices, many creative artists produced daring, eloquent, and groundbreaking works. Jazz and its gutsy improvisations flourished, along with bebop, Beat poetry (the original slam verse), and rhythm and blues. Rock 'n roll was born. Playwrights Tennessee Williams and Arthur Miller pulled away the skin of conventionality to lay bare the bones of individual, psychological tragedies. Martha Graham and Agnes de Mille broke the rules of classical ballet to create a heartbreakingly expressive modern choreography. Composers Leonard Bernstein and Aaron Copland elevated American themes and the common man. Writers Ralph Ellison and James Baldwin unmasked racism. Ray Bradbury skewered small-minded pack mentality. Edward R. Murrow reported on McCarthy's bully-boy tactics despite threats of reprisal.

Here's a quick background on historical events mentioned:

The Hollywood Ten: Much has been written about the ten screenwriters who lost their fight against the House Un-American Activities Committee (HUAC) by arguing their First Amendment rights. What happened in the entertainment business—literature, movies, radio, TV, live theater, magazines, and newspapers—reflects the ripsaw of changing politics and world circumstances that made so many vulnerable to McCarthy's smears.

Many of the creative artists blacklisted had indeed once been "armchair Communists"—liberals and progressives during the Depression's financial disaster, involved with trying to unionize and improve workers' lives, maybe passing petitions, perhaps attending political rallies or fund-raisers that had some association with the American Communist Party. At that point, in the 1930s, the American Communist Party was just another pro-labor political faction within American society. During World War II, the Soviets were allies, not trusted exactly, but admired for their stubborn fight, and certainly integral to Hitler's defeat.

All that changed after World War II with Stalin's aggression in Eastern Europe. But American citizens could not erase their own pasts and political statements. (Think about your tweets and Facebook posts.) Fanatical Red-hunters, or those who exploited the nation's fears simply in order to elevate themselves professionally or socially, used people's past opinions and activities against them.

Once blacklisted, entertainment professionals could not get jobs. Screenwriter Dalton Trumbo had to ghostwrite, hiding his identity for years, even after anonymously winning Oscars for *Roman Holiday* and *The Brave One*.

Anyone who spoke out in support of the Hollywood Ten might be investigated themselves. For example, when the Ten testified in front of HUAC, a group of actors formed the Committee for the First Amendment. They signed and ran a petition in newspapers, and traveled to Washington, DC, to sit in support in the audience. Many were later hauled in front of the hearings themselves.

The Venona Project and the Korean War: In Chapter 1, Don refers to decoded Soviet transmissions and evidence against the Rosenbergs that could not be entered into their trial for security reasons. Today, because of the Freedom of Information Act and the collapse of the Soviet Union in 1991, we know the program as the Venona Project—a counterintelligence office run by the Army's Signal Intelligence Service (SIS, the precursor to today's NSA, the National Security Agency).

In the chaos following the Allies' invasion of Germany, American soldiers discovered a cipher pad left behind by Soviet troops. It allowed U.S. cryptographers to read thousands of intercepted Soviet cables—revealing large-scale attempts at spying within the American government by KGB-handled operatives. The Army and the FBI knew, for instance, that the Soviets had code names for Julius Rosenberg (Antenna), and his brother-in-law, David Greenglass (Bumblebee).

Six weeks before the Soviets tested their first atomic bomb, our ability to decode Soviet messages "went dark." A Russian translator within Venona and a British intelligence officer posted in England's embassy in Washington, DC, were suspected of informing the Soviets that U.S. intelligence could read their messages. The Soviets immediately changed their codes.

This was long before surveillance satellites. Had Venona been able to decode the Soviet's military communications regarding its supply and training of North Korean troops, many experts speculate we might have been able to use diplomacy to prevent the Korean War. Instead, the Communist invasion into South Korea was a total surprise, killing 36,574 Americans, 620,000 North and South Korean soldiers, and 600,000 Chinese soldiers, as well as millions of Korean civilians.

Judith Coplon and the sting operation against her were as the character Abigail describes. Coplon worked in the Justice Department's Foreign Agents Registration division as the go-between with the FBI. When the bureau suspected her of leaking its cases to the KGB, it wiretapped her phone. Agents briefly lost her on her trip to her handler and arrested them before she had actually handed over the planted paperwork. Her conviction was overturned in appeals court because of the important civil liberties guaranteed to everyone by our constitution. The judge determined that her arrest was illegal because the FBI had failed to obtain a warrant beforehand and that the Bureau also lied about the wiretap.

The case broke Hoover's cardinal rule—never embarrass the bureau. Hoover was known to freeze out agents who received too much public credit for successes, and to punish agents who bungled investigations or didn't flatter him enough. He used agents to place bets for him at the racetrack, to do repairs on his house, and even to compile his tax returns. Given all this, the pressures I put on my character, FBI Agent Don Bradley, are fictional, as is he, but plausible given reported history. So too are his interactions with Hoover and McCarthy.

Advancing American Art: Right after World War II, the State Department tried cultural diplomacy to woo countries susceptible to Communist thought. (It was a tactic also used later by the CIA with jazz artist performances.)

The department purchased 79 abstract, expressionist, cubist, and realist paintings. Many of the works were created by liberal intellectuals, some born in Eastern Europe. The exhibit would travel to countries like Czechoslovakia, where a homegrown Communist party was sprouting. The idea was that the paintings would display— vividly—the freedom of thought and expression allowed in the United States, thereby refuting Soviet claims that American society was repressive. Many of the paintings depicted workers with haunting sadness, as did Gwathmey's *Worksong*.

The response in Prague was overwhelmingly favorable. Unfortunately, back home, a few conservative congressmen and radio commentators condemned the frank subject matter, dark color tones, and abstract forms as being critical of American life, thereby fueling Soviet claims that our society was decadent and cruelly materialistic. The exhibit was recalled.

Jane Bowles's career was brief, but influential. She was friends with writer Truman Capote and playwright Tennessee Williams, who also worked with her composer/author husband Paul Bowles (the author of *The Sheltering Sky*). The Beat Generation—Jack Kerouac and Allan Ginsberg, among many others—became devotees. Jane Bowles's writing was infused with wry, self-deprecating wit. I tried to replicate that in Chapter 8 by paraphrasing her quoted interviews.

William Oatis was the Prague AP bureau chief who employed the three Czech reporters—one of whom I *imagine* to be Teresa's cousin. All three were convicted of espionage and sentenced to 16, 18, and 20 years. The source of their stories, "the boy from Paris," was convicted in absentia as their ringleader. His name was Vladimír Kazan-Komárek.

Kazan-Komárek's story is the stuff of Cold War intrigue. During World War II, he was sent as slave labor to Germany. He escaped and was employed as a U.S. Army translator in Nuremberg from May 1945 to 1946. After Czechoslovakia's Communist coup, Kazan-Komárek escaped again, this time to Paris. He braved going back and forth to his native land, smuggling in radio transmitters and smuggling out people of interest to France's foreign intelligence service. Eventually, he married an American and became a U.S. citizen. In 1966, working as a travel agent, Kazan-Komárek went to Moscow for a business conference. But on the flight home,

Soviets forced the plane to land and kidnapped him. The United States negotiated his release, but six years later in Spain, Kazan-Komárek disappeared again. He was never found.

Pick Temple, the Green Feather Movement, the FBI sneaking into the Czech Embassy in a trash truck and making off with a decoding machine, LBJ and Hoover living within a few houses of one another, and the hollow nickel are wonderful truths that are far better than anything a writer could make up. (Look for a hollow nickel in the movie *Bridge of Spies* about Russian spy Rudolf Abel.)

The FAO Schwarz employee my fictional Natalia mentions when telling Richard about censored picture books was none other than Maurice Sendak, author of *Where the Wild Things Are*, who would go on to create some of the world's most imaginative and unconventional picture books.

My description of **Lolita Lebrón** and three Puerto Rican nationalists shooting 29 bullets into the House floor in protest of their island's status as a U.S. protectorate is pulled directly from news reports. Until that day, the gallery had welcomed any and all who wished to witness Congress passing the nation's laws. The only question guards had asked spectators was if they carried cameras.

Lebrón served 25 years in prison. She was released by President Jimmy Carter in 1979, in what many believe was a prisoner swap for CIA agents imprisoned in Cuba. Happily, the congressman shot in the chest survived. A lovely endnote to the terrible incident is the lifelong friendship of two teenage pages who helped carry congressmen out on stretchers. They became congressmen themselves, dear friends on opposite sides of the aisle:

Paul Kanjorski, a Pennsylvania Democrat, and Bill Emerson, a Republican from Missouri.

I'd like to end as Vladimir left Richard, quoting Philbrick and then Edward R. Murrow, the broadcast journalist who risked so much to investigate and expose McCarthy. First Philbrick: You might not expect a man who became such a 1950s icon for fighting Reds to be an advocate for calm reason and brave tolerance, but he was. Although his book refers specifically to communism, Philbrick warned his readers to resist fearmongering and not to descend into labeling and threatening those who have opposing philosophies or backgrounds. He echoed Murrow's plea that we not disintegrate into persecuting all because of the few.

Philbrick urged Americans to leave the battle against those who sought to undermine the United States to trained experts like the FBI, and added that acting with hatred or prejudice toward our detractors only strengthened their propaganda: "Ambitious politicians, demagogues, and rabble-rousers are no match for [them]. The fight . . . will not be won by flag-waving or name calling. . . . If we adhere to our traditional American dream of a society of freedom . . . of individual as well as collective intelligence . . . we will have disproved [our detractors'] theory. . . .

"[Our enemy] depends upon hatred, uncertainty, and fear. . . . The best answer for that is reaffirmation of the faith that ours is a nation and we are a people founded upon . . . the sanctity of each individual. Therein lies our strength."

On March 9, 1954, Edward R. Murrow and CBS' *See It Now* ran "A Report on Senator Joseph R. McCarthy." Murrow ended with these stirring words:

"The line between investigating and persecuting is a very fine one. . . . We must not confuse dissent with disloyalty. We must remember always that accusation is not proof. . . .

"We will not walk in fear, of one another . . . into an age of unreason. If we dig deep in our history and our doctrine and remember that we are not descended from fearful men—not from men who feared to write, to speak, to associate, and to defend causes that were, for the moment, unpopular.

"We cannot defend freedom abroad by deserting it at home.

"[McCarthy has] caused alarm and dismay . . . and whose fault is that? Not really his. He didn't create this situation of fear; he merely exploited it—and rather successfully. Cassius [from Shakespeare's *Julius Caesar*] was right. 'The fault, dear Brutus, is not in our stars, but in ourselves.'"

Bibliography

Texts:

Fried, Richard M. *Nightmare in Red: The McCarthy Era in Perspective*. New York: Oxford University Press, 1990.

Halberstam, David. *The Fifties*. New York: Ballantine Books, 1994.

Haynes, John Earl and Klehr, Harvey. *Early Cold War Spies: The Espionage Trials that Shaped American Politics*. New York: Cambridge University Press, 2006.

Haynes, John Earl and Klehr, Harvey. *Venona: Decoding Soviet Espionage in America*. New Haven: Yale University Press, 1999.

Kessler, Pamela. *Undercover Washington: Where Famous Spies Lived, Worked and Loved*. Sterling: Capital Books, Inc., 2005.

Miller, Douglas T. and Nowak, Marion. *The Fifties: the Way We Really Were*. Garden City: Doubleday, 1977.

Oshinsky, David M. *A Conspiracy So Immense: The World of Joe McCarthy*. New York: Oxford University Press, 2005.

Patterson, James T. *Grand Expectations: The United States, 1945–1974*. New York: Oxford University Press, 1996.

Ranville, Michael. *To Strike at a King: The Turning Point in the McCarthy Witch Hunts*. Troy: Momentum Books, 1996.

Shogan, Robert. *No Sense of Decency: The Army-McCarthy Hearings*. Chicago: Ivan R. Dee Publisher, 2009.

Theoharis, Athan G., ed. *Beyond the Hiss Case: The FBI, Congress, and the Cold War*. Philadelphia: Temple University Press, 1982.

Documentaries and Feature Film Biopics:

Bridge of Spies. Directed by Steven Spielberg. 2015. Universal City: DreamWorks Pictures, 2016, DVD.

Good Night, and Good Luck. Directed by George Clooney. 2005. Burbank: Warner Bros. Entertainment, 2006, DVD.

Guilty by Suspicion. Directed by Irwin Winkler. 1991. Burbank: Warner Bros. Entertainment, 2004, DVD.

The McCarthy Years. Part of the Edward R. Murrow Collection, narrated by Walter Cronkite, produced by CBS News, 2005.

Scandalize My Name: Stories from the Blacklist. Directed by Alexandra Isles. 1998. Seattle: Encore Media Group, 1999, DVD.

Trumbo. Directed by Jay Roach. 2015. New York: Bleecker Street, 2016, DVD.

Acknowledgments

Sometimes it takes a village to write a good novel.

I am blessed to have the brilliance and imaginative talents of my daughter, Megan, and my son, Peter—professional creative artists themselves—to guide my thoughts, to push me in the themes and issues I'll tackle, and to edit me when I falter. They add depth and humanity, pace and fluidity, and authenticity of character and dialogue to everything I write. Megan also waded through hundreds of newspaper clippings and photos at the Library of Congress to research this period's historical facts. And Peter helped me keep the voice and sensibilities of male adolescent protagonists natural, the plot trim and taut. He also wrote Richard's songs.

A former *Washingtonian* magazine colleague, Jay Sumner, edited the photo selection with her veteran eye, making it a wonderfully evocative set of images that Disney • Hyperion's Maria Elias then designed into a captivating sequence. The insights and gentle prodding of my editor, Kieran Viola, honed the novel's tone, character's personalities, and point of view.

My journalism background influenced my choice to organize this novel into vignette-style chapters, each starting with actual news events of that month. Interviewing people who were young during the 1950s but remember well the fears and triumphs of the decade made the story so much more palpable.

Particular thanks go to: Ken Yalowitz, former ambassador to the Republic of Belarus and Georgia, and his wife, Judy. They generously shared their memories of Ken's thirty-six years with the

U.S. Foreign Service as well as the fearmongering that terrorized the State Department and permeated the nation throughout their childhoods. Ambassador Yalowitz was also kind enough to read the manuscript in its various stages, greatly improving its accuracy and its depiction of the pressures put on ordinary people by sweeping political demagoguery.

Ben Lamberton—who grew up in Washington, DC, and whose father represented individuals in contempt of Congress cases brought against them by Senator McCarthy's committee—helped me really understand the anguish of the intelligentsia and artists targeted by the Red Scare. Terry Straub, former senior vice president of public policy and governmental affairs for United States Steel and special assistant for congressional affairs in the Carter White House, graciously read the manuscript as well, keeping me on track regarding political history and congressional procedures.

Without all these people's largesse and talents, I could not have adequately condensed such a complicated and alarming time in our political history into a compelling portrait. I am grateful beyond words. If you find worth in these pages, please attribute it to the group effort.

House Pages Bill Goodwin, Paul Kanjorski, and Bill Emerson carry a stretcher bearing wounded Representative Alvin Bentley of Michigan to a waiting ambulance on the East Front of the Capitol. March 1, 1954

Photo Credits

Chapter 1

Page 2 (top): *Julius and Ethel Rosenberg*, Library of Congress; page 2 (bottom): *Rosenberg children leaving Sing Sing after visiting parents*, © Everett Collection Inc / Alamy Stock Photo; pages 4-5: *Germans facing down Soviet tanks in Berlin*, © dpa picture alliance / Alamy Stock Photo; page 7 (top left): *Dorothy Parker*, Pictorial Press Ltd / Alamy Stock Photo; page 7 (top right): *Upton Sinclair*, Upton Beall Sinclair, Jr., unidentified artist, 1906, gelatin silver print, National Portrait Gallery, Smithsonian Institution; page 7 (center): *1954: A film still from the 1989 documentary* Comic Book Confidential *showing the burning of comic books*, Image From Cinecom Pictures / Michael Ochs Archives / Getty Images; page 7 (bottom left): *Ernest Hemingway posing with a marlin, Havana Harbor, Cuba. July 1934*, Ernest Hemingway Collection / John F. Kennedy Presidential Library and Museum, Boston; page 7 (bottom right): *Albert Einstein*, Library of Congress; page 8: *Herblock cartoon—"You Read Books, Eh?,"* a 1949 Herblock cartoon, © The Herb Block Foundation.

Chapter 2

Page 26: *A war-weary girl with her brother on her back trudges past a stalled M-26 tank, at Haengiu, Korea. July 9, 1951*, U.S. Navy; page 27 (top): *A grief stricken American infantryman,* whose friend has been killed in action, is comforted by another soldier. In the background a corpsman methodically fills out casualty tags, Haktong-ni area, Korea. August 28, 1950, National Archives; page 27 (bottom): *Korean War. A gun crew checks their equipment near the Kum River. July 15, 1950*, Signal Corps / National Archives; pages 28–29: *Map showing missile radius from Cuba*, John F. Kennedy Library and Museum, Boston.

Chapter 3
Page 48: *McCarthy pointing finger*, © Everett Collection Inc / Alamy Stock Photo; page 50: *Baker Bikini Test*, U.S. Military.

Chapter 4
Page 71: *Lucille Ball and Desi Arnaz together at a piano*, Moviestore Collection Ltd / Alamy Stock Photo; page 72 (top): *An eager school boy gets his first experience in using War Ration Book Two*, National Archives; page 72 (bottom): *Jackie and JFK wedding*, John F. Kennedy Presidential Library and Museum, Boston.

Chapter 5
Page 87: *Portrait of Dwight D. Eisenhower*, National Archives; page 89 (top): *First Lieutenant Milo J. Radulovich and his wife, Nancy, rejoice after learning that Secretary of the Air Force Harold E. Talbott had reversed a recommendation that he be discharged from the Air Force Reserve as a security risk, Nov. 24, 1953, in Dexter, Mich. Radulovich is a University of Michigan student. His case attracted national attention*, AP Photo / Detroit News; page 89 (bottom): *Edward R. Murrow*,

Everett Collection Inc / Alamy Stock Photo; page 90 (top): *Fahrenheit 451 book cover, a dystopian novel by Ray Bradbury,* World History Archive / Alamy Stock photo.

Chapter 6
Page 109: *How Red Is The Little Red Schoolhouse art,* public domain; page 110 (top right): *Portrait of Harry S. Truman,* U.S. Army / Frank Gatteri / Courtesy of Harry S. Truman Library; page 110 (bottom left): *Portrait of FBI Director J. Edgar Hoover,* National Archives.

Chapter 7
Page 126: Red Channels *cover art,* public domain; page 128: *Portrait of Langston Hughes,* © Everett Collection / Alamy Stock Photo.

Chapter 8
Page 145 (top): *Photo of Marilyn Monroe and Joe DiMaggio,* Pictorial Press Ltd / Alamy Stock Photo; page 145 (bottom): *Portrait of Ruby Dee,* Library of Congress; page 146: Nautilus *submarine,* U.S. Navy.

Chapter 9
Page 164: *Eisenhower / Nixon Campaign brochure,* Richard Nixon Presidential Library; page 166 (top): *Image of Dr. Jonas Salk holding up two medical bottles,* University of Pittsburgh; page 166 (bottom): *Image of nurse and two children with polio,* Centers for Disease Control and Prevention.

Chapter 10
Page 183 (top): *Annie Lee Moss, 48, was suspended from her Pentagon job in 1954 after she was accused of being a Communist*

Party member, Everett Collection Historical / Alamy Stock Photo; page 183 (bottom): *Senator McCarthy talking to attorney Roy Cohn*, Library of Congress; page 184 (left): *Gregory Peck and Audrey Hepburn from movie* Roman Holiday *1953, directed by William Wyler*, ScreenProd / Alamy Stock Photo; page 184 (right): *Portrait of author Arthur Miller*, Eric Koch / Nationaal Archief / The Netherlands.

Chapter 11

Page 202: *Herblock cartoon—"I have here in my hand,"* a 1954 Herblock cartoon, © The Herb Block Foundation; page 204: *Photo of Walt Disney*, © Disney Enterprises, Inc.

Chapter 12

Page 221 (top): *School integration, Barnard School, Washington, DC, 1955*, Library of Congress; page 221 (bottom): *Protest march against the segregation of U.S. schools*, National Archives; page 223: *A soldier in a trench during battle at Dien Bien Phu, May 7, 1954*, Keystone Pictures USA / Alamy Stock Photo; page 224: *Bill Haley and His Comets at the Guest Lodge, Oak Ridge, 1946*, DOE Digital Archive.

Chapter 13

Page 246: *Chief Senate Counsel representing the United States Army and partner at Hale and Dorr, Joseph Welch (left) with United States Senator Joseph McCarthy of Wisconsin (right) at the Senate Subcommittee on Investigations' McCarthy-Army hearings. June 9, 1954*, U.S. Senate Historical Office; page 248: *School kids hold a "duck and cover" practice drill and crawl under their desks*, Library of Congress.

Afterword

Page 266: *Herblock cartoon—"My next number will be—"* a 1950 Herblock cartoon, © The Herb Block Foundation.

Photo Credits

Page 286: *House Pages carry a stretcher on the East Front of the Capitol. March 1, 1954,* Collection of the U.S. House of Representatives.